THE GOLDEN WIND

THE GOLDEN WIND

by

L. Sprague de Camp

an imprint of

Rockville, Maryland

ISBN: 978-1-61242-204-6

Published by Phoenix Pick
an imprint of Arc Manor
P. O. Box 10339
Rockville, MD 20849-0339
www.ArcManor.com

***To* JIM CASSON,**

who as Professor Lionel Casson
knows more than anyone else
about classical ships and shipping.

CONTENTS

INTRODUCTION TO
The Golden Wind

by Harry Turtledove

The Golden Wind is the most recent of L. Sprague de Camp's historical novels, both in terms of when it is set and when it was written. It came out in 1969, four years after *The Arrows of Hercules*. In between the two, Sprague published *Spirits, Stars and Spells—the Profits and Perils of Magic*, the study on which he'd worked for many years (his wife, Catherine, has a coauthor credit), and *The Goblin Tower*, the fine novel that marked his return to original fantasy after too long an absence.

Along with being the last of his historicals, *The Golden Wind* may well be the best. De Camp himself thought it was. He told me so in a letter when I helped a friend—a professor of ancient history at California State University, Los Angeles, who also admired his work—get a copy from him. And he says the same thing in *Time and Chance*, his autobiography.

The novel, which takes the form of a father's fictitious memoir intended for his son, opens in 119 BC, so it is laid almost two centuries more recently than that of *The Bronze God of Rhodes*, the de Camp historical set next closest to the present. The Mediterranean world changed enormously between the two novels. When *The Bronze God of Rhodes* ends, Rome is a small but rising state. By the time *The Golden Wind* opens, Rome has grown into the greatest power in that world. This was not always an unmixed blessing. As our protagonist, Eudoxos of Kyzikos, notes in the third paragraph of the fictive memoir,

> *[A] small power like Kyzikos is well advised not to remind the Romans wantonly of its existence. The Romans are great ones for putting their noses into other people's business. It does not take much of a pretext—a tavern brawl between your sailors and theirs will do—to convince them that they owe it to the peace of the world to take you under their fatherly wing. Then you awaken to find a Roman garrison in your city and a Roman proconsul stealing everything not firmly nailed down and selling you and your family into slavery in Italy.*

Along with Rome, two of the kingdoms founded by Alexander the Great's generals after his death in 323 BC still survive at this time: a much diminished Seleucid state in Syria and, more important, Ptolemaic Egypt.

Eudoxos of Kyzikos, as de Camp portrays him, is a man with a problem. What that problem is, I will not say, since he explains for himself early on in the novel. Whether he actually had it, no one can say, not at a distance of upwards of 2,000 years. But he easily could have had it, which is as much as anybody can expect from historical fiction.

Thanks not least to his problem, Eudoxos is also a man of remarkable determination. In fact, we know he was. He was a real, if obscure, historical figure, like the protagonists of most of de Camp's historicals. What we know of his adventurous career and journeys is summarized in an extract lifted by the geographer Strabo from the works of the stoic philosopher Poseidonios. Eudoxos was the first sailor from the Hellenistic world to figure out how to use the monsoon winds to sail directly from the coast of southern Egypt to western India and to return when they reversed. Until his time, this trade had been in the hands of Arab middlemen. He cut them out, and the direct route remained in use till the Muslim explosion in the seventh century of our era drastically revised the political map.

This working out of the monsoon route is the growth in human knowledge at the heart of *The Golden Wind*, as the discovery of the okapi and the sources of the Nile lies at the heart of *The Dragon of the Ishtar Gate*, the invention of the catapult at the heart of *The Arrows of Hercules*, accurate knowledge of the elephant at that of *An*

Elephant for Aristotle, and the technology of sieges and of creating huge statues at that of *The Bronze God of Rhodes*. But, like its predecessors, *The Golden Wind* is as far from being a dry history book as it could possibly be. The people who inhabit it *are* people, doing what they do for love, for money, and for other recognizable human reasons. Amusingly, we also see in *The Golden Wind* faint echoes of the (fictitious or semifictitious) deeds of some of the characters from de Camp's earlier historical novels.

And, speaking of dry history books, it's occurred to me that one of the most enjoyable ways to learn ancient history would be to read a series of historical novels, and to go to the history books only afterward, to find out more about things in the novels that sparked your interest. Here is a suggested short course, from the most ancient to the most recent:

The Praise Singer, Mary Renault
The Dragon of the Ishtar Gate, L. Sprague de Camp
The Last of the Wine, Mary Renault
The Arrows of Hercules, L. Sprague de Camp
Fire From Heaven, Mary Renault
The Persian Boy, Mary Renault
An Elephant for Aristotle, L. Sprague de Camp
The Bronze God of Rhodes, L. Sprague de Camp
The Golden Wind, L. Sprague de Camp
I, Claudius, Robert Graves
Claudius the God, Robert Graves
Memoirs of Hadrian, Marguerite Yourcenar
Julian, Gore Vidal
The Death of Attila, Cecelia Holland
Count Belisarius, Robert Graves
Justinian, H.N. Turteltaub (pen name for Harry Turtledove)

This will take you from the sixth century BC to the beginning of the eighth century of our era. My own four Hellenistic historicals—*Over the Wine-Dark Sea*, *The Gryphon's Skull*, *The Sacred Land*, and *Owls to Athens* (all either issued or soon to be reissued by Arc Manor/Phoenix Pick)—fall between *An Elephant for Aristotle* and *The Bronze God of Rhodes*. Since each covers only one year, I don't presume to include them in a short course. If, however, you're looking for further reading …

(EXPLANATORY LETTER)

Epistolê Exegetikê

Eudoxos son of Theon, of Kyzikos, wishes his son Theon well. The gods willing, this letter and the manuscript with it will reach you by a trustworthy captain of my host in Gades, Eldagon ben-Balatar the shipmaster.

You may have heard hard things about me from your mother's kinsmen. Before you do anything rash—like throwing away these papers unread—I pray you to hear my side of the tale. Although we have not seen each other in nearly a decade, I hope the love that is proper between father and son be not wholly quenched. Furthermore, aside from such considerations, I want you to perform certain tasks for me, and you will be more likely to do so if I justify my course.

Not to make two bites of a cherry, the principal task is to edit the inclosed manuscript, taking out parts that would discredit me or reveal things better kept quiet. In writing it, I have let myself go. But age is upon me, and my judgment as to what should be said may not be so keen as once it was. Then, arrange for publication, that the fame due my deeds shall not be lost in the river of time. There used to be at least two good bookmakers in Kyzikos.

The source of the trouble between your mother and me was, basically, the difference in our ages. If young men be any more wont to take their elders' advice than in my youth—which I doubt—you may profit from my example.

Now, in my own youth, I could pleasure women with the best of them. In fact, I was known to the whores and hetairai of Kyzikos as a three-ball man. I speak in strict confidence of intimate family matters, and may a father's curse be upon you if you ever reveal what I am about to tell you.

I was well past forty when I began to tire of the sterile pursuit of pleasure women. My contemporaries were settled married men, some even grandfathers. To me, a peaceful domestic life took on a new attraction.

Discreet inquiries after a bride brought forth the daughter of my friend Zoilos the shipbuilder—your maternal grandfather. Your mother Astra was then twenty-two; she had been betrothed a few years before to a youth who had sickened and died.

At that time, my age—over twice your mother's—seemed a small matter. Moreover, at the start of our married life, I fell head-over-heels in love with her, like the hero of one of those sentimental novels that come out of Alexandria. I have never known a woman whom I desired so passionately, or whose company I so much enjoyed. I never expected to become an uxorious man, but there it is.

Nor did the feeling soon wane, as I have seen it do with other couples. I still feel that way about her, although she has been dead for years. While I do not really believe in the theologians' theories of a future life, the remote chance of being reunited with my darling Astra makes death seem almost attractive.

I am sure that your mother loved me, too, in spite of my broken nose and scars and pockmarks. When you were born, I thought my happiness complete. So, one would have said, what has Eudoxos to complain of? He is rich, respected, and famous, with a lovely girl for a wife and a lusty man-child. If he is no beauty, that does not matter, since he is not angling for lovers male, for whom he never cared. (My nickname as a boy was "ape," and a quarter-century of rough, adventurous life had done nought to better my looks.)

I need not tell you about the other sides of my career: the voyages I captained, the public offices I held, the missions and journeys I undertook for our city, the strokes of business that brought me the wealth you now enjoy, my adventures among the wild Scythians, and my scholarly researches in geography and exploration. All these things are well known in Kyzikos. But you must admit that, in my day, I was somebody. One would have said, some god must have cast his mantle over Eudoxos.

I fear, however, that the gods—if indeed there be gods—have an unpleasant sense of humor. Having been well taught by knowledgeable women, I introduced Astra with care to the arts of wedded love. Six years after our marriage, when you were three and I was just past fifty, she was as passionate a bedmate as one would wish.

But then, to my horror, I found my own lectual powers waning. My spear sagged like an overheated taper; my Egyptian obelisk began to turn from granite to putty at critical moments.

Slowly but inexorably this weakness grew. At first I thought little of it. Then, when I had to leave your mother unsatisfied several times in a row, I sought the help of physicians. Some said to drink more wine; some said to drink none at all. Some sold me powdered unicorn's horn and other rare medicines at fabulous prices. But nothing did any good. Once in a while I could still perform my husbandly duties; more often it was like trying to fight a battle with a length of rope for a spear.

Your mother became nervous and cranky, and I more and more frustrated. I loved her as much as ever. Moreover, I found that my decline as a lover was not matched by any wane in my interest in the act of love. I wanted her more than ever. My mind became preoccupied with memories of the last time we had enjoyed a good gallop and my hopes for the next one.

The most infuriating thing was that, in other respects, I was not prematurely aged. My hair was still black and thick, with only a little gray. I had all but two of my teeth. My belly bulged hardly at all, since I kept myself fit in the gymnasium. Few things so embitter a strong, vigorous, successful man as to find his masculinity failing him.

At last I poured out my distress to old Glaukos, the dean of Kyzikene physicians. He told me:

"Forsooth, best one, this weakness befalls most men sooner or later. In your case, the onset is a little earlier than usual, that is all. Some men are impotent all their lives; some become so in their thirties or forties. And, no matter what my colleagues say, no real cure is known. If you were a flabby, dissipated idler, I could tell you to drink less, keep regular hours, and get more exercise; but you already lead a healthy life."

Observing my hangdog expression, he continued: "Do not look so despondent, Eudoxos. A man feels about his loss of phallic vigor much as a woman feels about the loss of her beauty. But these things overtake all of us if we are fortunate enough to live so long. The life of an oldster is still better than its only alternative—death."

"Then what shall I do?" I cried. "By the Heavenly Twins, I'm not old enough to submit tamely to this fate! I have been as happily married as a man can be, but this is no longer the case. Things go from bad to worse."

He shrugged. "When I studied in Alexandria, I met an Indian, who assured me that Indian medical science was far ahead of ours. He claimed that the wise men of India could prolong life, revive the dead, and do all kinds of wonderful things. If these tales be true, they could doubtless stiffen your yard for you."

"Ah, but are they true?"

"Perhaps, perhaps not. I have never been to India and, save for this one man, I have never known anyone else who had, either."

"Nor I. It is said to be a fearful journey, the more so since the realm of the barbarous Parthians now lies athwart the land route to India."

"So they say," replied Glaukos, and we dropped the subject.

A few months later, Kyzikos made up an embassy to the court of King Ptolemaios Evergetes—Evergetes the Second, otherwise known—but not to his face—as *ho Physkon*, "the Sausage." Physkon staged a big spring festival in honor of Persephonê, and—she being our patron goddess—we sent a delegation of priests to take part in the rites and athletes to compete in the games. Since I had just finished my term as polemarch, and in view of my experience in such matters, I was appointed sacred ambassador and peace herald. I made the arrangements for the journey, governed the rest of the delegation, and represented the delegation in its dealings with the Egyptian court.

We traveled in the state galley. I took my slave, a Scythian named Gnouros. This was a quiet little man, who did as he was told and kept his thoughts—if any—to himself. This left Astra with only one servant in the house, our hired maid-of-all-work Dirka. But your mother preferred it that way. She felt secure, with daily visits to and from our many relatives, and she did not wish to have to break in a new slave or a hired servant in my absence.

As we headed out into the windy Propontis, I stood on the poop deck, waving to your mother, and she waved to me from the quay. I suppose you were too young at the time to remember that parting now. We waved until each was out of the other's sight. When Mount Dindymos sank below the blue curve of the Propontis, I wept tears as salty as the sea. Some of my fellow passengers spoke of this, and I made an excuse about the pain of leaving one's beloved city. It would not have done to admit that a mere woman had brought my feelings so visibly to the surface.

And so the tale of my later voyages, which has taken me months to dictate, begins. I hope you will find it beguiling for its own sake as well as an effective self-justification by your sire. Rejoice!

Book I

HIPPALOS THE CORINTHIAN

On the tenth of Mounychion, in the third year of the 165th Olympiad,[1] when Hipparchos was archon of Athens and Ptolemaios Physkon had reigned as sole king in Egypt for forty-five years, I, Eudoxos son of Theon, left Kyzikos in command of the delegation sent by my city to Alexandria for King Ptolemaios' Persephoneia.

As we coasted the south shore of the Propontis in the state galley *Persephonê*, we had not gone three hundred furlongs[2] before we passed the boundary of the Kyzikene lands and came abreast of those ruled by Rome. We made our overnight stops at those Ionian cities—Troy, Mytilenê, and Phokaia, for example—that the Romans had not yet raped of their independence.

Whilst our relations with Rome had been good, a small power like Kyzikos is well advised not to remind the Romans wantonly of its existence. The Romans are great ones for putting their noses into other people's business. It does not take much of a pretext—a tavern brawl between your sailors and theirs will do—to convince them that they owe it to the peace of the world to take you under their fatherly wing. Then you awaken to find a Roman garrison in your city and a Roman proconsul stealing everything not firmly nailed down and selling you and your family into slavery in Italy.

So we avoided the Roman-ruled cities of Asia Minor. As it was, a Roman fiver came boiling out of the harbor of Ephesos as we passed,

1 Approx. April 1, 119 B.C.

2 1 furlong (*stadion*) = 1/8 mile.

signaling us to stop. When the Roman galley drew close, an officer shouted across the water through a speaking trumpet, demanding to know who we were and what our business was. We told him and sailed on. Alas for the great days of Hellas, when the ships of a free Hellenic city went where they listed without anybody's leave!

Eighteen days after we set out, we raised the Egyptian coast near the Sebennytic Mouth of the Nile. I had been to Egypt twenty years before, as supercargo on one of the family's ships. The Egyptian shore showed the same dreary monotony: a land as flat as a marble flagstone in the temple of Persephonê, rimmed by a never-ending beach, and beyond it a mass of reeds and a hedge of palms against the sky.

We sailed westward, past Kanopos and Boukiris and little fishing villages, until the coast rose in the slight ridge that passes for a hill in the Delta. And so we came at last to the walls of Alexandria.

At the Bull Channel, a pilot boat, with the red-lion pennant of the Ptolemies whipping from its masthead, led us into the Great Harbor. To our right, on the isle of Pharos, rose Sostratos' colossal, gleaming lighthouse, towering up at least four plethra,[3] with a plume of smoke streaming from its top. On our left stood the fortifications and barracks at the end of Point Lochias, and then the temple of Isis.

Once we were through the channel, the Great Harbor opened out on all sides. On the right was the mole called the Seven Furlonger, joining the Pharos to the city, with scores of merchantmen tied up along it on both sides. Beyond lay the Old Harbor, or Haven of Happy Return, devoted to commercial and fishing craft. On the left, as we entered the Great Harbor, were the naval docks, with squadrons of Ptolemaic fivers and larger ships. Their hulls were black, and each bore a gilded statue of Alexander on its stern. Beyond and above the warships, the gilded roof tiles of the royal palaces glittered and their marble columns gleamed.

Near the palaces, a section of the harbor was marked off from the rest by a mole. In this inner harbor lay the king's private ships, which included three of the largest vessels in the world. These ships had all been acquired about a hundred years before, in the time of the fourth

3 1 plethron = 100 feet.

Ptolemy—Ptolemaios Philopator, the degenerate with whom the dynasty began to go to seed.

One of the ships was Philopator's pleasure barge. Another was a huge vessel built by Hieron of Syracuse. The tyrannos had meant to combine the virtues of a war galley, a merchantman, and a royal yacht in one hull; but the ship proved too slow for war, too costly for commerce, and too crowded for pleasure. So, in disgust, Hieron gave her to Philopator, who liked such nautical freaks.

The third ship was the largest war galley of all time, a fortier over four plethra long. Four thousand rowers, pulling ten-man oars arranged in four banks, propelled her. She had proved too slow for any practical use, and the hire of so many rowers would have strained the finances even of Egypt; so she had been tied up and neglected. Of the three, the barge was the only one that had been kept up. The two galleys lay forlorn, with most of the paint gone from their woodwork and no oars in their ports. I suppose the kings now and then had their bilges pumped out, or they would have sunk from simple leakage.

The pilot boat led us to a wharf to the right of the naval docks, near the temple of Poseidon on the teeming waterfront. Here several other sacred municipal triremes were drawn up. I recognized the Athenian *Salaminia*, having seen her several times on voyages to Athens.

* * *

We had not finished tying up when a naval inspector in gleaming cuirass and a couple of Greek civilians came aboard. While the inspector went down the line asking every man on board his name and business, and the two customs men poked amongst our baggage, I saw a dozen people hurrying from the mass of palaces to our left, with cloaks flapping and helmet plumes nodding. The nearer they came, the faster they went. At last they broke into a run, the soldiers clattering and the civilians clutching their garments.

As they straggled to the base of the companionway, a furious argument broke out. Fists shook; insults were shouted. Presently two—an army officer whose harness flashed with golden trim, and a tall, red-haired civilian—attempted to ascend the plank at the same time. Since the plank was too narrow for this purpose, they tried to shoulder each other off. Then they fell to pushing and wrestling, shouting: "Out of my way, you collared knave!" "You're mad, you temple-robbing sodomite!" "Go to the crows, you thickskin, or I'll cut your lying throat!"

While they strove in this unseemly fashion, another man quietly climbed up on the plank and proceeded to the deck. He was about my age, lean and swarthy, with a shaven head, wearing a long white Egyptian robe and carrying an ornate walking stick. As he approached, panting from his recent run, the other two ceased their battle and followed him up the plank, still muttering threats and insults under their breath. The rest of the party followed.

Stepping down to the deck and speaking good Greek with a trace of Egyptian accent, the white-robed man began:

"Are you Eudoxos of Kyzikos, sir? The peace herald and sacred ambassador of Kyzikos? Rejoice! I, Noptes, high priest of Sarapis, welcome you in the name of His Majesty—"

At that instant the other two, also reaching the deck, burst out: "Rejoice, worthy Eudoxos! I welcome you in the name of Her Majesty—"

Then each of the three tried to shout down the others, so that I could hear nought but an unintelligible babble. At last I banged the deck with my stick and roared:

"By Bakchos' balls, *shut up*, you three!" Their voices fell off, since I was larger than any of them and far from handsome. "Now," said I quietly, "you got here first, sir priest, so finish your speech. You two shall have your chance later. Go on."

With a flicker of a smile, Noptes continued: "I welcome you in the name of His Majesty, King Ptolemaios the Benefactor. During the Persephoneia, you and your party shall be lodged in apartments in the royal palace. If you will follow me, sir—"

"Wait!" cried the other two together.

"All right," I said and indicated the officer. "You next."

"Sir!" The gleaming soldier brought his heels smartly together. He was a good-looking man in his thirties, with a close-cut black beard, and on his head a black-crested, bowl-shaped Macedonian helmet, with a narrow brim all the way round and cheek pieces of boiled leather tied together under his chin. In a guttural Judaean accent, he began: "I am Ananias of Askalon, deputy commander of the regiment of Her Majesty, Queen Kleopatra the Wife. In the name of Her Majesty, I welcome you and your party to Alexandria for the Persephoneia. You shall stay in the guest house of Her Majesty—"

"My turn!" cried the red-haired civilian. He was almost as tall as I and about the age of the Judaean, with a sharp-pointed nose and slanting eyebrows that gave him the look of a Pan. With a charming smile and an Attic accent that was a little too preciously refined to be convincing, he said:

"My dear Eudoxos, allow me. I am Hippalos of Corinth, choragus to Her Majesty, Queen Kleopatra the Sister, and your servant. Her Majesty begs that you and yours stay in her portion of the palace, which has been redecorated especially for your pleasure—"

"So? The Wife's guest house is far more comfortable!" the Judaean officer broke in.

"I spoke first," said the priest, "and anyway my master is the king!"

All three began to jabber again, whilst their attendants in the background scowled at one another and muttered. It looked as if the deck of the *Persephonê* would become the scene of a brawl, when I shouted them down again.

"You put us in an embarrassing position," I said. "Why in the name of the Dog can't you settle these arguments before coming here? We would not offend any of your royal masters, but we cannot follow three mutually contradictory sets of orders at once."

The dispute went round and round until the Judaean said: "A story I'll tell you. Once my people were ruled by a wise and mighty king named Solomon, who had a case like this to decide. Two women each claimed a child. After listening to their clack all day, the king offered to cut the child in twain and give half to each—"

"If that be the Judaean notion of wisdom!" said the priest, Noptes. "It only proves—"

"You haven't heard the rest," persisted Ananias. "One woman agreed to this proposal; but the other said no, she would rather the other woman had the child than that it were harmed. So the king knew that the second woman was the true mother—"

"That is all very well," said Noptes, "but we cannot carve up our rulers' guests."

"I don't know why not," said Hippalos the choragus with a sly grin, whereat some of my delegation looked apprehensive. "I'll take the heads, and you two can divide—"

"Enough of your foolery!" said Ananias. "A joke of your mother's funeral you'd make. This is supposed to be a formal, dignified occasion."

"You've solved the problem, nonetheless," I told the Judaean. Turning to my delegation, I told off six men and said: "You six shall go with High Priest Noptes." To another six, I said: "You shall go with Colonel Ananias."

Then I realized that there were only five left, including myself. It would have been more foresighted to have included myself in the group to be lodged by the king, since he wielded the most power; but I did not want to change the arrangements at that stage. I assigned myself and the remaining delegates to Hippalos and told Gnouros to pick up my gear.

Walking along the waterfront towards the palaces, Hippalos chatted familiarly with me. "I say," he asked, "are you Eudoxos the geographer? The author of *Description of the Euxine Sea*?"

"Why, yes. Do you know it here?"

"I've read one of the copies in the Library. It is, I must say, a jolly good coverage of the subject."

"Most of my firm's trade is with the Euxine ports," I explained, "so I know Pantikapaion and the rest from firsthand acquaintance."

"Have you explored the great Scythian rivers?"

"I've been a fair distance up the Hypanis and the Tanaïs and the Borysthenes. There's not much to see—just a great, grassy plain to the horizon, whereon the Scythians roam with their flocks. I got this little scar—" (I touched my right cheek) "—from a Scythian arrow. I don't care what Homer and the other ancients say; the Scythians are not a notably just and upright race, nor is their climate mild and balmy. In fact, a less balmy one were hard to find."

"Have you ever thought of exploring in the other direction—south of Egypt? All sorts of fascinating mysteries await solution thither."

"I've read the arguments about the sources of the Nile," I said, "but I hadn't thought of trying to solve the problem myself. It's a fascinating riddle; but my exploring has been in the line of commerce, and now I'm getting a little old for roughing it."

"Why, how old are you?" asked Hippalos. When I told him, he exclaimed: "Oh, I say! You don't look a day over forty; just in the prime of life. By Herakles, I should like to make such an exploration! When I was a sailor, I visited all the main ports of the Inner Sea; but I should like to try something more daring and distant. Only, I lack the money and influence to mount such an expedition; the stars have been against me. Perhaps you and I could get together on such a project, eh?"

I raised an eyebrow. "Have you had any experience at that sort of thing?"

"I daresay I've traveled as much as you have, no offense meant. When I was a strolling singer, I jolly well had to learn to live by my wits in strange places."

"Well, it's worth thinking about," I said. In dealing with such people—especially in the East—one never gives them a flat "no"; they would be offended and try to do one ill. Instead, one says "perhaps" or "another time." Eventually they get the idea without hard feelings. At the time, however, I had no intention of haring off on some crack-brained jaunt with a professional entertainer, however charming and versatile.

We were let in the main gate of the palace area by a pair of Celtic mercenaries: big men with long, brown mustaches, wearing checkered coats and trousers and armed with huge, oval shields and long swords. The palace compound was a vast complex of buildings in ornate modern style, with gilded capitals on the columns and brightly painted entablatures. The area bustled with people coming and going, since these edifices contained the offices of the Egyptian government as well as the living quarters of the rulers.

The party broke up, the guests of each of the three monarchs being taken to a different destination. Hippalos led us into one of the buildings and to a two-room apartment. In the living room, a marble-topped table bore a small water clock which, as we entered, gave forth a sharp *ping* to signal noon. Hippalos showed us our beds and said:

"The bath is down the hall this way. You will be cleaned up, fed, and given a chance to rest. When the clock strikes the ninth hour, I shall lead you to the audience chamber for presentation to Their Majesties."

* * *

Our apartment in the royal palace had one delightful amenity. This was a tub or sink affixed to one wall. From the wall above it protruded a bronze pipe with a valve. This valve had a handle, so that, when one turned it one way, water flowed into the sink; when one turned it the other, the flow stopped. Thus one could wash one's hands and face without shouting for a servant to fetch a bowl and a ewer. Moreover, the sink had a hole in the bottom, closed by a conical pottery plug. From this hole, a pipe went down through the floor to carry off the dirty water. With all these marvelous modern inventions, I foresee the day when we shall all be waited upon by mechanical servants, such as some of the myths tell of.

Three hours after our arrival, freshly bathed, shaved, oiled, and scented, and wearing our best tunics, we were led into the vestibule of the audience hall. It was a day for receiving foreign visitors, since a group of lean, swarthy men from Numidia, with golden hoops in their ears and animal skins wound about their heads, were ahead of us. Ananias and Noptes brought in the rest of my delegation. A fat Egyptian led a group of trousered, bearded Armenians, wearing the distinctive caps of their country, out of the hall. The Egyptian took charge of the Numidians and led them in, while an assistant patted us for hidden weapons.

At last came our turn. Noptes presented us to the fat Egyptian, saying: "Sirs, this is Tetephras, chief usher to Their Majesties."

We murmured the usual courtesies, and Tetephras said: "You shall follow me into the audience hall, gentlemen, halting when I halt. As I state your names and titles, you shall bow individually to the king. Then, when I state the names and titles of the rulers, you shall bow collectively to each ruler as I name him."

"Must we prostrate ourselves?" asked Xenokles, the high priest of Persephonê.

"Nay; we ask that not of free Hellenes, but reserve it for Persians, Ethiopians, and the like, who are used to it. Now let me run over your names again. . . ."

At last Tetephras, fussing over us like a mother hen, got us lined up in a square and signed to the Macedonian mercenaries at the entrance to open the big doors. Tetephras stepped through the entrance, pounded the floor with his staff, and bellowed:

"The delegation from Kyzikos to the Persephoneia!"

We marched down the length of the hall behind the usher. It was a fine, big room, with many people lining the walls. There were soldiers in gilded accouterments. There were clerks at desks, with pens poised to take down any divine words Their Majesties might utter. There were servants standing ready with napkins, flasks of wine, and other things for the comfort of the rulers, ready to dash forward at a signal. There were several eminent foreigners, invited to the audience as a cheap way of entertaining them.

The torchères were not lit, since the brilliant sun gave enough light through the clerestory windows above. A dozen incense burners emitted a fog of blue smoke and an overpowering odor. A small orchestra twanged and tootled as we marched forward.

Down the hall we went to the far end, where Their Majesties sat enthroned. The thrones were, I am sure, of wood covered with gold leaf, notwithstanding that some Alexandrines claim they are solid gold.

Although I knew what to expect, I still goggled at the contrast between the pomp and glitter on one hand and Their Majesties' unprepossessing appearance on the other. On the central and largest throne sat King Sausage himself.

Physkon was in his middle sixties, bald as an ostrich egg and shaped like one, too. Although a short man, he must have weighed at least five talents and could hardly waddle without the help of servants. He wore Egyptian costume. A long-sleeved tunic of thin white linen reached to his ankles. A broad collar of gold and jewels, in the old Egyptian style, hung around his neck. On his bald head sat the towering double crown, of red and white felt, of Upper and Lower Egypt. Under this crown, his pale, blotched face was one vast roll of fat, through which a pair of sharp little black eyes peered out. His painted lips were as full and thick as those of an Ethiop.

Looking at Physkon's unlovely form, I found it easy to believe the tales about him. The fifth Ptolemy had begotten three legitimate children: two boys and a girl. In accordance with the local custom, the older son married his sister and succeeded his father as Ptolemaios Philometor. Then Philometor died. His younger brother, the present Physkon, had taken the throne as a youth of eighteen. He married the same sister, and—on his wedding night—killed the son of his bride by his brother. Not surprisingly, the two soon fell out, and the sister-wife's followers drove Physkon out of Egypt. Then, for nearly twenty years, he reigned in Cyprus. When he got his hands on the son that the queen had borne him, he had the lad killed and his head and hands embalmed and sent to her in a fancy casket, just to vex her.

Eventually, Physkon fought his way back to Egypt and was reconciled—on the surface, at least—with his wife. In the meantime her other child by Philometor, a girl, had grown up, and Physkon decided that he preferred the younger woman. He declared the mother divorced and married the daughter, but the mother refused to accept this proceeding. After another civil war, the three settled down to a wary but more or less peaceful coexistence, vigilantly watching one another for attempts at murder.

Since both queens were named Kleopatra, to tell them apart the mother was called "the Sister" and the daughter, "the Wife." I do not think we should have received so royal a welcome had it not been for the competition amongst these three monarchs, each striving to put one over on the other two. [O Theon: You had better cut out most of the above remarks about the Ptolemies before submitting this manuscript to Lathyros or any other member of the family. Father.]

Behind Physkon's throne stood another pair of Celtic mercenaries. To one side was an officer in Greek parade armor, who—judging from his swartness—must have been another Egyptian. Under the early Ptolemies, the Hellenes and Macedonians had formed the ruling class in Egypt, and no nonsense about it. Not getting on well with his Greek subjects, Physkon favored the native Egyptians. This enraged the Hellenes, who saw their privileges slipping away.

On the old monster's right—our left—sat Queen Kleopatra the Sister, about the same age as Physkon and almost as fat. The incestuous marriages of the Ptolemies had passed on, in full purity, the obesity they inherited from the original Ptolemaios, a general of Alexander of Macedon and the founder of the dynasty. The elder Kleopatra was another mountain of sagging fat, clad in a white gown of Hellenic cut, with a golden crown on her red-dyed hair and a veil of purple byssus over it. The paint on her face was so thick that I will swear it was peeling. Another officer stood beside her throne. Being deaf, she shouted at this man:

"What did you say? Who is that big, ugly fellow with the long, hairy arms, in front?" She meant me.

On our right sat Queen Kleopatra the Wife, a woman in her forties, plump but not so mountainous as her mother or her husband-uncle-stepfather. She wore a dress of gaudy red and white stripes in the Judaean fashion, and so much jewelry that she clattered every time she moved. Her officer was a muscular man with a graying beard. I learned that this was General Chelkias, Colonel Ananias' elder brother and commander of Her Majesty's Regiment.

Alexandria was inhabited by three races: the Hellenes, the Judaeans, and the Egyptians. Each tribe lived in its own part of the city. Since they differed widely in morals and customs, murder and rioting between one group and another were frequent. The only time the Alexandrines all acted together was when they rioted against some unpopular ruler, as they had done against Physkon in the early days of his reign. Physkon soon put a stop to that; he turned his mercenaries loose on the rioters. Soon blood ran in streams in the gutters, and heads were piled in man-high heaps in the public squares. This is not my idea of how to run a civilized country; but, with a populace as fickle and turbulent as that of Alexandria, it may be the only way that works.

Since Alexandria was so divided in population, each of the three rulers relied for support upon one of the groups. Physkon sought the sympathy of the Egyptians; the Sister, of the Hellenes; the Wife, of the Judaeans. They even had three separate armies. Physkon's soldiers wore red crests on their helms; the Sister's, white crests; the Wife's, black crests. Each color was represented in the audience hall, standing in squads where they could quickly come to the aid of their respective sovrans if the latter were attacked.

The music stopped. Tetephras halted and roared: "I present to Your Divine Majesties the illustrious Eudoxos son of Theon, peace herald and sacred ambassador of the city of Kyzikos and holder of many distinguished offices in that city; the Reverend Xenokles, high priest of Persephonê in Kyzikos; and the eminent members of his Board of Sacrificers: Master Hipponax, Master Kerdon, and Master Timaios; the athletes: Master Anaxis the wrestler ..." and so on. Then he turned to us:

"Gentlemen: I present you to His Divine Majesty, Ptolemaios Evergetes, the king of Egypt, Cyrene, Cyprus, and other outlying possessions; Her Divine Majesty, the Queen Kleopatra the Sister; Her Divine Majesty, the Queen Kleopatra the Wife; and the divine children: the Prince Ptolemaios Philometor, the Prince Ptolemaios Alexandros, and the Prince Ptolemaios Apion."

These last were three youths, who sat on small thrones flanking the three large ones. Ranging in age from twelve to eighteen, all had the short, tubby Ptolemaic build. The first two were the sons of Physkon and the Wife; the third, of Physkon and a concubine. The first, Ptolemaios Philometor, was the one we now call "Lathyros." Physkon also had two daughters by the Wife, who later married Seleucid princes, but neither was present. On our right, a lean, stooped, gray-bearded, tutorial-looking man stood behind the two youngest Ptolemies.

We bowed this way and that until we were dizzy. I presented the gifts we had brought: a golden-hilted sword for Physkon (albeit he could have wielded nothing more warlike than a toothpick), a bronze statuette for the Sister, and a jeweled tiara for the Wife. I made my speech, telling the rulers how wonderful they were and how honored we were by their gracious hospitality. Knowing that, for all their pomp and finery, all three were probably bored half to death, I kept the oration short.

Physkon nodded and said, in a voice that reminded me of gas bubbling out of a swamp: "Thrice welcome, gentlemen! Our Divine Majesties rejoice in the safe arrival of the distinguished delegation from the illustrious city of Kyzikos. We welcome you with Our most gracious cordiality and trust that you will enjoy your sojourn in Our glorious capital. It will be Our pleasure to have further intercourse with you as circumstances permit. Our servants will make the arrangements. You have Our gracious leave to withdraw. Be in good health!"

We all bowed again and backed down the hall, as Tetephras had instructed us. As we reentered the vestibule, another group awaited admittance. These were Parthians: proud, fierce-looking men in short jackets and long, baggy trousers, with bulbous felt hats on their long, curled hair and great, sweeping mustaches, waxed so that they stood out like the horns of bulls.

Tetephras told us: "Tonight you shall dine in the visitors' dining hall. Entertainment will be furnished. Father Noptes will take you in charge at the eleventh hour." He dropped his voice. "You, Master Eudoxos, are requested to keep tomorrow evening open."

"Oh?"

"Aye. No slight to your delegation is meant, but His Majesty wishes your advice on a question of geography, for which the presence of the others would not be useful. There will be an intimate supper, so be ready."

* * *

That evening, Noptes collected us and brought us to our places in the visitors' dining hall. Then he excused himself, saying he had duties in the temple of Sarapis.

The couches were arranged in groups, one for each set of visitors. These included delegations from other Hellenic cities and, in addition, the Armenians, the Numidians, and the Parthians whom I had seen earlier in the day. As head of my delegation, I felt it my duty to make the rounds of the other groups, introducing myself and passing a few words with each. The head of the Numidians, a tall, hawk-nosed man named Varsako, asked me in stumbling Greek:

"Master Eudoxos, pray—ah—please tell me: how can I get—get copy of play by great Greek playwrights? You know, Aischylos and—ah—Sopho—Sophokles? Our King Mikipsa, he say there should be more culture in Numidia, so he ask me get manuscripts. How to do?"

"Do you know where the Library is?"

"Nay. I have never been in city big like Alexandria."

"Well, I have never seen the Library, either; but I don't think it's far from here. Any Alexandrine can direct you. When you get there, apply to the Chief Librarian for the services of a copyist. Since it's a request from a king, he ought to assign you one without cost."

"Who is Chief Librarian?"

"One Kydas, I believe."

The next set of couches I stopped at were those of the Parthians. To my surprise, the chief Parthian greeted me in excellent Greek. After we had passed the amenities, he said:

"I heard your advice to the Numidian, Master Eudoxos. Do not tell him to apply to Kydas."

"Why not?"

"Because Kydas is a mere retired soldier, to whom Phys—ah—to whom His Divine Majesty gave the job as a sinecure. He knows nought and cares less about literature, and a request left with him will be simply forgotten."

"What, then?"

"Bid him apply to the Assistant Librarian, Ammonios. Then he'll get some action. Our king, who is also a tiger in the pursuit of culture, commanded me to get him some manuscripts on my last mission hither. So I know."

On my way back to my couch, I passed the word to Varsako, who was effusive in his gratitude. After the repast, our red-haired friend Hippalos brought in an orchestra and signed them to strike up a tune. He clapped his hands, and in came a squad of girls, who hung garlands of rare red and blue lotus flowers around our necks and went into their dance. As the wine was passed, Hippalos came in and sat on the end of my couch.

"You certainly have those girls well drilled," I said.

"I learnt the trick when I was a drillmaster in the army of Antiochos Grypos of Syria," he said with his satyrlike grin. "If you want one of those girls for the night, old boy, I can arrange it." When I hesitated, he dropped his voice and added: "Or, if you prefer boys, I can arrange that, too."

"Thanks, but I'm under a vow of chastity for the nonce." Naturally I was not going to admit my real reason for refusing.

"By the two goddesses, how utterly beastly!" said Hippalos. "But look, dear Eudoxos, I'm serious about this African venture. I know something about you and your shipping firm. By Hera, with your money and my wit, we could garner immortal fame—"

"My good Hippalos, you have a fine job right here. Why are you so eager to go galloping off on a hunt for gryphon's eggs? You'd probably only get yourself speared and eaten by the natives, or swallowed by one of those league-long serpents they tell about. What's the matter with your present situation?"

He smiled a sly, crooked smile. "You had a good look at my divine employer today, didn't you?"

"Yes."

"How long would you guess that she'll continue to shed her radiance on this earthly plane?"

I shrugged. "It's dangerous to guess about such things where you might be overheard. But I get your point."

"And, when the kingdom changes hands, many that were at the top of the ladder before find themselves at the bottom. A wise man foresees these things and makes preparations. But I'll talk some more to you about it. Now I must tend to my girls."

Hippalos turned back to his dancers, beating time with his hand and exclaiming:

"Come on, Lyka, you're slow on your turns! Get in step! *Ryp*-pa-pa-pai! *Ryp*-pa-pa-pai! That's better!"

The girls finished their dance, and a male singer took their place. Then more girls, then a snake charmer, more girls, a team of tumblers, and more girls. As the evening passed, the dancing became wilder and the girls, nakeder. I sighed for my youth, when to witness such a show would have made it embarrassing for me to stand up afterwards. Now my lance lay as limp as a dead eel. I saw Hippalos whisper in the ear of the Numidian, Varsako, who showed white teeth against his brown skin in a grin of eager interest. Not all the girls would be lonesome that night.

Book II

AGATHARCHIDES THE KNIDAN

Making preparations for the Persephoneia kept me busy all next day. At the appointed time, Father Noptes led me to the chamber that the king used for intimate suppers. A pair of guards at the door searched me for weapons. The chamber was larger than any commoner's dining room, although smaller than the visitors' banquet hall.

Present were Hippalos, representing the Sister; Colonel Ananias, representing the Wife; the gray-bearded Agatharchides of Knidos, tutor to the young Ptolemies; Kydas the Librarian, and his assistant Ammonios. Kydas was big, fat, and white-bearded; Ammonios, a small, slender, swarthy, clean-shaven man. There were also an admiral, a man from the Treasury, and Physkon's First Secretary.

As we stood around making talk, eating snacks of salt fish and sipping a light, dry wine, the king waddled in with a golden wreath on his egg-bald pate. A pair of slaves steadied him by the elbows. After him came ten Celtic mercenaries with long hair in various shades of yellow, red, and brown, to guard his precious person.

Physkon greeted us affably, flipping his hand and naming each guest. His servants lowered him, groaning, into a huge armchair; for, as he said: "With my bulk I find it too hard to eat from a couch. You will, my good Eudoxos, excuse the barbarism. Let me see—you are a shipowner, are you not? Then head of Theon's Sons of Kyzikos?"

"In name, O King," I replied. "I have lately left the routine of the firm to my brothers and my brother-in-law and my cousin. I travel to scout for new business and to gather material for my books."

"Do you find it difficult to write while being interrupted on business matters?"

"Extremely so, sire. That is why I have retired from active direction of the company."

"It is the same with me, Master Eudoxos. You know, I have published one book—a miscellany of observations on natural history—and should like to complete another before joining the majority. But whenever I try to devote a morning or an afternoon to my writing—*phy!* that is just the time some embassy arrives from the Romans or the Syrians or the Parthians with urgent business, or word comes of a frontier clash with the Ethiopians or the Judaeans, or one of the queens wants her allowance raised so she can buy a solid gold lamp stand. Away go the thoughts I had meant to commit to papyrus, and it takes me a ten-day to gather them again. Happy the man with a literary bent and no worldly business to distract him from it, like those featherless parrots in the Library! And now, tell me about your work in progress."

The king continued his probing questions throughout a repast of veal braised in a fish-and-raisin sauce, with onions and the disk-shaped loaves of Egyptian bread. A slave sampled each dish before the king partook of it. Physkon's comments showed him a very shrewd, intelligent man. I will not say that I liked him; his physical repulsiveness and the memory of his frightful crimes forbade. Nevertheless, I found myself making excuses for him. I told myself that the murder of one's kin was a matter of course in royal families. Besides, Physkon's crimes had been committed long ago, in his youth. For the last twenty or thirty years, his conduct had been no worse than that of most kings.

Afterwards, I decided that I had been so flattered by his attention that I had given him more credit than he deserved. His questioning meant, not that he found me especially wise or charming, but that I was the only man present whom he did not already know. Therefore, I was the one most likely to have something new and interesting to say.

Whatever Physkon's physical shortcomings, there was nothing wrong with his appetite. He ate twice as much as I did, and in those days I was deemed a hearty eater. Such, however, was his corpulence that his monstrous torso got in the way of his pudgy arms, and his servitors were kept busy wiping spilt food off the front of his robe.

* * *

When the food had been taken away and the servants had washed our hands, Physkon wheezed: "Gentlemen, I have called you here to discuss the plans for exploration that have been urged upon My Majesty, and if possible to choose amongst the alternatives." He snapped his fingers and said to a hovering flunkey: "Fetch Rama, will you?"

Then he turned to me. "This," he said, "is an Indian mariner whom my men rescued from shipwreck some months ago. His ship had lost its sail in a storm and drifted to the Ethiopian side of the Strait of Dernê, at the entrance to the Red Sea. Rama was the only survivor. My people brought him hither, and I have had men teaching him Greek, so that we could converse without an interpreter."

Physkon glowered at the two librarians, Kydas and his assistant. "You two keep wailing that you need more money for your polluted Library. Yet, when I ask a simple thing—for somebody who can teach Greek to an Indian—you're of no help at all. Your kept pedants can split hairs over the name of Achilles' dog, but none of them knows anything useful, like a foreign language. I had to dig an old Arabian sailor out of a waterfront grogshop. ... But here he comes."

The flunkey led in the Indian—a man of medium height and sturdy build, almost as black as an Ethiop. He wore a short-sleeved jacket and a long skirt pulled up between his legs in back and tucked in at the waist. His long, black hair was tied in a bun at the nape of his neck, and on his head a long scarf was wound round and round and tied in a huge bow knot. He had a square face with a sharp, hooked nose; like most modern Hellenes, he was clean-shaven. His lips twitched in a nervous little smile, while the expression in his eyes remained somber and sad. Arriving before the king, he placed his palms together before his breast, as if praying, and bowed over them, first to the king and then to each of the other guests in turn.

The king snapped a finger. "Fetch a cushion for the gentleman." To the Indian he said: "Now, my good Rama, tell these men your proposal."

Rama sat cross-legged on the floor on his cushion and spoke bad Greek in a strange and disagreeable accent: a staccato, nasal monotone. He said:

"My lords, I—I from city of Barygaza come. In dry time—what you call winter—we are sailing from Barygaza to ports in—how you say—Arabia. Wind all time that way blow. In summer, she blow other way and take us back home. Sometimes big storm is coming. He to other place blow us. That to me happen. All my shipmates die. Thanks to Lord Buddha, I live.

"Now, I like to go home. You like to sail to India from Strait of Dernê, all in one sail, not stopping in Arab ports. Arabs are taking your goods, are taking your money, are leaving you no profit. If you straight to India sail, you are not needing to pay money to Arabs. You can to India sail in summer with six-month wind and sail back in winter. You much profit are making. You are sending ship; I be your pilot. Everybody happy is."

The admiral spoke: "O Rama, if your people know about this direct passage from India to the Red Sea, why have they not put it to use?"

"Indian ships small are. Indians not great sailors are, except me. Little ships are good only for fishing or for sailing to Arab ports. You are having big ships; you can from Egypt to India sail without stop."

Agatharchides the tutor was unrolling a map of the world on the floor. The king nodded to Hippalos, who began:

"Now, I think we ought, instead, to mount an expedition to the sources of the Nile—"

Colonel Ananias broke in: "Yes, yes, we know, my dear Hippalos. So, what will you find, but desert land swarming with wild beasts and wilder men? There is no wealth in that country save ivory and slaves, and those we can let the king of Ethiopia gather for us. I say we ought to open up a direct route to India, and so does my royal mistress. For gems, the folk of the Inner Sea will pay well, and the kingdom can turn a pretty profit on the Indian gems that pass through it."

"Your divine mistress," growled the king, "is mad about jewelry; it must be the Judaean influence. She hopes to find an unlimited source of gewgaws and somehow get the monopoly of them away from me.

She should have been a Tyrian gem dealer. But I am not letting go of my exclusive rights to these goods for anybody. Go on, O Hippalos."

"Well—ah—there are several reasons for undertaking this expedition. As you have told us, sire, we must look to the south and southeast for expansion. In all other directions we are blocked by the might of Rome or of Parthia. Once we open up the lands to the south by exploration, trade, and road-building, the kingdom of Ethiopia will fall into our hands like a ripe fruit—"

"If you had ever fought Ethiopians, you would not so glibly compare them to ripe fruit," said Ananias.

High Priest Noptes seized the occasion to speak: "O King, the ancient records of the Egyptian priesthoods tell us that the Nile flows from the outer Ocean that encircles the world. Some modern geographers, thinking themselves wiser than their forebears—" (he looked hard at Agatharchides) "—deny this plain fact. If you will send Master Hippalos up the Nile, you will not only prove the wisdom of the Egyptian priests; you will also discover an alternative route to India. If a ship can sail from the Strait of Dernê to India, then it can also sail thither from the outlet, where the Ocean flows into the Nile."

"Rubbish!" exclaimed Agatharchides. "If the Nile flowed from the Ocean—as we Hellenes believed in the days of Homer—then the Nile, the Ocean, and the Inner Sea would all be interconnected. Now, Archimedes of Syracuse has demonstrated that, since water always flows downhill, the levels of any number of interconnected bodies of water, at rest, are identical. Therefore, the Nile could not flow from the Ocean to the Inner Sea, because it would exhibit the same level at both terminals and would hence remain stagnant."

"Water flows downhill only?" said Physkon. "How about when it is forced upwards through a pipe, as in the aqueduct system at Pergamon?"

"I should have said, water that has an upper surface open to the atmosphere, sire," said Agatharchides, flushing.

Ammonios, the Assistant Librarian, put up a timid hand. When the king gave him the nod, he said: "O King: there is a story that the Nile rises from a fountain somewhere in Ethiopia and flows thence in two directions: north to us and south to the Ocean." Bending over the map, whose corners were held down by slaves to keep it from

rolling up again, he illustrated his points with his forefinger. "If tru[e]
that would reconcile the ideas of the Reverend Noptes and Master Agatharchides."

Physkon: "Well, Agatharchides, which course do you advise?"

"Oh, sire, I favor the Nile expedition—if only to discredit the pretensions of our friend Noptes to the wisdom of his ancient priesthoods. It is time the enigma of the source of the Nile were settled. Such a journey would also prove my theory, that the annual rise of the Nile is occasioned by seasonal rains on mountains in the far interior of Africa. I am not much concerned whether the wretched river flows *from* the Ocean, or *to* the Ocean, or has nought to do with the Ocean. I only desire to ascertain the true circumstance."

"It's all very well for you," said the king, "to talk of sending expeditions hither and yon to settle your intellectual puzzles. But by Kyrenê's twelve postures, expeditions cost money, which I must furnish, forsooth! What tangible profit can you offer, to pay the cost of this project?"

The Nile party exchanged looks until Hippalos said: "As a matter of fact, O King, we have found some possible gains. Show him the scroll, Kydas."

Ammonios produced a battered roll of papyrus, which he handed to Kydas. The latter partly unrolled it and held it up, grunting: "You tell him, lad. I can't remember all these ancients' names."

"We have here," said Ammonios, "a part of the *Aithiopika* of Myron of Miletos, a work that we thought to have perished—"

"Who was he?" asked the king.

"An Ionian philosopher who served as tutor at the court of Xerxes, about three and a half centuries ago. King Xerxes sent Myron and a Bactrian cavalry officer named Bessas on a mission up the Nile. Unfortunately, the ends of the scroll are missing, so we do not know what the mission was, or even whether they reached their goal. I came upon this a few days past, when Hippalos and I were looking through the battered old books to decide which were worth recopying."

"What does he know about such things?" said Physkon.

Hippalos: "Oh, I was the buyer for the Library of Pergamon before the Romans took it over."

"So?" said the king.

pointed to the map. "Myron tells how, in passing ia, he discovered that the Nile flows from some great seas, flanked by snow-covered mountains. And he beside one of these lakes, built by the exiled Ethio-ta. In this castle, the story goes, was a vast treasure in gold and jewels."

"Did they find this treasure?"

"We don't know. The manuscript breaks off where the party leaves Tenupsis, the capital of the southern Nubae, and begins its struggle through the great swamps of that region."

"Perhaps," said Agatharchides, "the Nile flows hither out of these lakes, and another river flows out of them in the opposite direction until it encounters the Ocean. That would explain the belief of Noptes' old priests. I would give a lot to find out."

"Do you think the treasure might still be there?" said the king.

"It's a possibility, sire," said Hippalos.

"Then why did you not tell me of this manuscript before?"

"Why—ah—I wasn't sure what we had found at first, and I didn't want to raise Your Divine Majesty's hopes and then dash them."

"Ha!" said Physkon, wagging a fat forefinger. "I know better, my good Hippalos. You hoped I should authorize this expedition without your having said aught about the treasure, which you then hoped to find and keep to yourself, unbeknownst to me. Naughty, naughty!"

"Oh, no, sire! By Zeus on Olympos, no such disloyal thought—"

"Spare me your excuses, young man. I long ago learnt that men are a wicked, sinful lot, and that he who entreats them on any other assumption is only storing up trouble for himself." He turned to Kydas and Ammonios. "Well, what do my learned librarians advise?"

"We favor the Nile route," said Kydas. "If the expedition succeed, even to a small degree, it will prove the practical value of your Library and persuade you to devote more of the kingdom's resources to maintaining and enlarging it."

"Including, of course, higher salaries for you two," snorted Physkon, who then asked the remaining guests what they thought. The admiral favored the direct Indian voyage, because he thought it would be useful to establish a permanent Egyptian naval presence on the Indian coast. The man from the Treasury agreed, on the ground that it would be cheaper to refit a transport of the Red Sea fleet for the voyage than to outfit a land expedition through Ethiopia, with all its pack animals, soldiers, and equipment. The First Secretary also preferred the Indian voyage, because the Nile journey would involve diplomatic complications with Ethiopia.

"King Nakrinsan died within the year," he said, "and they have a new king, Tangidamani. We have not yet sounded out his attitude towards us. If we begin by demanding to send a well-armed party through his kingdom, he will at once suspect a threat. We must approach him gradually and cautiously."

"Well!" said the king. "Four of you have spoken for the Nile; four—not counting Master Rama—for the Strait of Dernê." He turned to me. "Now, my dear Eudoxos, you have heard the arguments both ways. As an unprejudiced outsider and a learned geographer, you can give objective advice. Will you speak?"

Poor Physkon did not know that I, too, had a personal interest to serve. As soon as Rama came in, I recalled the words of Glaukos, the old Kyzikene physician, about the possibility of an Indian cure for my masculine weakness. Then I knew that I had to get to India by fair means or foul. I at once began to muster arguments for the Indian voyage. At this I was so successful that, by the time the king asked my opinion, I had convinced myself that the Indian voyage was the only logical course to follow. [O Theon: For obvious reasons, the foregoing paragraph had better come out. Father.]

"There is much to be said on both sides," I began. "I, too, should like to solve the riddle of the source of the Nile. I must, however, point out that, for adding to human knowledge, India promises more than Africa. India is a vast country, as yet but little known. There are rumors of wonders like dog-headed men and mouthless folk who subsist by smelling the perfume of flowers. Doubtless many of these tales are false, but we shall never know for certain until we send trustworthy people thither to find out.

"Commercially speaking, India is a better choice than Africa. India has a large population of comparatively civilized folk, with great cities and skillful manufactures—"

Hippalos broke in, saying to Rama: "How about it, O Rama? Is it true that in India the roof tiles are of gold and the streets are paved with pearls?"

"You crazy are?" replied Rama. "This place here much richer than India is."

"You see, sire?" said Hippalos to the king. "These tales of the fabulous wealth of India are vastly exaggerated."

"Let Master Eudoxos continue without interruption, pray," growled the king. I resumed:

"Even if it be exaggerated, as Master Hippalos says, there is still far more profit in trade with such folk than with a thinly scattered race of bare-arsed savages, such as dwell in Africa beyond Ethiopia. And, they say, beyond India lies the unknown land whence comes our silk. For aught we know, the silk country may be as large and as populous as India; but no Hellene has been there to see.

"As regards the source of the Nile—since we know that the direct route is difficult, what of a suspicious Ethiopian king and boundless swamps—it were perhaps better to approach the region indirectly."

"How do you mean?" asked the king.

"How far have Your Majesty's ships pursued the African coast beyond the Southern Horn?"[4]

"A few leagues[5] only. They have a six-month, seasonal wind there, like that which Master Rama describes. That is why I am inclined to believe him. But around the Southern Horn, the wind blows north and south instead of northeast and southwest. My captains fear being trapped by the wind from the north, against which they would be unable to beat back around the Horn for months at a time. It is a barren coast, they tell me, inhabited only by a few naked black fisher-folk, without harbors or even roadsteads where one can be sure of food and water."

"Well, with these periodical winds, your men could sail down the coast at the end of the north wind and back on the beginning of the south one. If they explored the rivers that empty there, they might find the one that rises from the same source as the Nile. In the mean-

4 Cape Guardafui.

5 One league (*parasangê*) = 3.5 miles.

time, your trade with India by the direct route would pay for any number of expeditions elsewhere.

"As for the Nile journey," I continued, "I don't deny that it has points in its favor. I do not believe, however, that Your Majesty should count on paying for it by means of any treasure trove. Perhaps the tale was true—but more likely not; you know how people exaggerate. Even if it were, Myron of Miletos may well have won through to the treasure, in which case it is no longer there. Even if he failed, the existence of the hoard was known. So, during the last three centuries, somebody else may have made off with it. And even in the extremely unlikely case of the treasure's being still in place, do you think King Tang-what's-his-name would let us bring it back through his kingdom without grabbing it? No, sire, I should not count on finding any such gryphon's eggs at the end of our quest."

Physkon yawned. "Our Majesty thanks you, Master Eudoxos. I think that concludes tonight's discussion. I shall ponder the matter and make my will known in a few days. Good health, all!"

Physkon's servants heaved him up out of his chair and steadied his tottering steps out the door.

* * *

Next morning, Hippalos took the whole Kyzikene delegation in wagons to the Canopic Gate at the eastern end of the city. We passed through the barracks of the mercenaries and through the Judaean Quarter. The purpose of this journey was to prepare us for the next day's events. Besides the religious ceremonies and the athletic contests, the king meant to stage one of those monster parades whereby the Ptolemies and the Seleucids amuse and appease their subjects. We were to march in this procession. Several other delegations and groups were there also, as well as contingents from the three Ptolemaic armies and several elephants from the royal menagerie.

Hippalos was in the thick of things, giving orders right and left and answering the frantic questions of scores of paraders. He handled everything smoothly, joking with his questioners when they became upset at delays and contradictory instructions and what they considered dishonorable places in the procession. When it was all over and we were rumbling back to the palaces, I told him:

"I must say, you seem to have a knack for this sort of thing."

He laughed. "I learnt the trick when I was Superintendent of Festivals for King Nakrinsan of Ethiopia."

"Were those five elephants I saw all the king has? Doesn't he have a regular elephant corps in his army?"

"No, that's all. After the fourth Ptolemy won the battle of Raphia, the elephant-catching organization in the Red Sea was allowed to run down. Now we capture only one every five or ten years, to keep a few for parades."

"I wonder that the kings should let so fell a weapon rust from lack of care."

"There are two reasons," said Hippalos. "One is that the weapon isn't really so formidable. Northern barbarians like Celts and Scythians flee from the beasts, but we are not menaced by any such people. And civilized troops quickly learn to rout the elephants with noise, fire, and missiles. In the last century, the elephants have lost more battles than they won, by stampeding back through the troops of their own side."

"And the other reason?"

"As soon as we began to assemble an elephant corps, the Romans would be down upon us with demands that we slaughter the poor beasts, as they did in Syria. Nowadays we all dance to Rome's piping, and those heroes become frantic with fear when any other power has more than a feeble military force. So why beg for trouble for the sake of a nearly worthless weapon? I learnt the limitations of the beasts when I was elephantarch for King Mikipsa of Numidia."

* * *

After lunch and a nap, I ran into Agatharchides, sitting in the shade in one of the palace courtyards and making notes with a stylus on a waxen tablet.

"Rejoice!" I said. "Have you no royal pupils this afternoon?"

"No, they are all rehearsing for tomorrow's march past."

"You know, Master Agatharchides, I have never seen your famous Library. If you would care to show me …"

He shut his tablet with a snap. "Delighted, old boy, delighted. Wait whilst I get my stick. Alexandria has its allotment of savage dogs and tough characters."

"I'll get mine, too, and meet you here."

I fetched my stick—no dainty little cane, good only for punishing puppy dogs, but a solid, four-foot oaken cudgel—and gave Gnouros the afternoon off. A few moments later, we were walking south on Argeus Avenue on our way to the Library, which lay about ten furlongs southwest of the palaces. I asked the tutor:

"Has His Divine Majesty decided between the two proposals?"

"I saw him this morning, but he did not say. I suspect he has; but then, Physkon never tells one anything unless he has a reason for doing so."

"Which do you think he has chosen?"

"I suspect yours, from the tenor of his questions. He sought my advice on the organization of the party, and he seemed anxious that the commander have maritime experience. He even asked me if I should like to head the expedition."

"What did you tell him?"

Agatharchides: "I respectfully declined the offer. I'm a bit elderly—in my sixties—for anything so strenuous."

"I'm not much younger than you, but I feel I could command such a journey."

"You're a powerful man who doesn't look his age, but I know my physical limitations."

"Whom did you recommend for captain?"

"I told the king that Ananias the Judaean was the ablest of his commanders with whom I was personally acquainted, despite his lack of marine experience. Physkon was not prepossessed by the idea, since Ananias' first loyalty is to Kleopatra the Wife. Besides, he would probably not wish to go, because he suffers excruciatingly from seasickness."

"How about his brother? I thought he would be at the supper last night."

Agatharchides grinned slyly. "The same; and, anyway, I fear that Chelkias' royal mistress has too much use for him to let him out of her sight. He and she are like *that*—" (he held up two fingers pressed together) "—and also like *that*." (He rotated his hand until the two fingers were horizontal.) "Everybody is aware of it, including the king; but we don't mention it in the presence of Physkon, unless we are impatient to learn gold mining from the inside."

"I wonder that General Chelkias isn't breaking rocks in Nubia."

"Oh, Physkon doesn't mind; it keeps the Wife out of his way. He's beyond such interests, anyhow. So long as nobody brings the matter into the open, he prefers to turn a blind eye. There are other able royal servants; but most are adherents of one queen or the other, so Physkon doesn't trust them. His own entourage consists mostly of Egyptians, and your modern Egyptian is a peace-loving, stay-at-home sort of faintheart, no man for a daring expedition. And his naval captains, he feels, are too routine-minded."

"Whom, then, will he choose?"

"I don't know, but it wouldn't astonish me to see Hippalos get it."

"That entertainer?"

"Yes. He's a versatile individual, who has managed to keep in the good graces of Physkon and the Wife, despite being one of the Sister's faction."

"Has Hippalos really been all the places and done all the things he claims?"

"What he tells you is at least half true, I should say. As a mere boy, he escaped from the Romans' destruction of Corinth and has been living by his wits ever since."

At last we reached the Library section. This was a huge complex of buildings, not so large as the mass of palaces at the base of Point Lochias but still covering more than a city block. Actually, there were two groups of buildings. One was the Library proper; the other was the Museum, which housed the classrooms and laboratories of the professors of the various sciences. As we arrived first at the Museum, Agatharchides took me through it.

Despite the royal parsimony of which the scientists complained, some remarkable pieces of research were in progress. For instance, one man was working on a geared device—a kind of box, two feet high, with dials on its faces and a knob to one side. When one turned the knob (according to the proud engineer) the dials would go round and show the positions of the heavenly bodies on any chosen date.

There were models of catapults and other siege engines. There were elaborate water clocks and devices for measuring the angles of the stars. There were pumps for fighting fires and irrigating fields. Some engineers were trying to get power from flowing water; others, from rushing wind; still others, from heated air or boiling water.

Agatharchides introduced me until I could no longer remember names. Then we passed on to the section devoted to the life sciences. When I met Kallimachos, the head of the medical school, I jokingly asked:

"Well, when are you fellows going to find a cure for age?"

Kallimachos smiled. "That's a long way off, Master Eudoxos. Talk to some half-literate country doctor, and he'll assure you he knows the cause and cure of all your ills. Talk to one of us, who are really trying to push back the bounds of knowledge, and you'll hear a different tale. What we know about the human body is but a drop in an amphora compared to what we have yet to learn."

We commiserated with Kallimachos and crossed the street to the Library, where book rolls were stacked in their pigeonholes to the ceiling and the endless rows of bookcases receded far into the distance. We found Ammonios at work at a desk surrounded by a railing.

"Rejoice!" said Agatharchides. "How goes the world's intellectual ganglion today?"

Ammonios clutched at his head. "Do you know what that idiot wants to do now?"

"What?"

"He has some imbecile scheme for reclassifying the books alphabetically by the names of the authors' native cities: Athenians, then Babylonians, and so on."

"Many good-byes to him!" exclaimed Agatharchides.

"Who's the idiot?" I asked.

Agatharchides whispered in my ear: "His superior, the brave General Kydas. Kydas has two assistants: Ammonios to run the Library, and the Priest of the Muses to head the Museum. Being barely literate, he usually leaves them alone; but every now and then he thinks it incumbent upon him to earn his remuneration and issues some well-meant but witless instruction. Once he decided that the Library ought to dispense with everything composed before the time of Alexander the Great, on the hypothesis that it was obsolete. We talked him out of that; then he proposed that all books should be halved in length by deleting and discarding alternate sheets, so they shouldn't occupy so much space. Then—what was that other scheme, Ammonios?"

"He proposed that everything in the Library be rewritten in simple language, with all the long words and hard concepts left out," said Ammonios bitterly. "Making culture available to the masses, he called it. The originals were to be sold or burnt. And now this."

"Cheer up," said Agatharchides, clapping Ammonios on the back. "We'll circumvent him yet. I have brought Master Eudoxos for his first visit to the Library."

Cordially, Ammonios took us in tow. He showed us the principal sights of the Library, such as the original, autograph copies of the plays of Aischylos, Sophokles, and Euripides. The third Ptolemy had tricked the Athenians out of these manuscripts by borrowing them, promising to return them and posting a bond of fifteen talents. Then he kept them, sent back copies, and cheerfully forfeited the bond. [O Theon: Let this teach you never to trust a king! Father.]

A clerk came up to Ammonios, saying: "Sir, we have two noisy readers."

"Well, hush them up," said Ammonios.

"One—one is a fierce-looking barbarian, and I dare not."

Ammonios snorted and followed the clerk to a distant alcove, whither we accompanied him. We found Varsako the Numidian arguing over a map with a young man who, I learnt, was Artemidoros of Ephesos. This Artemidoros was making his first visit to Alexandria and cherished ambitions to become a geographer. When he learnt who I was, he practically fawned on me. He and the Numidian were disputing over the shape of Africa. Although Varsako did look a bit wild in his catskin turban and golden bangles, he quieted down peaceably enough when Ammonios spoke to him.

"Let me see that," said Agatharchides, bending over the map.

"The Numidian gentleman," explained Artemidoros, "claims that Africa extends much farther south than this map shows. I say that's impossible, because ..."

The three were off on a hot dispute, hissing arguments in an undertone. The Hellenes relied on quotations from Homer, Hekataios, and other ancient worthies, whilst the Numidian stubbornly insisted that the nomadic tribes south of his land told of vast plains and forests beyond the desert, which could never be fitted into the map. I had done enough actual exploring to distrust the ancients; but I had something else in mind than getting involved in this war of words.

"If you will excuse me for a while," I said, and walked Ammonios back to his desk. On the way, he showed me some of the oddities of the Library: a man composing a treatise on the use of the vocative case in Homer; a man who believed that the world was a hollow sphere with us on the inside; a man who was writing an epic on the fall of Carthage without using the letter *omega*; and a man who thought the world was about to end, when certain planets came into conjunction, and who wanted to do all the reading possible before that distressing event.

* * *

I hastened back to the Museum and found Kallimachos the physician. He was lecturing on the human skull, so I had to wait. When he had dismissed his class and put his skull away, I said:

"O Kallimachos, might I talk to you in strict privacy?"

"Dear me, what's up?" he said. "Let me see ..." We wandered about the building, but every room we passed was occupied. At last we came to a locked room, and Kallimachos took a quick look up and down the hall. Seeing nobody, he produced a key and unlocked the door.

"In, quickly!" he whispered. "I'm not supposed to show you this; but it's the only place available."

Inside the large room were models and drawings of cryptic devices and some of the devices themselves.

"Zeus, Apollon, and Demeter!" I said. "What's all this?"

Kallimachos explained the purposes of these strange machines; the temples of Alexandria used them to awe their worshipers. For instance, there was an arrangement of tilting and sliding mirrors to make spirits appear before the sitters at a séance. There was a magical pitcher that seemingly changed water into wine. I exclaimed:

"By Bakchos' balls, what shameless hypocrites the priests of those temples must be!"

"Why do you say that?"

"If they weren't atheists, they'd fear that the gods they pretend to worship would smite them for taking such liberties."

"Not at all, my dear fellow. Most are as pious as the next man. If the gods want worship and sacrifice, they ought to cooperate with their priests by doing a miracle now and then, to keep the flock faithful. When the gods shirk the job, the priests must need fake these miracles. Of course, a priest's idea of a god may differ from that of an ordinary worshiper."

"How?"

"Some of these priests, despite the nonsense they talk, are modern, educated men. Therefore they are skeptical about gods like Homer's, always getting drunk, seducing one another's wives, and clouting one another over the head like barbarian warriors. They conceive the gods as invisible, impersonal forces, whose nature can be grasped only dimly, if at all, by our fallible senses. Now, what did you wish to see me about?"

I told Kallimachos about my loss of virility, adding: "I thought that, if any new discoveries would shed light on this problem, this would be the place to inquire."

"I'm sorry to disappoint you, best one," said Kallimachos. "That is one of ten thousand things we ought to know about the human body but don't. *Ototototoi!* We are not making such progress in medicine here in Alexandria as once we did."

"Why? Lack of money for research?"

"It's partly that; but the main reason is the law against dissection."

"What's that?" I asked.

"Sixty or seventy years ago, when Herophilos and Erasistratos were cutting up corpses, they were really learning things. But the Egyptians insist that bodies should be embalmed and preserved forever. When they heard that the Museum was carving corpses for the base, blasphemous purpose of improving the health of mankind, they rioted until the then king forbade all dissection of human beings, alive or dead. And that law still stands."

"Couldn't you persuade the present king—"

"Not this king! He relies upon the superstitious Egyptians and will do anything to curry favor with them. That's one reason he has cut our appropriations down to a shadow of their former selves; the Egyptians have no use for the Library or the Museum, so he saves his gold and placates the natives at the same time." The old physiologist sighed. "Alas! The only things that people seem to care about in this degenerate age are weird new religious cults. About science, they know and care nothing and prefer not to learn. But to return to your flaccid member: Do you eat lots of snails, eggs, and sea food?"

"Yes."

"I suppose you have tried all the commercial aphrodisiacs?"

"Yes, and found them ineffective, save for irritating the bladder."

"As far as we are concerned, they are worthless; but we know of nothing better."

"I've heard that the wise men of India might know a cure."

He shrugged. "They might; they're said to do some remarkable things. The only way to find out would be to go to India."

* * *

Back at the Library, I rejoined Agatharchides, Artemidoros, and Varsako. We talked in hushed tones about questions of geography until Ammonios came to us, saying:

"I'm sorry, gentlemen, but it is closing time."

Sure enough, the sun had set. The light was dimming, and readers were streaming out of the Library. The four of us started towards Point Lochias, then decided to eat at a local tavern instead of returning to the palaces. As Agatharchides put it:

"It's pleasant to eat sometimes without the sensation that somebody is surreptitiously watching you from a secret passage."

We found a place that had enough food on hand to fill all of us, thus saving us a trip to a market to buy the materials. During the repast, Agatharchides bewailed the fact that he could not afford to publish several works he had written.

"I have composed a history of Europe, and a history of Asia," he said, "and a survey of the Red Sea. But Physkon has stopped all money for new publication."

"Could you ask him for the money as a personal favor, to show his appreciation of the splendid education you've given his sons?"

"I have, as often as I dared, to no avail. He seems to think that a scholar should subsist on barley porridge and beautiful thoughts."

After the meal, when the others were getting ready to leave, I said: "You two go on; I want to talk to Agatharchides in confidence. Where are you living, Artemidoros?"

"I have rented a room on the waterfront, near Cape Lochias. I'll show Varsako back to the palaces."

When they had gone, I ordered more wine and said to Agatharchides: "My friend, if the Physkon chooses the direct voyage to India—which you seem to think likely—I want the command of it."

Agatharchides gasped with surprise. "By Earth and the gods! You, an outsider, virtually unknown in Alexandria?"

"Yes, me. Think of my qualifications! I'm an old sea captain with plenty of experience, including the exploration of unknown coasts. I'm a competent geographer and not so unknown as all that; both Hippalos and Artemidoros know my work. Best of all, I don't belong to the faction of either of the Kleopatras."

"Ye-es; I see. Mmmm. Why do you desire this post, when you have a flourishing business back in Kyzikos?"

"I have my reasons. Say I lust for the explorer's immortal fame, if you like; or say that I've seen the entire Inner Sea and want to try something new. Say what you please, so long as you get me the job."

"Dear Herakles, man, what can *I* do about this?"

"Physkon may not appreciate your scientific labors, but he sets some store by your advice on personnel. The next chance you get, put my name forward."

"Well, I don't know—"

"I'm not asking something for nothing. You want to publish your books, don't you? Well, I may not have the wealth of a Ptolemy, but neither have I a court and a kingdom to maintain. Therefore, I can afford to subsidize your publication. Get me that captaincy, and publication is yours."

He took a long drink to cover his feelings, but I saw a hopeful gleam in his eye. Still, as a veteran of the Ptolemaic court, where there's a scorpion beneath every stone, he was going to scrutinize the bait before taking the hook.

"Will you return to Kyzikos with your delegation and then come back here?" he asked.

"No. These ceremonies will soon be over, and my colleagues can fend for themselves when they're back on board the *Persephonê.*"

"I shall have to consider this," he murmured. "For one thing, I ought to know more about you. If I advise Physkon, and he accepts my advice, and then things go badly, I shall be blamed."

"That's easy," said I, and began a tale of my adventures in the Inner and Euxine seas. If I slightly magnified the parts I played—well, I am sure I lied less than Hippalos had done to his many employers.

We finished our wine, paid up, and left. The streets were now fully dark, save for an occasional lantern or torch in front of some place of nocturnal amusement. Twenty years earlier, I should have made a night of it in these establishments, belike ending up with a free-for-all; but the years blunt one's taste for wine, women, and riot.

We found ourselves entering a block that was utterly dark, since it was the beginning of Thargelion and the night was moonless. We had to watch our step for potholes. I was telling Agatharchides how I had obtained Gnouros, a Scythian peasant about to be slain for some trivial fault by his nomadic overlords, when I heard a disturbance ahead.

"What's that?" said Agatharchides. "A robbery? My vision is no longer so keen at night."

As I came closer, I saw that several men had two others backed against a house wall. Shouting *"Help!"* the two victims were holding five attackers off with kicks and stabs.

"Let's run before they see us!" said Agatharchides.

"By Our Lady Persephonê, what sort of man are you?" I said, and charged the group.

A two-handed whack over the ear stretched one robber senseless, and a thrust in the stomach with the end of my stick sent another staggering off, bent double and clutching his middle. As a third thief turned towards me, one of the victims leaped upon his back, bore him to the ground, and twisted the rusty smallsword out of his hand.

Agatharchides came up, puffing. Seeing themselves outnumbered, the remaining miscreants fled.

"By the gods and spirits!" said the man who knelt on the robber's back. "Aren't you Eudoxos and Agatharchides?"

We had rescued Artemidoros and Varsako. It took us half the night to fetch the watch, drag our two prisoners to a magistrate, and answer endless questions. But then Physkon's justice worked fast. The magistrate heard our stories, asked the prisoners what they had to say, listened to their tales, and informed them that they were telling a pack of lies. He then sentenced them to life in the mines and ordered them taken to the torture room for questioning about their accomplices.

When we had been dismissed, Agatharchides said: "Well, this evening has taught me one thing. If ever I find myself in a tight predicament, I want Eudoxos of Kyzikos to come charging in to rescue me. If any representation of mine will effect it, you shall have the captaincy of the expedition!"

* * *

Since I had to march in the middle of the parade, I never did get a view of the whole thing. We formed up at the Canopic Gate, where thousands of paraders milled in confusion and Hippalos galloped about on a horse, straightening them out and sending them off, group by group. The procession was only two hours late in starting, which I suppose is pretty good for that sort of thing.

Xenokles and I marched at the head of our delegation, bearing poles between which hung a banner reading KYZIKOS. We trudged the whole length—thirty-five stadia—of Canopic Street, through the old Sun Gate and the main part of the city, breaking up at the Moon Gate at the west end of town. As soon as we had been dismissed, I hastened around the block to see those parts of the parade that were following us.

I was not sorry to miss the herds of Physkon's prize sheep and cattle, or the delegations from the other Hellenic cities. I did see the five elephants in their cloth-of-gold drapes and other animals from Physkon's menagerie: a two-horned African rhinoceros, a striped horse, several lions, leopards, and cheetahs, and antelopes of a dozen kinds.

There were also a number of freak objects carried in carts, which the Ptolemaic workshops had turned out to amuse the Alexandrines. These included a golden 135-foot Bacchic wand, a ninety-foot silver spear (made, I suspect, from a ship's mast), and a 180-foot golden phallus with a nine-foot golden star dangling from its end. The phallus, made of wicker work and covered with gilded cloth, enabled the reigning monarch to make a joke about having the biggest prick in the world. Needless to say, everybody went into gales of laughter on these occasions, although that joke had worn pretty thin from a century of repetition.

Back at the palace, I soaked my feet and relaxed over a jug of wine. Since my roommates on the delegation were out shopping for their womenfolk, I was alone when Hippalos came in, covered with sweat and dirt. I picked up an extra cup to fill it, then hesitated when he sat down opposite me, staring fixedly at me with a curious expression. He seemed to be smiling and scowling at the same time.

"Well?" I said at last, "what is it, man?"

"Furies take you, stinker!" he exclaimed at last.

"Oh?" said I, setting down my cup in case he wanted to make a fight of it. He had a twenty-year advantage of me, but I was still the larger of us and had been in enough rough-and-tumbles to think I could handle him. "What's on your mind?"

"The king took your advice on the expedition. It's going to India by Rama's route. And, by the gods and goddesses, *you* are to be captain instead of me. Oh, I could have buggered you with a hot iron when I heard it!"

"Herakles! I'm sorry you're disappointed, but we can't both win."

Then he broke into a broad grin, got up, and slapped me on the shoulder. "Don't look so solemn, old boy! I won't bite. Pour me a drink, as you were going to. True, I was as angry at first as a dog whose bone has been snatched. But then I thought: the stars probably intended things this way. Besides, I shan't miss the journey altogether; the king has appointed me your second."

"He *has*?"

"Yes, sir. You don't think he'd send an outsider like you off with a costly cargo, and nobody from the court to keep an eye on you, do you? So watch your step, old boy." He gazed dreamily off into space. "I have always wanted to study the wisdom of the mysterious East—not this Egyptian fakery, but the *real* East."

If he wanted to dabble in oriental superstition, that was his affair. I began at once to think of the practical aspects of the journey. "What goods do you think we ought to ship out, and what shall we try to stock for the return journey?"

"We shall have to ask Rama's advice. From what he's told me, I imagine glassware, textiles dyed with Tyrian purple, and wine are our best wagers. In addition, he says there's a ready market in India for copper, tin, lead, and antimony—and of course gold and silver coin, which fetch a jolly good rate of exchange."

"How about olive oil? Does the olive grow in India?"

"I don't know, but we might try it."

"And what goods should we try to buy there?"

"We must wait to see what they have to offer; but I think we can get some bargains in silk, cotton, ivory, spices, perfumes, and—ah—precious stones and pearls."

"Besides trading Physkon's cargo, can we do some dealing on our own account?"

"Zeus, no! At least, not if he finds out about it. He says we're just his hired men and shall therefore do no trading of our own. He guards his royal monopoly like a lioness defending her cubs."

"Pest! As usual, the potbellied backer who sits at home gets the loaf, while the fellow who does the work and takes the risk gets the crumbs. Isn't there any way around this silly rule?"

"There may be." He winked. "I'll discuss it with you anon, where there are no walls with ears in them."

Book III

RAMA THE INDIAN

In the games that Physkon staged, the Kyzikene team stood third in number of firsts, after Athens and Antioch. At last the Persephoneia was over, and I saw the delegates safely back aboard the *Persephonê*. I intrusted them with several letters, to my wife, my brothers, and other kinsmen, telling of my plans for the Indian voyage. When they had sailed, I settled down to the business of preparing myself, as thoroughly as I knew how, for this enterprise.

In my Scythian wanderings, I had found that books were practically useless for preparation, because they told so many untruths—for example, that Scythia had a mild, balmy climate. I shall never forget the shock I gave the family when I returned from Pantikapaion wearing a Scythian fur cap and trousers, having been forced to don these barbarous garments to keep my ears and balls from being frozen off. (I had been compelled to spend the winter there by a fall from a horse, which had cost me three broken ribs.)

Moreover, at my age I found it hard to focus my eyes on writing at less than arm's length. And I have always disliked being read aloud to; my mind wanders, and I miss half the message. (In Alexandria I was helped by Ammonios, who lent me a burning glass to read with. This glass was ground to such a perfect curve that, when one looked through it at a piece of writing, the letters appeared twice their true size. But most burning glasses are not so well made, and squinting through one of these things by the hour also tires the eye.)

In the case of India, however, I read the literature because there was so little other information to be had. Even Rama was not of much help. While he knew the ports of the Arabian coast, he had never been inland from his native Barygaza. As he explained:

"You see, Lord Eudoxos, Barygaza is city of reformed religion—religion of Buddha. You are knowing how peoples of India are split into—ah—how you say—colors?"

"You mean those classes, whose members are not allowed to marry or take jobs outside their class? Yes; I've been reading about it. There are seven classes, aren't there?"

"We call them colors. Five colors are: white for priests, red for warriors, yellow for merchants, black for workers."

"That's four."

"Fifth is no color—people who do not belong to any; mostly wild men hunting in woods. In reformed religion of Buddha, color not much matters; Buddha says: 'Any man is Brachman—that is, priest color—who is wise, patient, virtuous, pure, harmless, tolerant, truthful'—and so on—'no matter who his parents were.' But in old Brachman religion, color very important is. Among Brachmanes, a man who sails on sea loses color. Nobody will have to do with him, so he is starving. So we sailors are not visiting cities where Brachmanes rule. Always the Brachmanes are fighting followers of Buddha, and we might get killed."

Hence I read what Megasthenes and Onesikritos and Nearchos had to say about India, and I read about navigation on the African coast. I learnt that, according to Herodotos, a Phoenician fleet had sailed clear around Africa in the time of the Egyptian king Necho. Herodotos disbelieved the story, because the Punics asserted that, when they got to the southernmost parts of Africa, the sun stood to the north of them. But Agatharchides showed me by a diagram how the sun would, in fact, appear to the north at noon, south of the equator; and this claim, which made Herodotos doubt the tale, was really the best reason for accepting it. I suppose Herodotos did not know that the earth was round, because in his day this theory was just being broached.

I picked my boatswain with care, since Hippalos was not a professional ship's officer, and I had not captained a vessel for some years. I chose a burly, red-faced salt named Linos, with a bronzen hook in place of his right hand. He said he had lost the hand defending his ship against pirates. I suspected that he had been a pirate himself until his injury forced him into more lawful work.

* * *

What with one thing and another, we did not set sail in our refitted merchantman until the fourteenth of Hekatombaion,[6] at the start of the fourth year of the 165th Olympiad. The *Ourania* was the biggest ship in the Red Sea sailing fleet: a beamy 120-footer, like the grain or wine freighters of the Inner Sea. She was, in fact, too big for many of the shallow little coves that pass for harbors in the Red Sea; hence Physkon was easily persuaded to let me have her. She was old but sound. I had personally seen to her cleansing, scraping, caulking, and painting, and I had checked every bit of rope and sail that went aboard, at the cost of furious quarrels with Physkon's officials when they tried to palm off defective equipment on me.

It was a typical midsummer day at Myos Hormos, with a scorching sun glaring down from a steely sky, and the deck so hot that one had to wear sandals to keep one's feet from being burnt. The *Ourania* lay at the end of a rickety pier that thrust far out into the bay, the water near shore being too shallow for anything deeper than a raft. Anchored farther out were several black-hulled biremes and a few cargo carriers, similar to my ship but smaller, and a couple of little Arab coasters awaiting their turn to unload.

Nearer shore were tethered three elephant barges. A fourth, which had foundered from neglect—now that the Ptolemies no longer kept up a military elephant corps—was being broken up for salvage by a gang of local tribesmen, with black skins and hair in long, greasy braids. They splashed about, naked and yelling, in the shallows with mallets and crowbars, while a Greek foreman screamed orders at them.

In the other direction, a galley had been hauled out on rollers. A couple of workmen, supposed to be cleaning her bottom, slept in the shade of her hull. Further off, on the single shipway, carpenters languidly tapped at the hull of a new trireme.

Standing on the deck of the *Ourania*, I was checking the cargo of glass, wine, oil, copper ingots, and purple-dyed stuffs as the royal

6 Approx. July 5.

slaves, shuffling slowly along the pier, brought their loads aboard. They moved with all the liveliness of the pointer of a water clock, and even their overseer had not the energy to raise his lash to speed them up. Not trusting any slave to be careful enough, Hippalos and Linos personally carried aboard the gifts, wrapped in sacking, that we took for such kings as we might encounter. Rama the Indian, comfortable in his turban and skirt despite the heat, brought a cageful of small birds on board.

Beside me, little Gnouros held my inkwell and other writing gear. I had to enter the list of cargo on the papyrus manifest, awkward though this was, because the heat was such as to melt the wax right off a tablet. Although Gnouros kept his face blank as becomes a well-trained slave, I knew that, being subject to seasickness, he dreaded the voyage. He had already stowed my gear, including my sword and my Scythian bow, in the cabin, which formed part of the deckhouse aft.

When I had checked off the last amphora of Chian, I sought the shade of the freight shed and a big mug of Egyptian beer. Gnouros and I sat with our backs to the bulkhead, drinking thirstily to the snores of several sailors from Physkon's fleet, who lay in corners of the shed. I said:

"You don't like this voyage, do you?"

"I like whatever my master likes," he said. He had received a bad sunburn, and his shoulders, snub nose, and forehead were peeling. His little gray eyes peered at me from under his dirty mop of light-brown, gray-streaked hair.

"You don't fool me, boy. Look, you've been a good and faithful servant for—how long is it, now?"

"Nine years."

"Well, during that time you've obeyed every order, as far as you understood it; and you've hardly complained once. Not one slave in a hundred does his duty so well."

"Thank you, S-sir."

"Well, how would you like to be free? With the fare back to Scythia?"

He was silent for so long that I asked: "Did you understand what I said?"

"I understand all right, master. I am thinking." After another pause, he replied: "I like better to stay your slave."

"*What?*"

"*Arrê*, yes. What if I go back to Scythia? That knight who wanted to kill me would still kill me when he learn I come home."

"Perhaps he's dead or gone away."

"Maybe, maybe not. Somebody else has my land and my wife by now. She never liked me much, anyway. Used to say, I did not love her because I did not beat her. She a big strong woman, and I was afraid. So, is no way to make my living. I am farmer, not sailor or merchant or clerk."

"Suppose I gave you a farm near Kyzikos?"

A little lizard fell from the overhead, plop into Gnouros' beer. With a Scythian curse he picked the creature out and threw it away. Then he said:

"Thanks, but is no good. Farming different in each country: different weather, crops, soil. I only know Scythian farming. Too old and stupid to learn other kinds.

"Besides, I am not doing badly. I get plenty to eat, good clothes to wear, good place to sleep. You not work me very hard, not hit me, not call me names. With you I travel, see strange places. Peasants on Tanaïs River have much worse time. Starve in famines, freeze in winter. Say they are free men, but nomad lords are always robbing and beating and killing them, futtering their women, selling their children. I rather be slave of kind, softhearted master like you."

This was the longest speech I had ever heard Gnouros make. He caught my hand and kissed it with tears in his eyes.

"Well, grind me to sausage!" I said. "Me, the most ruthless, grasping, hard-bitten shipowner in the Inner Sea, kind and soft? Stop blubbering, or by Bakchos' balls, I'll beat you into a bloody mush!"

* * *

Hippalos and I rounded up the crew of Linos, nine deck hands, and the cook. We reported our departure to Physkon's officials and went aboard. I led the ship's company in prayers and sacrificed a chicken to the powers of the deep.

I also told them I had consulted a soothsayer, who assured me that the day was lucky and the planetary aspects favorable. I had not done any such thing; as far as I was concerned, all this mumbo-jumbo before sailing was a lot of nonsense. If the gods decided to kick up a storm—assuming that there were gods and that they caused storms—they were no more likely to notice some little bug of a ship crawling across the sea than you notice whether you step on an ant as you walk. But the sailors expected such mummery, and I thought it wise to humor them.

We warped ourselves out of the harbor with the ship's boat, hoisted the mainsail and artemon, and set off down this long, shallow, steamy sea called the Red. Myos Hormos, with its dust, flies, starving dogs, and snoozing sailors, shrank into the distance. May you never be stranded there!

For the first ten-day, we sailed along briskly enough with a fair north wind, stopping at Berenikê to top off our food and water. Then, however, the wind became fitful, veering and backing and betimes dropping away to a flat calm. We had to put out the dinghy on a tow line and struggle down this glassy, reef-bound sea by oar power. I wished that somebody had invented a sail by which one could sail, not merely at right angles to the wind, but actually against it more than a few degrees.

We stopped again at Adoulis, where a swarm of Ethiopians besieged us with offers to sell elephants' tusks, rhinoceros horns, and tortoise shells. Thenceforth we struggled against head winds until we got through the Strait of Dernê. The coast turned eastward along the Southern Horn, so that we had a beam wind.

We made another stop at Mosyllon, which—although it has nothing but an exposed anchorage off the beach—is still a lively trading center because of the spices and incense gums shipped thence. After loading up with all the fresh fruit and extra water we could find room for, we pointed our bow straight out into the unknown waters of the Arabian Sea, with the seasonal southwest wind filling our sails.

To show what perverse creatures men are, the sailors had behaved well during that first month, when they were sweating at the oars and struggling down the Red Sea through calms and adverse winds, in the hottest, stickiest weather I had ever seen. Now we were out on the ocean with a fair wind and plenty of fresh bread from the galley in the deckhouse. We had nought to do but stand watches, throw dice, and play "sacred way" and "robbers" on lines drawn with charcoal on the deck.

So the men got restless. The first sign of this was a fight between two of the older sailors over the affections of the youngest and prettiest of them. The boatswain knocked one fighter down, and I knocked over the other, so that for a while peace prevailed.

To pass the time, I had been getting Rama to teach me his language. The only foreign tongue in which I was fluent was Scythian. I offered to correct his barbarous Greek, in case he wished to try another voyage to Egypt. But he declined, saying that, once he got home again, an occasional voyage to Arabia would suffice him.

"Alexandria," he said, "is fine, big city. But I do not like place where everybody is hurrying all the time. Rush, rush, rush; no rest. You even have machines to measure time, those clip-clep—how you say?"

"Clepsydras?"

"Yes. Make me unhappy, just to look at them. If Lord Buddha help me back to India, I think I stay there, where people know how to live."

"O Rama," I said, "I've heard about the wisdom of Indian philosophers. Have you any such wise men in Barygaza?"

"I am thinking." Then he tipped his head from side to side, as Indians do when they mean "very well" or "as you wish." "There is one man of land we call *yogin*, who lives outside Barygaza. Name is Sisonaga. Why, you want to be his *chetaka*—how you say—"

"Pupil? Follower?"

"Yes, pupil. All right, you go see him. If he is not meditating, maybe he is taking you."

"And if he is meditating?"

"Then you wait for him to come out of trance. Wait maybe five, ten days. You say you want him to be your *guru—master*. He is giving you exercises and training for ten, twenty years. Then you can learn to live standing on your head for hundred years. He says he for hundred and fifty already has lived."

"Why in Hera's name should anyone wish to live standing on his head?"

Rama snickered. "How do I know? I am simple sailor man. If my ship does not run on rock or sink in storm, I am happy. No time to study wisdom of ancient sages."

At barren Dioskoridis Island, we stopped at the wretched Arab fishing village on the north coast. This is the isle's only settlement, the rest being given over to lizards, turtles, and crocodiles. Then we headed northeast once more.

When for a ten-day we had seen no sign of land, the sailors began to grumble. A delegation of three came to see me, saying:

"Captain, the boys have been talking, and we should like it mighty well if you'd turn back. The way we're going, we're sure to be swallowed by some sea monster or fall off the edge of the earth."

"The earth has no edge," I said. "It's round, like a ball."

"What a crazy notion—begging your pardon, sir! All the water would run off the bottom."

Not being too well up on the theory of gravity, I contented myself with saying: "Well, that's what all educated men believe, and you can see the curvature yourself as you sail away from land. Anyway, Rama is a wizard, and his spells will protect us. Besides, he has been over this track before and knows the way. So back to your posts."

All was quiet for a few days. Hippalos and I passed time by telling each other of our experiences in the Inner Sea. Although I suspected that many of his tales were fictions, I could not help enjoying them, for the Corinthian was a fascinating storyteller. One moonlit night he said:

"Eudoxos, old boy, I've known all along that you were going to India for some reason you won't tell. What is it?"

"Who, me?" said I, looking innocent—or as innocent as anyone with my scarred, weatherbeaten countenance can look. "I'm after fame and fortune, the same as you."

"Rubbish! I know better. You're already as rich and famous as any explorer has any right to be. And you've been asking about the wisdom of Indian philosophers. Are you after the secret of remembering your former incarnations, as some Pythagoreans claim they do?"

I should not have done it, of course; but I am not an especially taciturn man, and the monotony of a long, peaceful voyage can loosen one's tongue more than is prudent. I told Hippalos about my physical difficulties and my hopes of finding a cure in the East.

"*Oi!*" he said when I had finished. "So that's why you have not made the least pass towards that pretty young sailor laddie. Well, may the Genetyllides stiffen your yard. What you need is that woman I lived with when I was an actor in Syracuse. She could give an erection to a statue by Pheidias."

"Are you married, Hippalos?" I asked.

"Not really, although some of my girls' fathers seemed to think so and went hunting for me with hounds and boar spears when I moved on. If you form no ties, you'll have no regrets."

* * *

The days passed smoothly, and then the men began to grumble again. The sailors whispered in each other's ears, shooting wary glances at Linos and Hippalos and Rama and me. They obeyed orders, but grumbling under their breath.

After a ten-day of this, I called a council in the cabin. While we conversed, Hippalos and I cleaned and honed our swords—which we had taken out of their oiled wrappings—while Linos filed the point on his hook. I asked Rama:

"How long before we sight India?"

"Oh, we are seeing land very soon, very soon."

"How soon is very soon? How many days?"

"How many days since we left Dernê?"

"Let me see ..." I consulted the tablet on which I had been keeping a log. "Thirty-one."

"Then we soon are arriving; maybe one day, maybe ten. You wait; I find out."

"Are you going to work one of those spells I've told the men you do?"

Rama grinned and wagged his head, leaning it to right and left. "Maybe. You see." He left the cabin and went to the tent he had rigged on deck.

Presently he emerged from the tent, holding one of the little birds he had brought aboard. Then he went forward, uttering some sort of chant in his own language and making gestures with his free hand. The sailors gathered around, watching. After some more hocus-pocus, Rama cast the bird from him. It flew round and round the ship, climbing with each turn into the sky, which bore a thin, hazy overcast. At last it disappeared into the haze high overhead.

An hour later, the bird returned to the ship. It perched on the rigging for a while, then came down and landed close to Rama, who held out a handful of birdseed. It let him capture it and put it back in its cage. To the expectant sailors, he put on a solemn face and pointed ahead, saying:

"Land that way is."

"How far?" asked several at once.

"Little more than three days' sailing." To me explained, privately: "If bird see land, she is not coming back to ship. Bird can fly high enough to see land three days' sail away. Simple, yes?"

Three days later, he released another bird. Again it returned to the ship. The sailors began to grumble again. The tension on the ship grew by the hour. Linos muttered in my ear:

"I think those two—Apries and Nysos—are at the bottom of this. Shall I slug 'em and drop 'em over the side tonight, sir?"

"Not yet," I said. "We might need them in case of a storm or pirates. We'll kill them only as a last resort."

"Well, you're the captain," said Linos with a sigh.

Next morning, Hippalos stepped out of the cabin ahead of me. At once there was a yell and sounds of a scuffle. I grabbed my sword and rushed out.

At one rail, a knot of sailors held Hippalos by the arms and around the waist. A couple tried to grab Linos, but he knocked one to the deck with a back-handed blow of his hook, and the other shrank back from him.

"Stand back!" yelled the sailor Nysos, touching a knife to Hippalos' throat. Linos hesitated; so did I.

"Now," said Nysos, "we've had enough, sirs. The fruit is all rotten, the water's foul, and this ocean just goes on and on. So you'll please bring the ship about and take us back to Egypt. Otherwise, we'll kill your mate."

"How in Tartaros do you expect me to sail directly into the polluted wind?" I yelled. "This wind blows for half the year one way and half the year the other. The northeast wind doesn't begin for months!"

"You say that crazy Indian pilot is a wizard," replied Nysos. "Make him whistle up the northeast wind ahead of time!"

I looked for Rama, who was emerging from his tent with another bird in his fist. "Please, people!" he said. "Let me try my land-finding spell once more."

With everybody watching, he went through his ritual and tossed the bird away. The bird circled, rose, and disappeared. We watched and watched, but the bird did not come back.

"You see?" said Kama. "Land is less than three days' sail ahead. If wind hold and we are not reaching land in that time, you may cut off my head."

Under a thickening overcast, we plodded on towards the northeast, with big swells coming up astern and rolling past us. The sailors kept control of Hippalos, with three men holding him and a fourth with his knife ready.

Late in the day, a man went up the mast and shouted: "Land ho!"

The man came down, and I took his place. From the masthead, I could just make out a dark line on the horizon when the swells boosted us up.

"See what you make of it, Rama," I said.

Rama went up in his turn and came down with a sour expression. "Syrastrenê," he said, "northwest of Barygaza. He is all desert or water too shallow for ship."

"Isn't there a decent harbor?" I asked. "If we could get some fresh food and water, it would soften up my crew of temple thieves."

"Gulf of Eirinon is, but too shallow. No big city is; no good harbor. Must anchor half a league out from shore and row in with skiff. You are turning ship to starboard now, quick, before we run aground. Shoals stick out long way."

We swung a quarter-circle to starboard, furled the artemon, and braced the mainsail around to take the wind abeam. For the rest of the day we bobbed along, the roll making poor Gnouros seasick. The overcast thickened.

"Must feel for bottom and anchor," said Rama as darkness fell. "We cannot see stars and might run aground."

We found the water a mere three fathoms deep and put down two anchors. With dawn came a drizzle. By keeping the wind on our starboard beam and the low line of land to our port, we cut a fairly straight course along the coast.

At last the coast of Syrastrenê—which must surely be the lowest, flattest land on earth—curved around to the northeast, so that we could again run free. We anchored and spent another night in the pattering rain. The sailors released Hippalos and came aft to apologize. They practically licked the decks we trod upon in their eagerness to have us forget the recent unpleasantness.

Only Nysos and Apries hung back, looking scared and apprehensive. I had seen them whispering frantically to the other sailors, trying to keep command of the situation. But from then until we reached Barygaza, I never saw a more alertly obedient crew, jumping to obey our orders before we had finished giving them, as if they hoped we should forget their mutiny.

The next day we sailed up the Gulf of Kammonoi, between Syrastrenê and the Barygaza country. This gulf is so wide that, from the middle, one can barely see the two shores from the masthead. But it is no open seaway, being full of shoals and reefs. We brailed up our sails and felt our way, with Rama watching from the bow and a sailor from the masthead. Rama said:

"Captain, you tie a piece of white cloth to masthead."

"Why?"

"To tell pilot boat we into Barygaza are coming."

Accordingly, I flew a strip of white rag as he had said. The rain ceased, and in an hour a boat appeared to starboard. As it came closer, I saw it was a big twenty-oared barge, moving briskly. The naked, black, muscular rowers backed water under our bow, and a skirted man called up to Rama. I caught the words:

"Rama son of Govinda! Is that really you?"

"Yes, it really is," replied Rama, and the two went off into a long talk, too fast for me to follow.

At last the man in the barge threw up a rope, which Rama caught and made fast to the stempost. We furled our sails, and the barge towed us towards the eastern shore, avoiding shoals by a winding course. I saw that we were entering the estuary of a river, which Rama called the Nammados. The shores of the estuary narrowed, and the incoming tide boosted us along at a lively clip.

The sky had partly cleared and the sun, half hidden by clouds, was setting in the Gulf of Kammonoi behind us when we reached

Barygaza. The city was built around a low hill—a mere hummock, but conspicuous in that flat country. A fort or castle crowned this hill. The banks of the Nammados, clad in palms, stretched away to east and west.

The barge towed us to one of a number of tidal basins along the shore, a furlong below the city on the north bank. These basins were natural hollows in the river bed, which had been enlarged by the hand of man. As we anchored, a gang was finishing its day's work on the adjacent basin, hauling mud up from the bottom in buckets. Arab coasters, dwarfed by the *Ourania*, lay in others.

I asked Rama how much to pay the barge. Since the amount he named seemed reasonable, I paid. Later I learnt that he had named twice the going rate. No doubt he and the barge captain split the overcharge.

"He says," reported Rama, "we must stay on board tonight. Too late for inspectors."

I led the crew in the prayer of gratitude to Poseidon, and the cook got our dinner on board. During the evening, Rama coached me on how to behave ashore. "You must not," he said, "kill or harm any animal."

"What! You mean I can't even take a whack at a dog that snarls at me, or a cow that gets in my way?"

"Oh, no! Especially not cow. Indians are loving cows; man who hurts cow is worst kind of criminal. Brachmanes love cows even more than we Buddhists. They tear you to pieces if you hurt cow; but we think that is superstition. We just flog you."

"What's your king like?"

"I am not knowing. Naraina—barge captain I was talking to—says we have a new king, just elected."

"You mean you elect your kings in India?"

"In Barygaza, yes. Other places, king's son becomes king, or council chooses him, or candidates fight to death—every place is different. Two candidates were, one of merchants and one of sailors. Big election riot was; many people killed."

"Who won?"

"The sailor. He promised to lower harbor dues, but already he is raising them."

Somehow, that sounded familiar.

* * *

Next morning it rained again. The harbor master and his guards came aboard. I gave him a hearty greeting in Indian and a broad smile, but he only stared at me as if I were an insect of some repellant kind and proceeded to inspect the cargo. He collected his harbor tax, rattled off a sentence too fast for me to catch, and departed.

"What said he?" I asked Rama.

"He said you must call on king in middle of afternoon, today."

"I hope you'll come along."

"Oh, yes, he told you to bring Lord Hippalos and me."

I started to ask about court etiquette, but my words were cut off by a deep, booming roar. The tide was coming up the Nammados in a three-foot wave. I yelled to the sailors to loose the anchor cables but to hold them and brace themselves. They had hardly done so when the wave reached us. It split, foaming, into our little basin, and the *Ourania* was boosted into the air like a chip. The screaming sailors were jerked about the deck like dolls; one man almost went over the side. But, at the cost of some burnt hands, we had kept our anchors and cables. We pulled in and belayed the cables, while Rama bleated:

"Oh, Captain Eudoxos, I am so sorry! I meant to tell you about tide, but I am forgetting with excitement of getting home again!"

"By Bakchos' balls, must we watch for this thing twice a day?" I asked.

"It depends on time of month. When moon is at half, only little tidal wave is. When he is new or full, he even bigger than this one is. You see that all little ships have gone ashore."

I looked across the broad Nammados and, sure enough, the swarm of small craft that had plied it a half-hour earlier had vanished. Soon they began to reappear, creeping out from shore like so many water insects frightened by some splashing bather.

When the excitement had subsided, I made the sailors line up in front of the cabin to draw their pay, fining them two days' wages for the mutiny. As usual, some wanted the whole sum due them, to blow in one grand spree. Others, saving up for a house or a ship of their own, took only enough for small purchases and banked the rest with me. When the turn of Nysos and Apries came, however, I gave them their full pay for the voyage and told them:

"Take your gear and get off the ship. You're through."

Both spoke in shrill tones: "You can't do that to us, Captain. . . . You wouldn't maroon us here. . . . We might never get home. . . . We don't know the language or the customs. . . . You might as well kill us. . . ."

"You should have thought of that sooner," I said. "Now get off before I kick you off. If I find you hanging around the ship, or trying to stow away, I'll hang your heads from the yardarms."

If this has been a port of the Inner Sea, I should have dismissed the entire crew of mutinous rascals. But here, I knew, I should never find another Greek-speaking crew, so I should maroon myself as well.

When the rain let up, I gave Hippalos the deck and went ashore with Rama. The Indian's first task was to thank Buddha for his safe return. I accompanied him to a temple. This was a stone building of modest size, shaped like a kiosk.

Inside stood no statue, but a set of symbols of this sect, carved in stone. There was an empty throne, with an umbrella leaning against it. The prints of bare human feet were chiseled in the stone of the pavement before the throne. Behind the chair rose a pillar with a thing on its top that looked like a flower, but which I was told was a wheel with twenty-four spokes. Looking at these symbols, one had the uneasy feeling that the demigod (or however one should class the Lord Buddha) had just gotten up and walked out and might return any moment.

"We do not believe in making statues of Enlightened One," Rama told me. "Ignorant people would worship statues, as they do gods of Brachmanes, instead of trying to lead right lives."

Rama bought a bunch of flowers from a flower seller at the entrance. Inside the temenos, he spoke to a couple of shaven-headed priests, clad in robes of thin yellow cotton wrapped round and round them. He laid his flowers before the statue, clapped his hands, and stood, palms together and head bowed, praying in a high, nasal voice.

The priests looked curiously at me, standing at the entrance. As he turned away from his devotions, Rama called out:

"Come on in, Captain Eudoxos. Every good man is welcome." He introduced me to the priests, who smiled, bowed, and spoke. "They are saying," he translated, "'Peace to all beings!' You like to hear teachings of true religion?"

"Yes," I said. So, with Rama translating, the senior priest spoke somewhat as follows:

"My son, when the Enlightened One received his illumination, four hundred years ago, it was disclosed to him that all existence is misery. Birth is pain, life is pain, and death is pain. Nor is death the end of misery, because one is then reborn into another body, to begin again the wretched round of existence."

"As the Pythagoreans believe among us," I put in. But the priest merely looked annoyed at the interruption and continued:

"Now, the cause of misery is desire, which in the nature of things always expands beyond what can be satisfied and is therefore always thwarted. The only way to avoid misery is to extinguish desire. This can be done by following the eightfold path, namely: right views, right intention, right speech, right action, right occupation, right effort, right alertness, and right concentration.

"Practice these things, my son, and in time—not, perhaps, in this life, but then in a future one—you, too, will become enlightened. Then, when you die, you will not be reborn but will achieve the supreme bliss of nonexistence."

There was more of it, about the Four Noble Truths and so on. But this gives the gist of the doctrine, which has many points in common with Stoicism. When the priest had finished, I said:

"That is all very fine, Reverend Father, for those who find life a burden. But I enjoy it thoroughly. I've traveled to far lands and seen strange beasts and people. I've hunted and fished, galloped and sailed, gorged and guzzled, reveled and mourned, lain with fair women, and told tall tales. I've loved, hated, and fought with bloodthirsty foes. I've consorted with the great and the humble and found the same proportion of rascals among both. I've served my city and made money from my voyages. I've made new discoveries, written a book about them, and heard it praised by qualified critics. I've had narrow escapes from maiming and death, and I've rejoiced in every moment of it."

"But, my son! The pain of wounds and sickness—and I see from your scars and pockmarks that you have sustained both—far outweigh the pleasures of this material life, to say nought of the loss of dear ones and the waning of physical powers with age. Is it not so?"

"Not for me, it isn't. True, life has its pains and adversities. One of them, in fact, impelled me to come to India. But they merely add spice to the stew. If I were to perish painfully tomorrow, I should still say that life on the whole has been great fun."

"What adversity brings you to Bharata?" (For so the Indians call India.)

I told the priest of my masculine weakness and asked: "Now, you people are supposed to be full of the wisdom of the ages. None of the physicians of my country can help me; can you?"

The priest looked sadly at me and sighed, as if he were trying in vain to explain some obvious truth to a half-wit. "Oh, my dear son! Have you not heard what I said? Your loss, as you call it, is one of the luckiest things that could have befallen you. It will help you to suppress all attachment to mundane objects and beings. It will aid you to cultivate a benevolent indifference to earthly matters. It will enable you to extinguish all desire and thus to reach the true happiness of nonexistence. I cannot revive your fleshly lusts and give you the means of gratifying them, nor would I if I could. I see that you are not yet ready for the higher wisdom. Perhaps the *yogin* Sisonaga can help you, although we deem him a mere vulgar magician.

"Is it true that you have come thousands of *yojanas* across the Black Water, out of sight of land, in that great ship of yours?"

"It is. I wonder that you Indians, knowing of this seasonal wind, hadn't built ships to ply this route long ago."

"Ages ago, my son, we of Bharata had ships that flew through the air, magical weapons that blasted like lightning, medicines to give eternal youth, and other ingenious devices. But our wise men found that these earthly things are not important. They do but bind one to the material world and retard one's escape to blessed nonexistence. So the sages ceased to care about childish things like ships and weapons."

After some more small talk, I bid farewell to the priests. We entered the outer wall of Barygaza: a feeble affair of mud brick. I suppose that in case of attack, the people counted on withdrawing to the hilltop castle. Rama turned off into a side street.

"Now I go," he said. "I am seeing you this afternoon on ship."

"Why not come with me as guide and interpreter?" I said. "I'll stand you a drink."

He grinned. "I am sorry; must get home to see wives and children. I have much lovemaking to catch up on."

"Well, don't make love so hard that you can't stay awake this afternoon."

* * *

I left him and walked on into Barygaza. The streets were wandering tracks in the mud, lined by squalid little thatched mud huts set at every angle among palms and other trees. Monkeys chattered and scampered in the branches.

The town was as filthy as a Scythian peasant village, which is saying a lot. Dung—animal and human—lay everywhere; one could not walk without stepping in it. Barygaza was a good-sized center, whose streets swarmed with oxcarts, laden asses, carriages, chariots, gentlefolk being borne in litters, two men riding an elephant, and other traffic. Crying their wares in a nasal singsong, peddlers trotted through the mud with wide, shallow baskets of goods balanced on their heads. But there was no real shopping district, only an occasional hut with an open front and the goods laid out on a board in the street in front of it. There did not seem to be any sort of inn, tavern, or wineshop in the entire place. The more I saw of Barygaza, the more convinced I became that it was not really a city at all, but an overgrown village.

Like Rama, the folk were very dark of skin, if not quite so dead-black as the Ethiopians of Adoulis and Mosyllon. The men wore dirty waist garments like his, although with many the skirt was a mere breechclout. Buddhist priests wore yellow robes like those I had already seen and carried staves with iron rings loosely strung on them at one end; the clatter of these rings, when the priest shook his staff, was their way of begging alms.

Dodging among the ubiquitous cows, which were nosing in the heaps of garbage in competition with beggar women, I passed an elderly man, completely naked, with long, matted hair and beard and his body smeared with ash. He was rolling his eyes and shouting incoherently. I took him for a madman but later learnt that he was a particularly holy ascetic.

The women wore longer—if equally soiled—skirts but, like the men, left their upper bodies naked save for necklaces and other ornaments, and a veil of thin stuff draped over their hair. A common ornament was a golden plug, often set with a precious stone, inserted in one side of the nose. Among the more prosperous-looking younger women, their bare breasts were often attractively full and rounded; but the more numerous working-class women were skinny little things, no bigger than a well-developed Greek girl of twelve.

As I strolled, people turned to stare at me from all sides. When I paused at a crossroads, where women were drawing water from a well, several children stopped to stare at me. Then older persons, seeing a gathering crowd, stopped also. In fifty heartbeats a hundred Indians, all staring sullenly with big, sad, black eyes, surrounded me. To have two hundred glassy white eyeballs staring fixedly at one out of black faces makes one uneasy, to say the least. But one must put up with it in India, for they stare thus at a foreigner wherever he goes. When Hippalos came ashore, his red hair aroused even more and harder stares than I received.

When a swarm of beggars came creeping and hobbling forward, displaying stumps and scars, I thought it time to move on. I wandered through a street of coppersmiths, and a street lined with the cribs of courtesans, who called invitations in soft, childish voices. These last would not have attracted me, even if my strength had been upon me; it would have been too much like mounting a small child.

At last, along the river front, I found a tavern with an inn attached: small, cramped, and dirty, as everything seemed to be in India, but still a tavern. I squeezed into a seat and looked about me. Most of those present were Arabs with beards, head cloths, and hooked noses; there were only a few Indians, and those mainly of lower degrees.

A boy appeared, whom I asked in my best Indian for a mug of wine. He looked blank. I repeated the request, slowly and carefully. The boy went away, and soon a short, fat Indian appeared. I made the same request. Again that blank stare, with a mutter that I could not understand. Then I heard a shout from a corner:

"*Ô xene, legeis ta hellênika?*"

"Well, thank all the gods and spirits!" I cried. "There's somebody I can talk to. Who are you, sir?"

The man responded: "Come on over; we have room. Your servant is Otaspes son of Phraortes, of Harmozia in Karmania. This is my friend, Farid son of Amid. And you, sir?"

I introduced myself. The Persian who had spoken crossed his hands on his breast and bowed; his Arab companion touched his fingertips to his breast, lips, and forehead. The Persian was a stout man of medium height, with a long, straight nose in a square face, black hair growing low on his forehead, heavy, black brows that met above his nose, and a close-cut black beard. He said:

"You thought you were asking for palm wine; but you really asked for 'the black one.' They do sound alike, and our host was naturally puzzled."

Otaspes spoke to the taverner, who brought my mug. It was the horrible concoction, made from fermented palm juice, which they drink in India; but at times any drink is better than none.

"How," I asked, "do you come to speak Greek, and what are you doing in India?"

"That is a long story," said Otaspes. "But your servant traded for many years in Seleuceia and so came to know Greek. Then I returned to Harmozia with a Babylonian bride. The family took umbrage at that. Then the syndicate to which we belonged decided they needed a resident factor to handle the Indian end of our trade, so I took the post."

"How do you like it here?"

He shrugged. "It's India, even though it pays well. I shan't be sorry to retire on my gains. This is the unhealthiest damned coast in the world during the rainy season. We have lost all three of our children, one after another."

"Is this the rainy season?"

"This is the fag end of it. A month ago it rained all the time; now it only rains half the time. But about you: is it true what I've heard, that you have sailed directly hither from the Strait of Dernê?"

"Where did you hear that?"

Otaspes gave a silent little laugh. "My dear fellow! What earthly good should I be as a factor if I did not learn such things? The story of Rama's return from the dead was all over town within an hour of your arrival last night." He turned to the Arab. "It occurs to me, friend Farid, that we are seeing the opening of a new commercial era in the Arabian Sea. If Captain Eudoxos can do it, so can others; so will others. So think not to avert the new competition by cutting his throat or burning his boat." The Persian laughed silently again and translated his remark to me, while the Arab looked at me with such a venomous glare that I knew he had been thinking just that.

"Much better," continued Otaspes, "to build yourselves bigger ships and get in on the new trade at the start. I might be tempted to try a bit of throat-cutting myself, but I hope soon to leave for home. So this Egyptian competition won't concern me. Come to dinner at my house tomorrow, Captain, an hour before sundown. My house is near the Souppara Gate. Anybody will point it out; just say: *'Kahang Parsi ka ghar hai?'* Agreed?"

"You're extremely kind," I said. "Agreed."

* * *

Inside the hilltop fortress, the king's house—one could hardly call it a palace—was larger and better built than those of the common folk, but it was of the same mud-brick construction. Along the front of the house ran a terrace, shaded by a thatched roof upheld by wooden pillars. The king used this terrace for audiences, since it never gets cold enough in this part of India to force people indoors.

Protocol at this court was highly informal. Eight soldiers attended the king; but these were merely men in loincloths, with a spear and a buckler each. Instead of standing at attention, they squatted or lounged, and one was peacefully snoring against the house wall. A small crowd of petitioners and litigants milled on the muddy ground in front of the terrace.

To one side, near the end of the terrace, four musicians sat, twanging and tootling. Their music had a nervous, apprehensive sound, as if the musicians were about to burst into hysterical tears. Two dancing girls swayed and spun.

They were comely wenches, altogether nude save for strings of pearls and other ornaments around their wrists, ankles, necks, and waists. Their dancing consisted of slow little shuffling steps, while they jerked their necks and arms so that their bangles clashed.

To one side of the king stood a flunkey holding a white umbrella, ready to hoist it over the king's head in case His Majesty chose to walk out from under the roof of the terrace. I found that all Indian kings are accompanied by such umbrella carriers, since in India a white umbrella is as much a symbol of royalty as a crown is in more westerly lands.

On the other side squatted the royal timekeeper. His clock was a basin in which floated a bronze cup with a small hole in its bottom. When the cup filled and sank, the timekeeper whacked a drum or blew a blast on a horn made from a conch shell. Then he emptied the cup and started over. The Indian hour is only three quarters as long as ours, so that a day and a night comprise thirty-two hours instead of twenty-four.

As the king finished each case, his minister or major domo pointed to somebody in the crowd and shouted to him to come forward. There would be arguments and counterarguments, which became shouting matches, until the king shouted down both parties and gave his decision. People wandered in and out, and nobody thought anything of interrupting or contradicting the king.

We listened to one such case, and then another—a criminal case, this time, wherein a merchant was accused of poisoning a competitor. The king heard the stories and sentenced the culprit to be trampled by one of the royal elephants. Then the minister beckoned us forward.

Sitting on a heap of cushions on the floor of the terrace, King Kumara of Barygaza was a small, cross-eyed man with a skin wrinkled by years of seafaring. He wore the usual skirt, a couple of ropes of pearls around his neck, and a turban with a spray of peacock feathers stuck in the folds. He chewed a cud made of the nut of an Indian palm, wrapped in leaves. Now and then he spat a crimson stream into the royal spittoon. This habit stains the Indians' teeth black, which gives an odd effect when one of them permits himself a rare smile.

With Rama translating, we uttered our greetings and presented our gift: a handsome silver cup set with garnets. I said grandly:

"I, Eudoxos of Kyzikos, am the ambassador of the mighty king of Egypt, Ptolemaios Evergetes. My master greets his brother king—"

"Peace to all beings! Where is this Egypt?" said the king, giving me a haughty stare from one of his crossed eyes.

"Two months' sail to the west, sire. It compares in size and population with all Bharata. To further the prosperity of our respective realms—"

"What is this story of your sailing straight across the ocean, without stopping at the Arabian ports?"

I explained as best I could. Beside me, I could see Hippalos suppressing a guffaw at my description of myself as an ambassador. While Rama was translating, I muttered out of the side of my mouth:

"If you laugh, by Herakles, I'll break your fornicating neck!"

"Well," said the king at last, "tell your master I am glad to have his friendship. As for sending his ships to trade, I am glad of that, too—provided he gives us equal privileges in his ports. That is all, except that I shall ask you to receive some small gifts from me."

He snapped a finger, and a servant came out with a tray on which lay a rope of pearls, like that which the king wore, and a couple of other pieces of jewelry.

"The pearls," said King Kumara, "are for your king. You may have the first choice of the other gifts."

I chose a silver bracelet set with three small pearls, leaving a silver brooch with a big turquoise for Hippalos. The bracelet was of no use to me—a Hellene does not wear such things, and I could not have gotten my big fist through it anyway—but maybe Astra would like it. They were nice gauds, although one can find the equal in Alexandria for fifteen or twenty drachmai. I thought that, counting the pearls, we had gotten the better of the exchange. But doubtless King Kumara thought he had, too, because pearls were so much cheaper in India than in Egypt.

* * *

When we returned to the ship, we found four Barygazan merchants standing at the foot of the plank. Displaying his hook, Linos said:

"They wanted to come aboard to look over the cargo, sir: but I figured if they stole anything you'd take it out of my hide."

"Quite right," I said and led the merchants aboard.

Since my sailors had gone ashore, Gnouros, Linos, Hippalos, and I had to haul the samples up from the hold ourselves—a procedure that the Indians found extraordinary. They poked and fingered and smelt, as solemn as owls. Naturally, when one is about to make an offer, one does not display enthusiasm, lest one's eagerness stiffen the price. But these men, it seemed to me, carried disdainful indifference beyond reasonable bounds.

They finally muttered a few offers, as if they were doing us a great favor even to look at our garbage. The olive oil they would not consider at any price. Even when I had explained, through Rama, the many uses to which we put it, he reported back:

"They say this oil smells foul and tastes dreadful, and it is not customary to rub oil on themselves or to cook with it. In India, we cook with butter."

"They could burn it in their lamps."

"We burn butter in lamps, too. Oil lamps stink."

"Well then," said I wearily, "tell them we won't sell anything today. We shall have to learn the Indian market better. Ask them if they'd care to join us in a round of drinks."

"So sorry," said Rama, "but they are not drinking wine. It against their religion is."

"Well then, how would they like to have supper with us?"

When Rama translated this offer, the faces of the merchants, hitherto as blank as virgin papyrus, took on expressions of stark horror.

"Oh, sir!" said Rama. "Indians never eat with strangers, or with people not of their color. It would be a—how do you say—poll—"

"Pollution?"

"Yes, pollution. Why, if the shadow of person of lower color on your food falls, you must throw it away."

"I notice you ate with the boys on the voyage."

"Oh, but I am traveled man, used to funny customs of foreigners. But these men could not eat your food anyway. Members of high colors are not eating meat."

"I thought your wise Buddha taught that color was not important?"

Rama shrugged and spread his hands. "Even Enlightened One cannot change all old customs."

* * *

That evening, when the blue haze and pungent smell of cow-dung fires hung in the air, Nysos and Apries appeared, begging to be taken back aboard ship.

"You're murdering us, Captain," wailed Nysos. "These barbarians won't hire us for even the dirtiest work. In this dunghill of a country, all jobs are inherited, so there's no place for a foreigner. We shall have to live by stealing, and they'll catch us and have us tramped by those polluted elephants."

"Go to the crows!" I said. "I wouldn't let you temple thieves back aboard, if you were the only sailors in India."

After the pair had wandered despondently off, I returned to Hala's tavern; but the Persian factor was not there. As before, there were many Arabs and a few Indians.

I hung around for a while, trying to strike up acquaintances. But the Arabs only glowered and fingered their daggers. I tried them in my bad Syrian, which is similar to Arabic and which most northern Arabs understand, but without success. My rudimentary Indian was no more successful. As for the Indians, they stared coldly at me and made remarks, meant to be overheard, about the uncouth appearance and disgusting habits of this crazy foreigner.

I do not think my failure was entirely due to a poor command of the languages. I have struck up acquaintances in pothouses all around the Inner and Euxine Seas without any trouble, when I knew even less of the lingo. Doubtless the Arabs had decided that I represented a threat to their coastal shipping business, while the Indians were just being Indians.

I gave up at last and set out for the ship. Since it was almost the end of Boedromion, there was no moon. As I walked, I thought I heard the patter of feet behind me, but I could not be sure. When I stopped, the sound stopped; when I went on, it resumed.

Having been through this sort of thing before, I slipped around a corner and waited. Presently three shadowy figures appeared, slinking along. Even in the feeble starlight that filtered through the palm fronds, I could tell an Arab cloak and head cloth from the skirt and turban of an Indian.

"Well?" I said.

The three whirled with guttural exclamations, and I caught the gleam of a curved dagger in the starlight. I sprang forward and brought my stick down on the arm that held the knife. I heard the bone snap and the knife skitter away. A rap on the pate sent a second man sprawling. The unhurt man dragged his felled companion to his feet, and the three scuttled off.

When I got back to the *Ourania*, I told Linos to post a double watch, since there might be trouble. Everybody was aboard save Rama, who had gone home, and Hippalos, who was out whoring. In the cabin, I unwrapped my Scythian bow.

I had hardly been asleep for an hour or two when a yell brought me out. On shore, twenty or thirty paces away, a group of Arabs stood around a man with a big torch, by which they were lighting fire arrows and shooting them at the *Ourania*. Several had already stuck in the woodwork. My men were running about, wrenching them out and throwing them over the side, or knocking them loose with boathooks.

I stepped to the rail and sent a Scythian arrow whizzing towards the group. I missed, but range is hard to judge by such lighting. A second shaft was luckier. The Arabs gave a wild yell and scattered; the torch bearer threw his torch at the ship, but it only struck the side, fell into the water, and went out with a sizzle.

Linos, a couple of sailors, and I went ashore and found an Arab with my arrow through his brisket, spitting bloody foam with each breath. We carried him, feebly begging for mercy, aboard. By threats of finishing him off in interesting ways, I got his name and the name of his ship. Linos said:

"Captain, I've been looking these Arab ships over. They're made of little pieces of scrap lumber tied together with strings. If I took a gang of the boys, we could board one and knock a hole in her bottom in no time."

"Not yet," I said. "We don't want to start a feud between all the Hellenes and all the Arabs that may use this port forever more; bad for trade. Leave this to me."

Hippalos, returning, whistled when he learnt what had happened. The Arab died at dawn. I went ashore, hunted up the harbor master, and made him understand that I wanted Rama. He gave me the usual insolent stare, rattled directions at me, and—when I did not understand—sent a guard to show me the way. The guard found Rama's house, but the sailor's two little wives informed us that the master was out.

* * *

I was wandering aimlessly about the town, looking for Rama and followed by the bored harbor guard, when I heard a hail. It was Otaspes the Persian, who said:

"Well, well! I did not know you were a hero like the Persian Thretonas and the Greek Achilles rolled into one."

"What have you heard?"

"Only that you beat all the Arabs in Barygaza in pitched battle, single-handed."

"That's a slight exaggeration." I told him what had really happened.

"Since when," he asked, "has any Hellene been able to shoot like a Persian?"

"This Hellene learnt how among the Scythians. Now, I don't want to make too much of this brawl, but I should like to lay a complaint before the king, to stop it before it gets out of hand. Can you help me?"

Thus it came to pass that, late that afternoon, we stood again before the king's house. The corpse lay on the ground on a stretcher, and the crews of the two ships involved—the one to which the dead man had belonged, and that of the man whose arm I had broken—stood before the terrace with their hands bound and soldiers guarding them.

"Now hear this!" said King Kumara. "Master Eudoxos does not wish to go to extremes in this matter. But, lest any of you be tempted to disturb the peace again, I will keep *you* and *you*—" (he pointed to one man from each crew) "—as a hostage until your ship is ready to sail. If aught befall Captain Eudoxos or any of his men in Barygaza, you shall be trampled by elephants. And I have doubled the waterfront patrol. Court is dismissed."

As Otaspes and I walked to his house through the rain, the Persian said: "I am sorry you had trouble, but that's the way of things. These Arabs are an emotional lot: good friends but bad enemies, and one never knows which tack they will take. Luckily, most are friends of mine, and I'll try to smooth things over. And, if I may make a suggestion, do not wander the streets at night without high, thick boots."

"Why? To kick marauders with?"

"No; serpents. This land swarms with them. People are always going out to visit their uncle Krishna at night, treading on a venomous serpent, and being found dead in the morning. That is what befell that former sailor of yours, the Egyptian."

"Apries? Is he dead?"

"Yes; had you not heard? The harbor patrol found him this morning; he was trying to break into somebody's house when he trod on this serpent."

"Lovely country," I said. Startled by Otaspes' news, I had paused in my stride. While I hesitated, staring Indians began to collect in a circle around us. Annoyed, I pushed through the circle and resumed our walk, moving more briskly.

"Not so fast, old man!" said Otaspes. "I do not have legs like tree trunks, as you have."

"Sorry," I said, "but this constantly being stared at bothers me. Have these folk never seen a man from the West before?"

"There have been no Hellenes here for decades. Half a century ago, they tell me, Apollodotos, who was a satrap of the Greek king Demetrios, marched down here from Syrastrenê and demanded submission. The Barygazans gave it on condition of retaining their local self-government. So for a time the city had a Greek garrison, first under Demetrios and then under the great Menandros. But after Menandros died, about thirty years ago, these Greeks marched away to take part in the struggle for his empire; for God has given you Hellenes all the virtues save the ability to work together. Hence you and your shipmates are the first Hellenes seen here in a score of years and are naturally objects of curiosity."

As we walked, I became aware that two Indians, who had formed part of the crowd we had escaped, were following us, stopping when we stopped and pretending interest in the nearest display of merchandise. After we had rounded several corners, so that there could be no mistake, I called Otaspes' attention to this escort. He only gave his little silent laugh and explained:

"Those are the spies from Magadha and Andhra."

"How do you mean? Where are those lands?"

"I see you are not up on Indian politics. Well, a hundred and some years ago, a mighty king of Magadha, one Ashoka—named for one of these flowering trees—conquered most of India. Then he turned Buddhist and discovered that conquering and slaying people was wrong. In fact, he came to believe in no killing whatever and ordained that no man should slay even an animal, on pain of death. This does not make sense to me, but perhaps your Greek logic can explain it. Of course, Ashoka did not free all the hundreds of tribes and kingdoms he had conquered, but I suppose that were too much to ask.

"After Ashoka died, his empire broke up. At the moment, the strongest powers are Magadha, *that* way—" (he pointed northeast) "—and Andhra, that way." (He pointed southeast.) "As Ashoka's successor, King Odraka of Magadha claims to be the rightful ruler of all India. But the king of Andhra, Skandhastambhi, says *he* should be the rightful ruler. So they fight, and each sends agents into other nations, to subvert the local rule in favor of some puppet of their respective masters. The Brachmanes love to harp on the virtues of harmlessness and pacifism, but at the same time they tell each king he has a moral duty to enlarge his realm until it comprises the whole earth. So, naturally, the Indians fight among themselves just as much as do the less enlightened peoples, like yours and mine."

"If you know these knaves, why not tell the king?"

"Kumara knows all about them, but he prefers to let them live and watch them. They are singularly stupid, inept spies, as you can see from the fact that you noticed them. If Kumara had them squashed by his elephants, Odraka and Skandhastambhi might send a pair who were more skilled and less easily watched."

"Is it true that descendants of Alexander's generals still rule parts of India?"

"Aye. They ruled the mountainous country to the northwest and, when Ashoka's empire fell, moved down to the plains to set up kingdoms there. Lately they, in turn, have been beaten by the Sakas and have lost much of their power."

"Who are the Sakas?"

"What you would call Scythians—the eastern branch of that race. Subdued by Mithradates of Parthia, many Sakas have moved eastward, seeking lands and fortune on the marches of India."

We reached Otaspes' house, and I met his charming Babylonian wife Nakia; for Persians, like Egyptians and Romans, are perfectly willing to let their wives meet strangers. I could talk to Nakia to some extent in Syrian. The pair had suffered much from the loss of their children to India's deadly diseases but were too well-mannered to dwell upon the subject. Otaspes merely said:

"You can see why I am eager to get back to Harmozia, to a clime where, if the Lord of Light grant us some more, they have a chance of growing up healthy. For, as you see, Nakia is still a young woman."

When I was taking my leave with profuse thanks, Otaspes said: "Think nothing of it, old boy. In India, we palefaces starve for human contacts. Indians have little to do with those outside their own families, less to do with those outside their colors, and nought to do with foreigners. So, for a foreigner in India, there is no social life. Come back again soon."

I picked my way home with caution, watching for serpents and listening for Arab assassins. As I neared the *Ourania*, my attention was attracted by a small, jabbering crowd around one of those giant fig trees which, by lowering auxiliary trunks from its branches, becomes a whole grove in itself. A man was hanged from one of the branches. As I got close, I saw by the flickering torchlight that it was Nysos, the other mutineer.

Linos came up, saying: "He climbed up the main trunk with the rope around his neck, while a score of these barbarians stood and watched. Then he tied the rope to the branch and let go."

"Didn't anybody try to cut him down?"

"No. Rama—where is the little dog-face? He was here a moment ago—Rama explained it to me. In India, if somebody wants to kill himself, that's his business. Maybe he'll do better in his next life, so nobody interferes. Anyway, nobody cares what becomes of a foreigner."

"Well," said I, "this simplifies things for us, anyway. If he'd kept on coming around and begging for a berth, I might have weakened."

Book IV

OTASPES THE PERSIAN

Two ten-days after the attack on the *Ourania*, I had sold most of our cargo. I could speak enough Indian to get around, although it is a long way from saying: "Two fowl's eggs, a loaf of bread, and a mug of goat's milk, please," to carrying on an intelligent conversation.

I had bought some cargo for the return voyage—mainly cotton cloth, silk, ivory, pepper, cinnamon, ginger, perfumes, and spikenard. I bought several knife and sword blades of Indian steel, which is finer than any steel one can purchase in the Inner Sea. Indian smithery and carpentry are exceptionally skillful. Indian pottery, on the other hand, is crude; there might be a market there for fine Athenian decorated ware.

I learnt some of the peculiar techniques of Indian commerce. Some of their coins are round, some square. Coinage is nowhere standardized, so that every purchase requires weighing the coins as well as the goods. For small change the Indians use, not coins at all, but little sea shells shaped something like walnuts. They count on their fingers, as we do, but begin by extending the little finger instead of the thumb or the index finger. To bargain, one sits cross-legged beside the shopkeeper and conveys one's offers by a kind of dumb language, touching his hand with one's fingers. Thus onlookers are kept from following the course of the chaffer.

The rains were dwindling. We had, however, another month to wait for the seasonal northeaster. With Otaspes as intermediary, I tried to make my peace with the Arabs by telling them that their little ships could still fetch cargoes to Barygaza from shallow ports like Barbarikon and sell them to the Hellenes. But it was no use.

The Arabs had decided that they had a feud with me and would not give it up.

Arabs are funny that way. Without some enemy to hate and feud with, an Arab finds life too dull to bear. So, if he has no enemy, he goes out and kicks somebody in the balls in order to make one. The fact that there is nothing much else to do for fun in the Arabian desert may have something to do with it. If they try to rob or murder you and you hurt one of them in resisting, they become as furiously indignant as if you had been the aggressor.

I have had good friends among the Arabs of Syria, but not with this crowd in Barygaza. After they had stabbed and wounded one of my sailors, I made my men go armed and in pairs ashore. I also got permission to carry my sword, a keen Persian blade, longer than the usual Greek smallsword. From Otaspes I bought a shirt of fine Parthian chain mail, made of little interlocked iron rings, and wore it under my tunic.

I survived the attack of some local disease, with flux and fever. When I had recovered, I tried to hire Rama to stay on with us as interpreter, but he refused.

"I am shipping out day after tomorrow to Souppara," he said. "Must save enough to buy share of another ship."

"At least," I said, "before you go, take me to meet that wise man, that Sas—Sisa—"

"Sisonaga?" He wagged his head. "All right, we go in the morning."

I invited Hippalos, too, but he declined. He had taken a hut with one of those little Indian women, a girl of fourteen. I suppose the paltry price he paid her father was more than the old man usually saw in a year.

Sisonaga lived in a hut in the woods, a few furlongs from Barygaza. When we came upon him, he was sitting naked in front of his hut with his eyes closed, enjoying the morning sun, which slanted through the leaves. He was very black, with a mane of white hair and beard. In this part of India, as in the Hellenic lands, a beard is usually the badge of a philosopher. (I had let mine grow on the voyage, because I have always hated to shave or be shaved on shipboard, fearing lest a roll of the ship result in a slashed throat. Moreover, if its gray streaks made me look older, it also hid some of my pockmarks.)

"Peace, O Rama," said Sisonaga as we approached. "And peace to your foreign guest. He would, I take it, learn wisdom?"

"That I would, O Sisonaga," I said. "Permit me, sir ..." And I laid down the loaves of bread and the hamper of fruit and greens that I had brought, as Rama had directed, for my lecture fee.

Sisonaga ignored the food and spoke: "You have come to the right place, my dear pupil. For I, and only I, have found the one true means of uniting oneself with the world-soul. Where the foolish Buddhists and Brachmanists still grope in ignorance, I alone know the truth. Sit before me and I will explain my system."

So, with Rama interpreting the hard parts, Sisonaga told of the three categories (energy, mass, and intelligence); of the equilibrium between soul and consciousness, whence the ego evolves; of how activity causes the ego to differentiate into the six senses, the five motor organs, and the five potentials, which in combination with the five elements and the soul make up the twenty-five realities ...

"Speaking of the five motor organs," I said, "it is about the last of those—the generative organ—that I wish to consult you." And I told him of my troubles. He said:

"Oh, my dear pupil, how wrong you are! You seek to continue experience; but experience involves pain. This pain results from the five errors: inference, illusory knowledge, imagination, sleep, and memory. To attain concentration and thence to unite your individual consciousness with the cosmic consciousness, you must correct these errors. To correct the five errors, you must suppress egotism and self-esteem, which includes all desire and aversion, even the desire for self-preservation. To achieve this, you must first adhere to the negative ethic. That is, you must renounce injury to any being, falsehood, theft, incontinence, and the acceptance of gifts. This is followed by the positive ethic of vegetarianism, austerity, and irresponsibility. So, obviously, your desire—"

"Yes, yes," I interrupted. "This is very much what Rama's Buddhist priest told me. But suppose I undertake all this, what do I get? That priest's bliss of nonexistence?"

"Not at all; that is where they err. You unite your individual consciousness with the cosmic consciousness, and the powers of the cosmic consciousness become yours."

"What powers?"

"An accomplished yogin can do things on this material plane that ordinary men cannot—levitate himself, pick up an elephant, push over a city wall, or raise the dead back to life. Of course, these acts must all be done from purely altruistic motives. The slightest trace of self-interest, and the powers vanish."

"Well," I said, "I have known a multitude of men. Many claimed purity of motives; but when I considered their actions, I saw that all of them acted from self-interest, at least most of the time."

"Precisely, my dear pupil, precisely," said Sisonaga, beaming. "That is why so few yogins can perform these acts, although there are many liars who falsely claim all sorts of wonders. Beware of them. In my own century and a half of seeking—in this body, that is—I have been privileged to achieve such feats on but a few occasions: two revivals of dead persons, for example."

"How shall I acquire these powers?"

"First, there are the six postures: the lotus, the inverted, the pan-physical, the fish, the plow, and the serpent. Then there are the breathing exercises, with their cycles of inhalation, exhalation, and holding, and the control of the nose, mouth, and throat passages. The final stage comprises the exercises in concentration, whereby one learns to control one's own thoughts, to observe them with complete detachment, and to induce a mental vacuum. Eventually, one achieves the cosmic trance. Let us try the first and simplest posture, the lotus. Sitting erect, place the left foot, with the sole up, on the right thigh. … Come on, my good pupil, pull!"

"I fear I am a little old and creaky for such gymnastics," I muttered, straining to get my leg into the position indicated. At last I got my foot up on the opposite thigh.

"Now," continued Sisonaga, "push your left knee down so that it lies flat on the ground, as mine does. Push harder! Harder!"

Feeling like a suspect being questioned on the rack by the Ptolemies' police, I tried to carry out the yogin's commands. But, though I strained until my joints creaked, sweat ran down my brow, and the two Indians lent their help, I could not get my left knee down to the grass. Until I did, there was no hope of hoisting my right foot up so as to lay it upon my left leg in the lotus posture.

After a struggle that may have lasted a quarter hour, although it seemed much longer, the yogin gave up. When I tried to straighten out my bent left leg, I found that I could not. The leg was stuck, with the foot pressing into the right thigh. I had to ask the Indians to pull the foot loose. Although I am no stranger to wounds, the pain of this operation fetched a groan from me. When I tried to stand up, I collapsed like a toddler just learning to walk. Rama had to steady me until my limbs recovered from the wrenching they had received.

"With one so stiff in the joints as yourself," said Sisonaga, "we must draw nigh to these things bit by bit. I will prescribe exercises for the thigh joints. Performed once a day, these will enable you to begin your regular course of postures within a month."

"In a month," I said, "I shall, Lady Luck willing, be on my way back to Egypt. Whilst I do not doubt the value of your treatments, I have no wish to go into a cosmic trance or to pick up an elephant. What I really want is to make love to my dear wife once more."

Sisonaga clucked. "Nay, I fear I cannot help you to seek sensual gratification. I do, however, have a colleague: the *vanaprastha*, Jaivali of Mahismati. Although I deem his doctrines riddled with error and his practice hardly more than witchcraft, it is said that he can help earthbound persons like yourself to attain their mundane goals."

"Where shall I find this Jaivali?"

"Go up the Nammados about twenty-five yojanas to the city of Mahismati and ask for Jaivali the hermit. Anybody can direct you to his forest dwelling. In fact, it is deemed a pilgrimage of great merit to walk the entire length of the Nammados afoot, up one side to the source and down again on the other to the mouth. If you would fain cleanse your karma thus ..."

"No, thank you. Time does not permit, and anyway I fear that your spiritual exercises have crippled me for life." I took my leave of Sisonaga and, leaning on Rama's shoulder, hobbled back to Barygaza.

I sought out Hippalos' hut and found my versatile first officer sitting in front of it in the very lotus posture which I had tried in vain to assume and from whose effects I was still limping. Moreover, he was amusing a circle of Indians by conjuring tricks, making square Indian coins and other small objects appear and vanish and plucking them out of the ears and nostrils of his audience. Rama said he had to go, so we bade him a final farewell.

"Walk to the ship with me," I told Hippalos. The spies from Andhra and Magadha fell in behind us. Being sure they did not know Greek, we ignored them.

"I'm going up the river for a couple of ten-days," I said. I told Hippalos about Jaivali, adding: "I shall have to leave you in command of the ship. Now, this would be the time to do a little trading on our own. It seems obvious what sort of goods to buy, to avoid old Fatty's monopoly."

"Pearls and precious stones, of course," he replied with his satyr-like grin. "We can hide them next to our skins on our return. I'm with you, Captain. I should say for me to try to buy pearls locally, since they will be cheapest along the coast, while you see what you can do in the way of rubies and sapphires inland."

"Agreed."

"When should I expect you back?"

I thought. "Sisonaga said Mahismati was twenty-five yojanas up-river, which according to Rama is about sixty leagues. But one can never be sure of distances in a foreign land. Besides, I might fall ill or have to come back by another route. You'd better give me at least two months. If I'm not back by then and haven't sent word, take the *Ourania* back to Egypt."

Then I sought out Otaspes the Persian and said: "You hope to leave during the coming dry season, and you'll want to make a last killing before you go. Why not go to Mahismati with me and try to pick up some bargains? You can help with the local dialects, while I can help with the fighting if it come to that."

"What sort of trip had you in mind? A simple round trip, up and down the river?"

"I don't know. I might make a side trip if something interested me. I must, however, be back when the northeast wind begins to blow."

"If you are going to travel about the interior of India, you had better choose nations under Buddhist rule to visit."

"Why?" I asked.

"Because Buddhists are generally friendly to Hellenes, whereas Brachmanists are hostile. This goes back to the days when King

Menandros and King Pushyamitra of Magadha were fighting up and down the Ganges. Being a devout Brachmanist, Pushyamitra persecuted the Buddhists, so the latter sided with Menandros and looked upon his Bactrio-Greeks as saviors. Besides, Brachmanists hate Hellenes because the latter do not take their system of colors seriously. In their eyes, to permit 'confusion of colors'—that is, intermarriage among people of different color—is one of the wickedest sins a ruler can commit."

"I'll bear that in mind. But are you coming?"

Otaspes thought a moment and said: "I'm with you, Eudoxos. Your servant is getting too fat, sitting around the pothouses picking up gossip, day after day."

* * *

Two days later, Otaspes, Gnouros, and I were on our way up the Nammados in a river boat. Under my tunic and mail shirt I carried my money, in golden Ptolemaic staters, folded into a cloth, which was tied like a belt around my middle. Otaspes brought a man-load of Persian rugs and other trade goods besides his money.

During the wet season, the traffic on the Nammados, like that of the Nile, benefits from the fact that the water goes one way while the wind goes the other. One merely hoists sail to go upstream and lowers it to come down again.

The jungle-clad banks on either side of the river rose by stages, like steps, to low ranges of hills or plateaus. Now and then we passed a village in a clearing, or a temple, or one of those huge domes of brick, covered with white stucco, which the Buddhists build to house the relics of their holy men. There was constant traffic along the roads on each side of the river: single wayfarers, family groups, caravans of traders, pilgrims and holy men, and religious processions. There were men afoot, on asses, on horses, in carriages, in ox wains, in buffalo carts, and on elephants. We had thought of using horses, too, but the river promised greater comfort and safety.

At night, there always seemed to be a religious ceremony within earshot. We heard their singing and their musical bands, sometimes slow and solemn, sometimes fast and frenzied.

"The real business of India is religion," said Otaspes. "If you wonder why they act like such idiots, the reason is that their minds are not on this world, which to them is a mere illusion. Instead, they are trying to think up some new and quicker way to unite themselves with God—or at least with some god or other, for this land has more gods than it has men."

"How about you?" I said.

"Me? I worship the one Good God, Oramazdes, the Lord of Light. If these people wish to divide God up into ten thousand aspects, incarnations, demigods, and so forth, that is their affair."

In nine days we reached Mahismati. As we disembarked, Otaspes hired some skinny little porters to hoist our baggage on their heads and follow us into the city. As we climbed the path from the landing to the river gate, we saw a crowd of people around a funeral pyre. As we drew closer, I saw that an elderly woman sat on top of the pyre beside the corpse. She was not bound; she simply sat there until the flames roared up and hid her from view.

"By the gods and goddesses!" I said, "what's that?"

"A widow burning herself," said Otaspes. "Among the upper colors of the Brachmanists, it is a point of honor for a widow to sacrifice herself on her man's pyre. She thus expiates all their sins, so they shall spend the next fifty million years in paradise. If she failed to burn herself, she would be deemed an outcast—a person of no color, treated worse than a dog."

"*Phy!* What a country!"

We walked on to the city—a town of much the same size and character as Barygaza, but with a more substantial wall of brick. A gay assortment of flags flew from the walls, and Otaspes learnt that the king was celebrating the birth of his first son by his legitimate wife. The massive wooden gates were studded with large iron spikes to keep elephants from breaking them down with their heads. Before each gate was a kind of triumphal arch, consisting of a pair of wooden pillars joined at the tops by several wooden cross-pieces intricately carved into figures of elephants, dancing girls, creatures half woman and half serpent, and other beings.

At the river gate stood a pair of soldiers whose bronzen cuirasses, horsehair-crested helmets, and long pikes looked familiar. As I approached, I said:

"*Ô hoplitai! Legete ta hellênika?*"

They looked startled; then the bearded faces split in broad grins. "*Malista!*" they shouted. In no time, the whole duty squad was swarming around me, wringing my hands and pounding me on the back. Their strangely accented Greek was sprinkled with Persian and Indian words.

"By Zeus the Savior, have the Hellenes at last reached this god-detested part of India?" asked one.

"Just this one Hellene, a trader from Egypt," I said. "But how did you fellows get here? You're as far from Hellas as I am."

The speaker explained: "We're Bactrian Hellenes—born and reared in the mountains of Gandaria. We soldiered for King Antialkidas, but lately the polluted Sakas have wrested most of Antialkidas' lands from him. The other big Hellenic king, Straton, saw a chance to stab Antialkidas in the back, so he attacked his rear.

"When the fighting stopped, Antialkidas had so little land left that he couldn't afford to keep us all, so several thousand left to take service elsewhere. Some went over to King Straton, but we wouldn't work for the treacher. So we came hither."

"How do you make out?"

He shrugged. "It's India, but we might be worse off. But look, sir, you must let us give you a feast, so you can tell us the news from the West."

"I shall be glad to." I turned to Otaspes. "Where are we staying?"

"At Sudas' inn, unless he's full. Tell your friends to leave a message for you when they get their party organized."

So it was agreed. Having paid a tax on our goods to the customs officer at the gate, we passed on into the city, ignoring as best we could the stares of the Indians. When we were settled, we went to pay our respects to the king. Since His Majesty was busy at rites connected with his son's birth, we were received, instead, by a lean, bald, dour-looking, elderly minister, who wore the sacred thread of the Brachman color about his neck. He welcomed us with brief sentences and told us to come back two days later, when the natal ceremonies would be over.

"But you need not waste your time tomorrow," he said. "The king is giving a fête to conclude the celebrations, and you shall be invited." He signed to a clerk, who produced a piece of dried palm leaf on which something had been scribbled in ink. "That is your pass. Present it at the public park outside the East Gate at sunrise tomorrow."

By now it was too late for trading or for seeking out the hermit Jaivali. A couple of Bactrio-Greek soldiers appeared at Sudas' inn and invited us to the party at the barracks. A fine, festive affair it was, with naked dancing girls and real wine from Persia—a great rarity in India—on which Otaspes got drunk and slid quietly under the table. King Girixis' whole company of Greek mercenaries jammed into the mess hall.

I told the soldiers about events around the Inner Sea, and they told me how King Odraka of Magadha was already collecting tribute from the next neighboring kingdom to the east, that of Vidisha. It was only a matter of time, they said, before he fastened his grip on Mahismati and Avanti as well.

"I don't think our little king will resist very hard," said one. "So long as he has his girls and his jug and his hunting, he doesn't care who collects tribute from whom."

"Oh, come!" said another. "You're unfair to the little bastard. He's a real sport, always ready to give us a big bonus. It's that dog-faced minister who's always telling him he can't afford to do the generous thing."

"He'll do the generous thing once too often, and then there won't be any regular pay left for us," said the first soldier. "Remember last year, when he ran short? He'd have sent us on a raid into Vidisha to refill his coffers, except that he was afraid it would bring Odraka down on him. So he had to grind it out of his starving peasantry, as usual. What he should do is to play off the kings of Magadha and Andhra, one against the other. ..."

And they were off on an argument over foreign policy. Like onlookers everywhere, each was sure he could manage the government with infinitely more skill and address than those who were faced with the task.

While these two argued, a third soldier said: "Master Eudoxos, among your trade goods, you didn't by chance bring any Greek girls, did you?"

"Why, no," I said. "I never expected to find a market for them here."

"I think you might. We all have women—except those who prefer the love of other men—but they're native women and don't count as lawful wives. What we want are real Greek girls, so we can marry them properly and beget legitimate children—"

"Now, look here!" said another. "My wife is a respectable Bactrian girl, of a good landowning family, and I won't have anybody saying our children are bastards—"

"All right for you," said another, "but most of us have to make do with whatever dames we can pick up. Solon's right. If Master Eudoxos will load his ship with Greek girls—either slave or free; we'll free the bonded ones and wed 'em anyway—we'd make it well worth his while. . . ."

And so it went, far into the night. I took note of the idea for possible future use. When I finally got to bed, I had the fright of my life when I disturbed one of those giant mice, as large as a half-grown kitten, which infest this land. Luckily, the beast dashed into its hole without attacking me.

* * *

We presented ourselves at the park at dawn, with supplies of food and drink for the day. Despite having awakened with four heads instead of one, Otaspes had wisely thought to bring this provender with us. We were shown to an inclosure reserved for foreigners, heretics such as Buddhists and Jainists, and persons of low color. The other colors all had their proper inclosures. I grumbled a bit at being so classified, but Otaspes merely shrugged and smiled.

"It's India," he said.

Around us, thousands of Indians sat or squatted on the grass, while the action took place in a cleared space in the center of the crowd. The king made a speech, which did not much enlighten me because he spoke with his back to us. Then his band played and his dancing girls danced.

Next, a company of actors staged a play, about a noble hero whose king was turned against him by the plots and slanders of a wicked minister. The actors, in gilded armor, strutted about the low platform that served as a stage, shouting verses in the ancient Sanskrit tongue, of which I understood not a word. I was startled to see actors performing unmasked, with their faces bare save for paint and powder. I have heard that the Italians put on plays in this manner. I also learnt that women's parts were actually taken by women instead of by boys. I suppose it was foolish of a widely traveled man like me, but I could not help feeling uncomfortable, as if this spectacle were somehow indecent.

After the heroine had stabbed herself and thus, in some manner I never understood, proved to the stupid king that the hero was really a monster of virtue and valor, other acts followed. There were acrobats, tight-rope walkers, jugglers, animal trainers, wrestlers, storytellers, and conjurors. There was a chariot race along a path cleared through the crowd.

As the sun set, another troupe staged a play. This was a comedy, which I had little trouble in following. For one thing, the actors spoke ordinary modern Indian; for another, the plot was much like that of the comedies of Menandros and his kind. It told about a pair of young lovers kept apart by the benighted obstinacy of their parents but united at last by the crafty advice of a holy hermit.

* * *

Next morning I called upon Jaivali. I took the usual offering of food and found the hermit a stout, jolly-looking fellow, naked and bearded like his colleague downstream, and living in a cave. He, too, assured me that he had the only true system of attaining the higher wisdom.

"Sisonaga means well," said Jaivali, "but he is lost in a swamp of ignorant atheism."

"Does he not believe in gods?"

"Well, he calls himself an agnostic, saying there is no proof whether gods be or not."

"We had a fellow named Protagoras, who said something like that," I said. "The men of Athens—a great city in the West—exiled him and burnt his books on that account."

"What a wicked thing, to force a belief upon a man by persecution! But that, I suppose, is to be expected in your barbarous land. In Bharata we believe in tolerance; nobody would dream of interfering with another's beliefs.

"But as to the gods, I can assure you that they do exist. By austerities and spiritual exercises, I have induced a vision wherein the gods appeared to me in person and explained it all. If you would submit to my discipline, I could double your physical powers and the acuteness of your senses within a year."

Jaivali described his system, which sounded much like Sisonaga's, save that it entailed the worship of many Indian gods. It also involved some disagreeable-sounding exercises, such as swallowing and vomiting up a rag to cleanse one's stomach. Lacking a translator, I repeatedly had to ask Jaivali to slow down and to repeat, but I think I got the gist of it.

"Well," I said, "I fear I shall not be in Mahismati long enough for your full course. Actually, I came here in hope that you could cure me of one specific physical weakness ..." And I told him.

His response was just like those of the Buddhist priest and the yogin Sisonaga. "My poor man!" he exclaimed. "Know you not that, for long life and health, you must retain your semen instead of wasting it in copulation? If retained, this secretion is carried by invisible ducts to all parts of the body, nourishing and lubricating it. Besides, of all forms of physical pleasure, that of copulation is the most intense. Therefore it must be forsworn by the seeker after higher wisdom, since it ties one by the strongest bonds to attachments and desires on this material plane."

"Well, that is what I am after and nothing else. If you cannot help me, who can?"

Jaivali closed his eyes for a space. When he opened them, he said: "There is a philosopher in Ozenê, Gupta, who might do something. His repute is not of the highest, but he may have what you seek."

"Where is Ozenê?"

"Eight yojanas north of here, over the Paripatra Hills. It is the capital of Avanti."

I got directions for finding Gupta and took my leave. Otaspes had spent the morning trading in Mahismati and had bought a bolt of turquoise-colored silk. I told him that my next goal was Ozenê.

"By the Holy Ox Soul, you do have the traveler's itch!" he said. "Here in Mahismati, the Brachmanist dynasty enforces tolerance between its Brachmanist and Buddhist subjects. But in Ozenê, the two factions are always fighting for supremacy. The Brachmanists (or

Orthodox, as they call themselves) are more numerous, but the Buddhists have more wealth and power."

"Jaivali tells me that Indians never do that sort of thing. They believe in tolerating one another's opinions, he says."

Otaspes gave his silent laugh. "My dear Eudoxos, have you been around for half a century without learning that men say one thing and do another?"

"I know what you mean. But are you coming to Ozenê?"

"To hear is to obey! One can make even better buys there, and no true Persian merchant ever quailed at the prospect of a hazardous journey. But we shall need horses."

I made the rounds of the gem merchants, picked up three sapphires, and marked for purchase a ruby and an emerald if I could beat the price down far enough. These five gems would have been worth a king's ransom in the Inner Sea, but for a hundred drachmai one can buy a gemstone in India that would fetch a thousand in the West.

* * *

In the afternoon, we at last made our duty call on King Girixis. The sour-looking Brachman minister informed us that the king was late for the audience; he was out hunting in the royal park east of the public park we had seen the day before.

"But you need not waste your time whilst awaiting His Majesty," he added. "I will have one of our officials show you through the royal art gallery."

This was an unexpected diversion. The gallery was a separate building full of paintings of astonishing lifelikeness and liveliness. Most of them illustrated scenes from Indian myth and legend, such as the churning of the Sea of Milk, the slaying of the demon Bali by the god Indra, and the adventures of the scholar Utanka in the underground world of serpents. The official pointed out some paintings by the king himself, which to me looked neither better nor worse than the rest.

Back before the porch of audience, we found King Girixis seated on his terrace and judging a minor lawsuit. This king proved a short, plump young man who nibbled sweetmeats and watched his six naked dancing girls more than he did the litigants.

When our turn came, he graciously accepted our gifts and seemed pleased to see us. When I told him—truthfully—that the paintings in his gallery were better than anything I had seen in my native western lands, and less truthfully added that his own paintings were by far the best, he beamed all over and hoped we should have a long and profitable stay in Mahismati.

"I thank Your Majesty," I said, "but we must shortly leave for Ozenê. I should not like my ship to sail for home without me."

"That beastly place?" said King Girixis, yawning. "Full of fanatical sectaries? Know, sir, that I am Orthodox, as was my sire before me. But I do not force my beliefs upon others, and I treat my Buddhist subjects the same as any others. You will find things otherwise in Ozenê. But then, meseems, you merchants must needs face such risks. If you can cross the dreadful Black Water, you can do anything." He snapped his fingers, and a servant appeared with a tray of gifts.

"I regret that I can offer you but one small gift apiece," said the king. "Our treasury has been straitened of late."

Otaspes chose a silver ornament. When the tray was proffered to me, I picked up a little bronze statuette with a ring at the top and a fine chain for hanging it round one's neck, as Phoenicians do with glass statuettes of their Pataecian gods. The statuette was that of a pudgy man with an elephant's head, seated on a flower.

"Would Your Majesty mind telling me what this means?" I asked.

Girixis smiled. "That is the Lord Ganesha, one of the most popular minor gods among the Orthodox. He is the patron of literature and commerce. With that statue in your possession, you should be able to sell anybody anything, since Ganesha gives you the power to make people believe whatever you say."

"Well, I am a merchant, and I have written a little for publication, so this statue should be the perfect amulet for me."

"May it prove so. You came hither by boat, did you not? How will you get to Ozenê?"

"We had thought of buying horses, sire."

"My dear barbarians! That will never do; the Paripatras swarm with tigers and brigands. The only small parties who can cross the hills in safety are holy men, so poor they tempt not the robbers and so pure that even the tigers let them be."

"What, then, Highness?" I asked.

"If you could tarry …" Girixis turned to his minister. "Munda, when leaves the next caravan for Ozenê?"

"At the next full moon, sire, fifteen days hence."

"Can you wait until then?" the king asked me.

"I fear not, sire."

"Well, then …" He snapped his fingers. "I have it! Permit me to lend you an elephant. Thus shall you be safe from attack. Let me see—there are you, and your Persian friend, and your slave. Old Prasada can easily bear the three of you and your trade goods. See to it, Munda."

"But, Your Majesty!" protested the minister, "that elephant is too precious to risk—"

"Not another word, Munda. Prasada is my elephant, and if I am fain to lend him to these foreign gentlemen, that is that."

* * *

Thus it happened that, two days later, Otaspes, Gnouros, and I hoisted ourselves and our gear aboard the biggest bull in Girixis' herd. Prasada was certainly a monster, as tall as two men, one atop the other, with tusks half again as long as my arm. He was also elderly, as was shown by the deep hollows on the sides of his head and the ragged edges of his ears. He moved slowly and ponderously, refused to be hurried for long, and did not get excited over trifles as, I was told, younger elephants were wont to do. He had formerly been the Royal Elephant, regularly used by the king for war and parades. But a few years before, Girixis had retired him from this post in favor of a younger and more spirited beast.

* * *

Our saddle was not one of those box-shaped affairs, with benches for two or four riders, which Indian kings occupy for hunting, war, and processions. It was a less pretentious but more practical structure. First, on the elephant's back were two long rolls of padding, extending the length of the animal's torso, one on each side of its spinal ridge. Atop these rolls was laid a huge plank, also as long as the animal's back. From this plank, a footboard was hung by ropes on each side. The whole assembly was held in place by a girth of ropes, which went around the elephant's body just aft of the forelegs, and a crupper around the base of the tail.

At each end, the plank bore an iron staple, a span high and as wide as the plank itself, which served as a handrail for those seated at the ends of the plank. Those in the middle had loops of rope to hold on by. When I first clambered aboard, I tried to sit astride the plank, as if I were riding a horse. But the plank proved too wide for this purpose, and the elephant's barrel too thick. After a half hour of torment like that which I had undergone in trying to assume the lotus posture, I turned sideways on the plank, with both feet on one footboard, and made out much better.

Prasada was lying down when we mounted him. The plank proved amply long for the three of us. The driver or *mahavata*, a little gray-bearded man named Koka, scrambled up to Prasada's neck and picked up the two-foot iron goad, which he had hung over Prasada's left ear. He spoke to the beast and whacked him over the head with the goad. The blow made a sound like a drum or a hollow log, but the elephant did not seem to mind.

The driver called back: "Beware!" Up went Prasada's foreparts. Gnouros yelped with fright and clutched the rear staple. Then the hindquarters rose in their turn, and Prasada plodded out of the elephant yard. He had an easy gait: a gentle, back-and-forth, rocking motion. A bell hung from his neck tolled with an irregular rhythm.

We shuffled through the winding streets, out the Ozenê Gate, and along the muddy road to the hills. A drizzle hid the rising sun.

We were still riding through cultivated fields—mostly of poppies, whence the Indians extract an intoxicating juice—when Prasada stopped. A little man in breechclout and shawl, with a pair of baskets slung over his shoulder by a yoke, stood in the road before us. He and Koka engaged in a long colloquy, but I could not follow their speech. Otaspes confessed himself likewise baffled.

"I think," he said at last, "that the man in the road is asking Koka to give him a ride."

"Well, now, we won't have anything like that—" I began, when the man in the road scuttled around to Prasada's rear and scrambled up like a monkey, baskets and all, using the elephant's tail and the ropes of his harness. Before I knew what had happened, he had squeezed in between Gnouros and the after end of the plank.

"Koka!" I cried. "We do not wish another passenger. He crowds us. Put him off, at once!"

"Sorry, my lord," said Koka, "but this man has forced me to let him board the elephant."

"What do you mean, forced you? Nobody can force you except Master Otaspes and me."

"He has compelled me by his reasoning. Giving him this ride will gain me merit in my next life."

"You heard me!" I yelled. "Put him off, do you hear?"

"I am sorry, my lord, but I cannot."

"You do as I command, or by all your ten-armed Indian gods I'll wring your scrawny neck!"

"Then who will drive the elephant?" said the driver, helplessly spreading his hands.

"You might as well calm down, old boy," said Otaspes, who had been slyly grinning. "This is India, where people who ruffle easily don't last long. We are not really crowded. I'm wider than you, and I do not mind. Besides, it never hurts to do a favor that costs nought."

"You're too good-natured," I grumbled. "By the time we reach Ozenê, we shall have these knaves hanging from the elephant's ears."

"Besides," persisted Otaspes, "this man may give us news. One never knows what one may pick up. Koka, find out who he is and what he does."

There was more speech in the dialect I did not know. Then Koka announced: "His name is Bhumaka, and he is a snake charmer. He came to Mahismati to earn a pittance with his snakes during the natal fête."

"Snakes!" screamed Otaspes. "Mean you that he has serpents in those baskets?"

"Only in one of them, my lord. The other contains mice to feed his serpents on."

"Arimanes take them! Get rid of him! Throw away those baskets! I am terrified of serpents!" The Persian had turned deathly pale.

"Now who's getting excited?" I said. "The lids of the baskets seem to be well tied down, so the serpents can't get at you. Now I'm glad we have Master Bhumaka with us; I have always wondered how one charms a serpent."

"Then you shall change places with me," said Otaspes, "to put me as far as possible from those accursed reptiles."

When this had been done, Koka whacked his beast on the head, Prasada resumed his shuffle, and we breasted the long slopes that led up into the Paripatras.

* * *

As we wound higher into the hills, the villages and cultivated fields became smaller and fewer, until we were plodding through dense jungle, dripping from the morning's rain. A herd of deer bounded across the road before us. I snatched at my bow case, which dangled from one of the footboards along with the rest of my gear.

"Better not," said Otaspes.

"Why not? We could have a venison dinner—"

"I think there is some law that only the king may hunt. Besides, these people are mostly Buddhists, who consider it wicked to slay even an animal."

"If it's wicked for me, why isn't it wicked for King Girixis?"

"He is a Brachmanist, and in any event the king may do as he likes."

We passed on. A piercing scream made me start until I realized it was only a peacock. An immense pile of dung by the road caused me to ask what monster could possibly have dropped it.

"Rhinoceros," said Otaspes.

"Then your Indian rhinoceros must be thrice the size of this elephant!" said I in some alarm.

"No, it's much smaller than an elephant. But it has the habit of coming to the same place to relieve itself every day."

We stopped for lunch in an open space, while Prasada wandered through the nearby woods, stuffing greenery into his vast pink maw. A monkey stole up, snatched Gnouros' piece of bread, and ran away with it, chattering in triumph.

Bhumaka opened one of his baskets to exercise his serpents, while Otaspes moved as far away as he could without leaving the clearing altogether. Bhumaka's troupe comprised three serpents: a six-foot python, a four-foot snake of an extremely venomous kind they call a *naga*, and a smaller snake of some harmless species.

All were torpid from having been lately fed, but by flapping a cloth Bhumaka persuaded the naga to rear up and spread its hood. Then he played his tootle-pipe to it. swaying his body in time to the music. The naga swayed likewise. It is said that the music compels the serpent to sway, but it looked more as if the creature were sighting upon its owner in order to make its deadly lunge. Every time its target moved, it had to move also. After a while the naga got bored, shrank its hood, and sank back into its basket. Bhumaka seized it by the neck, dragged it forth, and pried open its jaws.

"What is he doing?" I asked Koka.

"He is looking to see if the naga's fangs have grown in."

"How do you mean?"

Koka: "A charmer from time to time makes his naga bite a piece of cloth and then jerks the cloth to break the serpent's fangs. But, when a naga loses its fangs, a new pair grows in. Hence the charmer must assure himself that a new pair grow not in unbeknownst to him, lest he lose his life."

Bhumaka spoke angrily. Koka said: "He says I give away his trade secrets."

"Tell him we won't tell a soul," I said.

"I do not want any more lunch," said Otaspes, looking green.

"Well, you came on this journey to lose weight," I said.

The afternoon passed pleasantly, with glimpses of the swarming wild life: buffalo, deer, antelope, wild pig, and once a rhinoceros, standing a few paces from the road and staring at us, as unmoving as a great, gray boulder. The Indian kind has but one horn on its snout. Birds and monkeys chattered overhead.

When night came, we found another open space, ate, and told stories around the fire, which attracted a vast swarm of moths. Koka and Bhumaka performed a ritual to keep ghosts and goblins away, and we lay down, wrapped in our cloaks, on beds of leaves. I spent the first watch in tramping around the clearing with bow and arrow in hand, hearing the distant toot of a wild elephant and the rhythmic snarl of a hunting tiger, which sounds like a man sawing wood. Koka assured me that the presence of Prasada, prowling around the camp and gorging on green stuff, would discourage any dangerous men or beasts from molesting us.

Otaspes, who also had brought a bow, took the second watch. Then came the turn of Gnouros. Although the little man swore afterwards that he had been wide awake the whole time, I think he must have dozed. For, the next thing I knew, I was awakened by a chorus of yells, and several men landed on top of me. I kicked and punched but was never able to shake off more than one at a time.

I was lined up with the rest of our party in front of our campfire, all battered and disheveled. Our captors were a wild-looking, ragged crew of fifteen or twenty Indians, thin as skeletons and armed with only crude spears. The tall, gaunt chief wore a turban and carried a sword.

Several Indians held each of us by the arms while a man with cords began binding us. While he was tying Gnouros' wrists, Koka spoke to the chief.

"What is all this?" I asked Koka. "Just thieves?"

"Nay, my lord," said the *mahavata*. "This is a religious sect. Besides robbing us, they believe they can achieve union with God by a ritual, wherein they torture us to death. That is why they have not yet slain us. They will tie us to yonder trees ..."

There was no sign of Prasada, who had discreetly withdrawn. The chief was looking at Bhumaka's baskets near the fire. He cut the cord of one and knocked off the lid. Up popped the heads of Bhumaka's serpents, which, having been warmed by the fire, were in a lively mood.

The chief gave a wild yell, backed up, tripped, and fell into the fire. With a shriek he bounced out, scattering coals and beating at his burning skirt and shawl. The serpents began to slither out of the basket. One of the men holding me let go and, shouting his alarm, backed away. In the excitement, the others loosened their grasp.

A quick wrench freed my arms; a blow knocked one of my captors sprawling and a kick in the crotch doubled over another. A glance showed that Otaspes had freed himself likewise and was laying about him with his sword.

I still wore my sword, too; but Hermes sent me a better idea. I sprang to the basket and picked up a serpent, the naga. The reptile struck at my arm but failed to draw blood in its fangless state. I tossed it into the faces of the nearest Indians, who scattered screaming. The harmless serpent followed.

Then I grabbed the python. The beast gave me a nasty bite on the knee, tearing the skin with its many needle-pointed teeth. But I gripped it by neck and tail, whirled it around, and let fly at the chief, who had torn off his shawl and was stamping out the flames.

When the brigand saw the huge serpent whirling through the air towards him, he threw up both hands before his face, covering his eyes. Otaspes stepped forward with a mighty backhand swing. The chief's head leaped from his shoulders and went bounding and rolling across the clearing, while the body, spouting blood, fell. Then there was only the backs of Indians, fleeing into the forest. I caught one and sworded him to death. Otaspes pursued them, too, but he was too stout to catch them.

Back in the clearing, I had to lean against a tree to get my breath. Koka cut Gnouros' bonds. Bhumaka wept and bewailed the loss of his serpents, all of which had vanished into the darkness.

"Tell him I'll buy him a new set of serpents," I bade Koka. "And round up that accursed elephant of yours before these scoundrels recover their nerve and come back."

Book V

TYMNES THE SCYTHIAN

The road descended with many bends and turns from the Paripatras to the plains of Avanti. From the height of land it followed a small stream, which grew into the northward-flowing Sipta River. Thirty or forty years before, Avanti had formed part of the short-lived, ramshackle Indian empire of King Menandros but had quickly reasserted its independence after his death.

As Prasada trudged along, the character of the country changed. On the northern slopes of the Paripatras, the jungle was smaller, becoming scrubby or bushy. As we descended into the plains, cultivation—mainly of wheat and poppy—again became frequent. We passed oxcarts and men riding camels and asses.

At a village, Bhumaka left us. I gave him a drachma of King Menandros, which I had taken in change in Barygaza, to make up for the loss of his snakes, and he happily wagged his head and took his leave. I suppose I paid too much, but I was not up on the current prices of serpents.

The sun hung low in the red-banded western sky as we neared Ozenê. Then came a drumming of hooves behind us. A troop of cavalry galloped up, shouting for us to halt. These men were taller and lighter of skin than the Indians whom we had seen hitherto, with beards dyed red, green, and blue. They wore large turbans and tunics not unlike the Hellenic kind, all gaudily colored. They carried lances and small bucklers and rode in a curious way. A ring was attached to the girth on each side, and the rider hooked his big toes into these rings, thus giving himself a steady seat.

The leader, wearing the largest turban and a shirt of scale mail, shouted incomprehensibly up at us until Otaspes, shouting back, found a tongue they had in common. After more speech, Otaspes said:

"He asks what we mean by riding an elephant. Know we not that it is forbidden to all but royalty?"

"Tell him King Girixis—"

"I have already told him. He will escort us to town, to do us honor if we are telling the truth; but if not—" Otaspes drew a finger across his throat. "We must be careful with these fellows. They are Arjunayanas, who would as lief spear you as not."

"What people is that?"

"They come from a great desert northwest of here. I believe the lands of the Indian Hellenes lie beyond this desert, but I have not been there to see. Anyway, these rascals are mercenaries, serving the king of Avanti—or rather the queen mother, who really runs the country."

We resumed our plod towards the city, while the sun set and the Arjunayanas cantered restlessly back and forth. They never rode at a walk or a trot. The silver sickle of a new moon hung above the red band of sky that surmounted the western horizon.

A little way from the road, a grove of huge old trees rose ahead of us. As Prasada carried us closer, I saw that this grove contained a small temple. There were lights and movement, and the next instant our escort was streaming away, galloping up the path to the temple. One of them shouted to us to follow.

A crowd, fitfully revealed by the yellow glow of butter lamps, was gathered before the temple. The cavalrymen dismounted. Leaving a few to hold the horses and lances, the rest mingled with the crowd.

Some ceremony was going on. Seated on Prasada beyond the fringes of the crowd, we were too far away to see clearly in the fading light; but a turbaned man handed something to a shaven priest. There was a racket of drums, gongs, and howling chants. Something flashed in the lamplight, and the audience gave a gasp and burst into song.

We waited, but the Arjunayanas seemed to have forgotten us. At last I told Koka to resume our way to Ozenê. I also asked Otaspes what we had seen at the temple.

"An Arjunayana gave his baby daughter to be sacrificed to Shiva," said the Persian. "Thus they dispose of their little girls when they cannot afford their dowries."

"Beastly barbarians!" I exclaimed.

"Oh, yes?" said Otaspes with his silent laugh. "Your servant has heard that Hellenes expose unwanted daughters. Here they sacrifice them to a god, whereas you throw them on rubbish heaps like so much garbage—unless that be a vile slander against the noble Hellenic race!"

I could only chew my lip in silence, since everybody knows that my fellow Hellenes do just that, so that the population of mainland Hellas is much less than it once was. To change this embarrassing subject, I asked Otaspes:

"Are the worshipers of Shiva a kind of Brachmanist?"

"The Orthodox," he explained, "are divided into two main sects or cults, as well as many minor ones. The two main cults are the worshipers of Shiva and of Vishnu. These two groups get along amiably enough, since each believes that the other's god is but an aspect—whatever that be—of its own. But they are united in detestation of the Buddhists and the Jainists, whom they deem wicked heretics."

The Jainists are a reformed sect, whose doctrines, I believe, are somewhat like those of the Buddhists; but, since I never had a chance to investigate them in person, I will not attempt a description of their cult.

As at Mahismati, a squad of Bactrio-Greek mercenaries guarded the city gate. There was the same jovial welcome, the same promise of entertainment in exchange for news, and the same import tax. Ozenê proved a larger and more imposing city than Barygaza or Mahismati, with a well-built wall and straight streets crossing at right angles; but it had the usual filth and swarms of beggars. A beggar trotted alongside the elephant, holding up a hand without fingers. Another hobbled after him on a crutch, displaying a twisted foot that dangled uselessly.

"They form a hereditary guild here, like every other occupation," explained Otaspes. "Their parents mutilate them—cut off their fingers, or dislocate a joint—so they can beg better."

* * *

The three rulers of Avanti sat on their cushions on their terrace of audience. In the middle was King Ariaka: a youth of not yet twenty years, small and sallow. He sat unmoving and unspeaking, staring straight before him with eyes that seemed to have no pupils.

"He is in a poppy trance," whispered Otaspes. "Tuck that statuette inside your shirt; we don't want them to think you a Brachmanist."

On the king's right sat his mother, the widowed Queen Indrani. This was a good-looking woman of perhaps forty, with well-filled bare breasts and a voluminous skirt. She wore a single rope of pearls and a few bangles, but no more gewgaws than any prosperous Indian matron; Indians care little for appearances.

On King Ariaka's left crouched the minister, a lean, vulture-faced Buddhist priest in yellow, named Udayan. He and the dowager queen ran the land between them, since the king was such a slave of poppy juice as to be useless as a ruler.

Here were no music or dancing girls. Although this court was not quite so informal and disorderly as those I had seen before in India—the Bactrio-Greek guards actually stood at attention—the gods know it was loose enough. People came and went, chattered loudly, and shouted: "O Queen!" or "O *mantrin*!" (minister) whenever one of them thought of something to say.

As we arrived, the queen and the minister were interviewing a band of Sakan mercenaries, who had come to Avanti seeking employment. They comprised a score of light-skinned men dressed in Scythian fashion, in long-sleeved, belted jackets, snug breeches tucked into the tops of high boots of soft leather, and caps that stuck up to a point on top and were prolonged down at the sides into a pair of tails that could be tied under the chin. The Bactrio-Greek guards scowled at their hereditary foes.

The Sakas' leader was a handsome fellow in his thirties. Bareheaded, he had his hair cut short in the shape of an inverted bowl. He shaved his chin but sprouted a huge, up-curling black mustache. He wore russet breeches, an emerald-green coat embroidered with golden thread, and a russet cloak to which green roundels were sewn. Golden earrings and bracelets and a necklace of amber and bear's claws completed his outfit.

I remarked to Otaspes: "I suppose I ought to consider those fellows as enemies, since they are fighting my fellow-Hellenes in the North."

"Be your age, old boy," replied the Persian. "After all, the Sakas pay tribute to Mithradates of Parthia. So does King Tigraios of Karmania, which makes me and the Sakas fellow-subjects of Mithradates. But Oramazdes forbid that you and I should quarrel on that account!

Everybody seemed to be waiting for something. Minister Udayan drummed on the floor of the terrace with his fingers, while the Sakas spoke among themselves. I found I could understand the Sakan dialect of Scythian quite well—better, in fact, than the local Indian, which differed from that of Barygaza. At last I approached the nearest Saka and asked:

"What causes the delay, friend?"

The man smiled at the sound of the Scythian speech. "Men are searching for somebody who speaks Sakan, to interpret." He called to the leader: "Ho, Tymnes!"

"What?"

"Here is our interpreter! He speaks our tongue, and I suppose he speaks this Indian chitter."

"Well, that is a mercy!" Tymnes approached me with a lordly nod. Despite his finery, I was forcibly reminded of the Scythian abhorrence of bathing. "Know, stranger, that I am Tymnes the son of Skopasis, the son of Ariantas, the son of Oktamazdas, of the noble Saulian clan. We trace our ancestry back for thirty-six generations, to the supreme god Papaios. This makes us the noblest clan among the Sakas, who are the noblest folk of the Scythian race, who are the noblest race on earth. Hence the Saulian clan, as is generally known, consists of the world's bravest men and fairest women. And who, may I ask, are you, sir?"

I could have replied to the Saka's haughty courtesy in kind but could not be bothered; I wanted to get our audience over with. "I am Eudoxos, a Hellene," I said, "and I shall be glad to help you as far as I can. Your Majesties!"

I turned to the rulers and explained. With me translating, the Saka began his speech. After repeating his boasts of his noble ancestry, Tymnes got down to business.

"A feud arose amongst the Sakas," he said, "and our clan became embroiled on the losing side. Having been vanquished in battle by overwhelming numbers, we must needs flee. We passed through the lands of the Ionians—" (in the East they call all Hellenes Ionians) "—who were hostile to us, and came to the Great Desert. Here were no rich kings who might hire us, but only scattered robber clans, which attacked us. But we drove them in rout by our archery, which, as is well known, is the world's deadliest. Skirting the desert, we came at last to this fair land to offer our services. This is no trivial offer, for we are, as everyone knows, brave and fierce beyond the imagining of any sedentary folk.

"The rest of our clan, under the leadership of my noble father, Skopasis son of Ariantas, is camped two days' ride north of here on the fringes of the desert, near the boundaries of Avanti, with their women, children, and flocks. When Your Majesties give the word, we will fetch them hither. I have spoken."

The sour-looking minister, Udayan, spoke: "I am sorry, but we already have all the mercenary horse we can afford."

"Mean you those Arjunayanas who escorted us hither? It is rascally jackals of that sort whom we scattered in the Great Desert, with a mere whiff of our deadly arrows. You, sir, err if you consider these thieving poltroons in the same breath with us. …"

The argument raged back and forth, with me interpreting as best I could and Otaspes helping out with the Indian end when I got stuck. Tymnes said:

"It need cost you nought. We do but ask the right to plunder certain of your towns each year."

Udayan looked shocked. "Licensed robbery? Kali smite you! We are a civilized folk, who do things decently and in order."

The argument dragged on, but Udayan and Indrani did not mean to hire the Sakas. At last the latter were made to accept this fact.

"There are kingdoms to the east, west, and south," said Udayan, "where your peerless courage will be appreciated. I suggest the kingdom of Vidisha, southeast of here."

"If we succeed in this Vidisha," said Tymnes, "will you grant a passage through Avanti for our clan?"

"So long as they behave themselves and rob or molest not our folk. We will send an escort to make sure."

The Saka began another argument but was interrupted by the metallic thud of the timekeeper's cup's striking the bottom of its bowl as it sank. The timekeeper pounded his drum four times and blew two blasts on his conch. Udayan said:

"And now, Master Tymnes, your audience is over. Your interpreter and his companion, I believe, have the next turn."

We presented our gifts and were proffered a trayful of trinkets in return. Udayan said:

"From King Girixis, eh? We like not Girixis, for that he is a lewd, sensual pleasure-seeker. But I suppose it were unjust to blame you gentlemen for his lapses. Here in Avanti we hold to the highest moral standards. There is only one way to deal with evil, and that is to scotch it at the source. Hence we allow no winebibbing or meat-eating—"

"And no fornication or adultery!" put in Queen Indrani. "Here, for the first time in the history of this wicked human race, we have utterly abolished sin!"

I was tempted to ask about poppy juice, to which the young king was evidently addicted and which must have furnished Avanti with most of its revenue. It seemed, however, more tactful to say nothing about it, albeit it surprised me to learn that any government would dare to meddle to such a degree in the private lives of its subjects. People who complain about the tyrannical rule of the Ptolemies and the Seleucids, I thought, should visit Avanti to learn what real tyranny is. I asked if we might engage in normal trading.

"Buy and sell what you please," said the queen, "so long as you deal not in goods that lead men into sin, such as intoxicating liquors, or the flesh of beasts, or pretty young slave girls. You are, I trust, persons of good morals—not liars, thieves, drunkards, meat-eaters, or lechers?"

"Surely, madam," I said. "We are as pure as a mountain spring."

"You have not come hither to stir up the superstitious Brachmanists?"

"Nothing is further from our minds than to mix in local religious quarrels."

"Very well; you are welcome to Avanti. But bear in mind what we have told you. How did you ever get to Bharata from your distant land?"

"I sailed across the ocean."

"The Black Water?" exclaimed Udayan with a shudder. "Are you a man or a demon?"

"A man, as far as I know. Why, sir?"

"To cross the Black Water—how ghastly! Pray go about your business; the mere sight of you makes us quail."

"One more thing, may it please Your Majesties," I said. "Know you of a philosopher named Gupta hereabouts?"

Udayan scowled. "That vile materialist! Any contact with him will only besmirch your karma and lead you astray from the Eightfold Way to the bliss of nonexistence. I will not take upon myself the responsibility for telling you where he lives; you will have to seek him out yourself."

As we took our leave, I asked Otaspes if the minister was crazy, to carry on so about the ocean.

"No," he said. "These people have never been out of Avanti and have heard only dim, dreadful rumors of the sea. They are full of such fancies, and it is useless to try to disabuse them."

* * *

We saw to it that Prasada was housed in the royal elephant stables and, ignoring the stares of the townspeople, returned to our quarters. On the way, we learnt a curious thing about Ozenê. Besides the usual beggars, people kept sidling up to murmur offers of forbidden goods. One would whisper of a supply of palm wine; another, of a repast of roast mutton; still another, of his nice, clean sister who would be delighted to entertain us. Had I been so minded, I could have spent my entire stay in Ozenê in enjoyment of these pleasures.

I attended another Bactrio-Greek party and learnt that Avanti was a seething cauldron of hostility between the ruling Buddhists and the Brachmanist majority. These Bactrio-Greeks, like those in Mahismati, urged me to bring some nubile Greek women on my next voyage.

I bought more gemstones, until my Ptolemaic staters were nearly all gone. These stones included several fine rubies and a couple of emeralds, as well as minor stones like agates, jaspers, chrysoprases, and onyxes. I also bought one diamond. This stone has always seemed to me a waste of money, since it is too hard to cut and hence never looks like anything but a glassy pebble; but there are those who believe that wearing it confers upon the wearer some of its own hardness and will pay accordingly. The Indian tale is that diamonds come from a vast range of mountains, the Hemodos, to the north of India. Diamonds are made, they say, of water frozen so hard by the intense cold of those heights that it is permanently fixed in the solid state and cannot again be melted.

I also prowled the shops, asking the prices of everything—even goods I had no thought of buying—to become familiar with the market. This was not a pleasant business, because of the Indians' intense dislike of foreigners. Every one of them believes that Indians are the only good, well-behaved, decent, civilized folk on earth, and they miss no chance of letting the stranger know it. This is of course ridiculous, since every well-informed person knows that, if any people is superior to all the others, it is we Hellenes.

* * *

Three days after my arrival, I knocked on the door of Gupta the philosopher. Gupta proved a small man with a long, gray beard, very lively, cordial, and effusive.

"Come in, come in!" he exclaimed, when I had told him who I was. "Everybody who earnestly seeks the truth is welcome here, regardless of creed or color. I have heard rumors of your arrival in this city. If I give you a sip of forbidden palm wine, you will not tell on me, will you?"

"Of course not!"

"Who is the other man?"

"Gnouros the Scythian, my slave."

"Ah, yes, a slave," said Gupta. "We have little slavery in Bharata, although I have heard that it is much practiced in the western lands. Slavery is a cruel, unjust custom."

I shrugged. "Somebody has to do the dirty work. And from what I have seen, the members of your lower colors are no better off than slaves are among us."

"There is that," he said. "And do not think, because I criticize slavery, that I praise the system of colors. That is the most fiendishly clever method of making the lower orders content with their lot that our wicked species has yet devised."

"How so?"

"Why, the men of the upper colors tell them that, if they suffer from oppression and starvation, it is only a just punishment for misdeeds in some former life. To shine up their karma and get promoted in the next incarnation, they must bear their troubles humbly and obey the higher colors without complaint. Most of the poor fools believe it, too."

"You take a critical view of your own land, sir," I said.

"What is the good of having intelligence if one use it not? What Bharata needs is a complete overthrow of the present social order, if justice shall ever prevail. They need persons like myself, without vested interests or superstitious preconceptions, to manage their affairs. Have another! Dear me, where did I put that jug? Ah, there! So you have been to Sisonaga and Jaivali, eh? Well-meaning wights, I doubt not, but oh, so misguided!"

"How so?"

"They suffer from the curse of our land, which is subjectivism. Everybody in Bharata thinks that, by contemplating the tip of his nose and ignoring the real world around him, he can dredge up eternal truths out of the depths of his own mind. All they get are a lot of mutually contradictory fancies. Now, I follow the great Ajita and Kanada—two of the few clear thinkers that Bharata has produced—in believing that all is made of atoms, moving in space. You and I are made of atoms. When we die, these atoms scatter, and that is the end of us."

"We had a Hellene, Demokritos, who I believe advanced similar theories."

"I am glad to hear that even in foreign lands there are men of sense. All this talk of the soul and immortality and karma and reincarnation is sentimental rubbish, invented to comfort men who fear extinction."

"Do you believe in gods?"

"Show me a real, live, miracle-working god and I will own to belief in that god, at least. I suspect they were invented by the clever to exploit the simple. When the first fool met the first knave, they started the first religion, with the former as the worshiper and the latter as the priest ..."

We went on for hours. Gupta was an interesting talker, full of daring impieties and unorthodoxies, which he had no hesitation in avowing. I judged him to have two main faults. First, he caustically condemned practically everything and everybody. Every person mentioned was either a fool, or a knave, or a bit of both; every belief was superstitious nonsense; every institution ought to be destroyed and replaced by something more rational. Such a man would never be satisfied with any system run by real, fallible human beings. He might, moreover, be extremely dangerous if he got power, because he would want to destroy everything and everybody that did not come up to his own impossibly high ideals. Second, I thought him more dogmatic in denying the existence of the spiritual or supernatural than was warranted by the present state of man's knowledge.

Nonetheless, he was a relief after the woolly-minded speculations of the other thinkers whom I had lately heard. I finally got around to the real purpose of my visit. When I had explained, Gupta said:

"I must think about this. Unlike some of my mystical colleagues, I see nought wrong in enjoying mundane pleasures in moderation, but your problem presents difficulties. Howsomever, I doubt not that by the application of proper scientific methods we shall succeed. Thousands of years ago, before they wandered off into the swamp of subjectivism, the wise men of Bharata achieved great scientific triumphs, such as flying chariots and elixirs of youth, as anybody can perceive from an enlightened reading of the *Rigveda* or the *Ramayana* or—"

"Yes, yes," I said. "I have heard of those. Of course, we Hellenes can make the same sort of claim. Thousands of years ago we had an artificer named Daidalos, who could fly through the air. He made a mechanical bronzen giant, which guarded the isle of Crete. Another epic tells of the mechanical tables of the god Hephaistos, which served repasts without the help of human servants—"

"Hm, hm, very interesting," said Gupta. "But let us get back to business. Have you done nought but wander the face of Bharata, asking one wiseacre after another how to stiffen your *lingam*?"

"I have also done a bit of trading, to make the journey pay for itself."

"Have you had good luck?"

"Not bad at all. You see, the price of gems in the western world is much higher—"

I could have bitten my tongue for blabbing so indiscreetly, but the harm had been done. The palm wine and Gupta's garrulity had between them loosened my tongue. I finished lamely:

"Well, anyway, I hope to end up with some small profit."

"Good for you! And now I think I know how to cure your weakness. Have you ever attended an orgy?"

"I have enjoyed many women, surely; but a real orgy—no, I think not."

"You would be surprised at its stimulating effect."

"Do you mean you have orgies in India? Indians have impressed me as the most straitlaced and sobersided lot I have ever encountered."

Gupta giggled. "The Brachmanes strive to impose all these ridiculously rigid rules of conduct upon the rest of us, but not everybody takes them so seriously as they would like. Now, I head a little group of advanced thinkers, who meet betimes on the banks of the Sipta to enjoy an evening of philosophical discourse and good-fellowship. The next meeting of our club is—let me think—by the nonexistent gods, it is tomorrow night! Meet me here at sunset, and we shall see what we can do for you."

* * *

There were fourteen in the club, including Gupta and myself: seven men and seven women. We met in a little hollow in the banks of the Sipta, half a league north of Ozenê. They did not use the public park, Gupta explained, because it was too close to the city and hence too likely to draw hostile attention. This place was well hidden by trees and shrubbery from the Modoura road.

I was there alone, having given Gnouros the evening off. Otaspes was entertaining the Sakas, who had lingered in Ozenê to sample the joys of what seemed to them a big, glittering city. He and they could understand each other, for the Scythian tongue is much like the Persian.

Gupta hung a garland of flowers around my neck and introduced me to our twelve fellow-celebrants. A comely woman named Ratha had been chosen as my partner. They questioned me about my native "Ionia" and its customs, which they found barbarous and revolting. I thought it inexpedient to tell them what I thought of some of their customs.

We grilled beefsteaks and washed them down with palm wine. We drank to the nonexistent gods. We drank confusion to the meddlesome Buddhists and the superstitious Brachmanists alike. By the time we had drunk to the downfall of all of Gupta's pet abominations, my head swam.

One man, a merchant, had lately returned from a journey to Palibothra, the capital of mighty Magadha. To judge from this traveler's account, King Odraka's capital must be a metropolis the size of Athens or Alexandria, and the magnificence of its royal palace would make the palaces I saw in Barygaza and Mahismati and Ozenê look like peasants' huts by comparison.

At Palibothra, this merchant had encountered a cult that worshiped, with extravagant rites, the "female creative principle." Producing a small drum, he explained these rites, rhythmically tapping his drum. There were, for instance, *mantras* or incantations, of which he gave us a few samples. Soon all fourteen of us were chanting the mantras, such as "The jewel is in the lotus," in unison.

Then there were dances. We danced in circles and drank some more and chanted mantras and danced and drank. . . .

I fuzzily noted that the others seemed to have cast off their few garments and that the dancing was taking on the character proper to an orgy, with writhing embraces, lascivious fondling, and intertwining of limbs. Ratha tugged at my tunic, which I allowed her to pull off.

Other couples had thrown themselves down in the long grass, which quivered with their exertions. Ratha tried to spur my sluggish passions, at last it seemed that she would succeed. I felt my old strength flow into my loins. Then she indicated the belt of cloth containing my gemstones and my remaining cash.

"Take it off!" she said from the ground on which she lay, supine and expectant.

"No," I said. "It will not be in the way."

"Take it off, or you shall never put your jewel into *my* lotus!"

"I will not!"

"What is the matter?" said Gupta, who had risen from his woman. "You cannot enjoy the pleasures of love with that ugly thing around your waist. Do it off, as she says!"

"I will not. Take your hands off it!" For Gupta had seized the belt on one side while Ratha, having risen, tried to grasp it from the other.

I jerked free from the pair of them, thoughts of love banished by a lively suspicion of my new friends. I cursed my stupidity in not having left the girdle in the care of Otaspes or Gnouros.

"Seize him!" yelped Gupta.

The five other men, all of whom had finished their rites, threw themselves upon me. I swung a blow at one that, had it landed, would have knocked him arse-over-turban into the Sipta. But in my drunken state I missed, and two of them threw themselves at my legs and brought me crashing to earth. I struggled, kicked, bit, and tried to get up, but they were too many.

"Turn him over," said Gupta. "One of you untie that belt."

"Cut his throat first," said an Indian, holding on to my right arm for dear life. "He is too dangerous; he might break loose."

"I fear you are right," said Gupta. "Dear me, where did I put that knife?"

"What kind of philosopher do you call yourself?" I yelled.

"A practical one," he replied, producing the knife and testing its edge with his thumb. "Since reason has led me to disbelief in the supernatural, it follows that morals are a human invention, to be observed only as a matter of expediency. With the folk among whom I live, I observe their code of morals faithfully enough to keep me out of serious trouble. This does not apply, however, to a foreigner like yourself, who will never be missed. Hence, since you have something I want and would not give it to me for the asking, my only logical course is to slay you and possess myself of your wealth."

"Was this whole party a plot to entrap me?"

"Why, of course! This meeting was not planned, as I implied to you, in advance but was made up on the spur of the moment. A clever move, if I do say so—"

"In the name of Shiva the Destroyer," cried one of the others, "slay him! You two would talk and argue all night, but we are tired of holding this monster."

"Ah, me, I suppose you are right," said Gupta. "It is a pity in a way; this giant barbarian is not without the power of reason. Tip your head back, my dear Eudoxos—"

A chorus of yells interrupted Gupta, and the next instant my limbs were freed. A mass of men in the yellow robes of Buddhist priests rushed out of the shrubbery and fell upon the erstwhile revelers, whacking them with bamboo clubs and screaming: "Base materialists! Vile sensualists! Cow-murderers!" and other epithets that only an Indian would think to use on such an occasion.

The seven women, who had resumed their skirts, ran off up and down the river. The men, however, were compelled to flee naked except for their garlands, leaving their meager garments behind, for they had not donned them before assaulting me. As I rolled to my feet and snatched up my tunic, I said to the nearest priest:

"I am the Ionian, Eudox—"

Whack! went the priest's pole, making me see stars. A couple of other blows landed before I broke out of the mellay. I think they caught Gupta and one other, but I did not wait to see. Albeit already winded from my struggle with the orgiasts, I ran for all I was worth. Here my long legs were my salvation, for, panting and staggering though I was, I still outdistanced my pursuers.

It was nearly midnight when I talked my way past the Bactrio-Greek guards at the Modoura Gate and rejoined Otaspes in our room. The Persian lit a lamp and exclaimed:

"By the Holy Ox Soul, Eudoxos, what happened to you? You have a beautiful black eye—"

"And other lumps and bruises," I growled. I told him a little about the orgy, without confiding my ultimate reason for seeking out Gupta. My flapping tongue had gotten me into enough trouble already.

Otaspes gave his silent laugh. "You certainly get into the damnedest things! But harken. We must leave Ozenê, early tomorrow."

"Why?"

"I have picked up more gossip. The hatred between Brachmanist and Buddhist is at the boil here, and it needs only a small event to make it spill over. If the Brachmanists revolt, the Bactrio-Greeks might be able to put them down. But I would not trust the Arjunayanas, who are Shiva-worshipers and brigands to boot. If they turn against Queen Indrani or if the Bactrio-Greeks desert—well, I shan't care to be here when it happens."

Gnouros snored heavily in a corner. "Is he all right?" I asked.

"All right except that he is sleeping off a hemp spree. You know Scythians; they burn the stuff and sniff the fumes. My Sakan friends put on a little orgy of their own."

* * *

It seemed that I had hardly fallen asleep when a thunderous knocking awakened me. A feeble pre-dawn light came through the shutters. Otaspes had opened the door, in which stood our landlord.

"You must leave this place, fast," said the landlord. "There is trouble in the city. Mobs are killing all foreigners. They will search this place, and if they find you—" The man drew a finger across his throat.

"What has happened?" I demanded.

The landlord explained: "The story is that some worshipers of Vishnu had gathered on the banks of the Sipta for private devotions, and the Buddhist priesthood set upon them with clubs and cruelly beat them all to death."

"That sounds like my party," I muttered to Otaspes, "after the rumor-mongers had been at it."

The landlord continued: "So all the Orthodox have joined to rid Ozenê of heretics." The man smiled one of those nervous, flickering, mirthless little Indian smiles. "I concern myself not with sects and philosophies, sirs. I am only a poor man, striving to make a living. But for you to be caught here would do none of us any good."

"He has a point," I said. I kicked Gnouros awake and helped him to pack up our modest possessions. Whilst we were thus engaged, an outcry from the street outside drew our attention. Otaspes cautiously opened the shutters and peered out. He hissed at me and beckoned.

This inn was one of the few two-story structures on Ozenê, and our window commanded a good view of the South or Mahismati Gate and the avenue leading to it. A dull roaring came to our ears, now near, now far.

Suddenly, a man rounded a corner several crossings away, running hard with the yellow robes of a Buddhist priest fluttering behind him. After him pelted a couple of score of breech-clouted, wild-haired Indians led by a naked holy man covered with cow-dung ash, who rolled his eyes, foamed at the mouth, and screamed some phrase I could not catch, over and over.

"What is he saying?" I asked Otaspes.

"*Gao hamara mata hai*—the cow is our mother."

"A strange war cry," I said. "I thought Indians were born normally to human mothers—look!"

Almost under our window, the mob caught the running man, who disappeared beneath a tangle of bodies. There was a moment of screaming confusion, and then the mob set up a chant, in unison, of "Die, detestable heretic! Die, confuser of colors!"

The severed, shaven head of the priest was jammed down on a sharpened pole and hoisted into the air. Behind this banner, the mob trotted off to other mischief.

"We had better get our elephant," said Otaspes.

I slipped on my mailshirt and strapped on my sword. "There's no point in our all going to the stables with the baggage. I can go thither as safely alone. When I return with Prasada, you two shall be ready to leave."

They started to argue, but I slipped out without answering. I made the three blocks to the stables without meeting a soul. At the stables, however, I was told that Koka and Prasada had already left. At the first hint of disturbance, the elephant driver had fled the city with his pet.

Back at the inn, I broke the news to my companions. We were trying to form alternative plans when more noises brought us again to the window.

"Great Oramazdes!" breathed Otaspes.

Down the avenue to the South Gate, marching in step to the tune of flutes, strode the three full companies of Bactrio-Greek mercenaries in full battle array, pikes at the ready and kilts aswing. Their women and children scuttled along in the intervals between the companies.

A mob of Indians raced around a corner in front of the troops. The soldiers in the first two ranks lowered their pikes and plowed through the rabble like a ship through water, leaving a score of trampled bodies. Other knots of Indians dashed screaming at the Bactrio-Greeks from the sides and rear, to be likewise repulsed. It was amazing to see the ferocity these little, underfed brown men, usually submissive and timid, could work up when they tried.

Some Indians climbed to the roofs of the houses lining the avenue and hurled stones and tiles down upon the marchers. I could hear the clang as these missiles struck helmets and body armor. When the companies had passed, a couple of light-skinned figures in bronzen cuirasses and plumed helmets lay in the mud with the stricken Indians.

The Bactrio-Greeks marched on. The gate opened, and out they went, never breaking step. The mob churned about the avenue, screeching and mutilating the bodies of the fallen Bactrio-Greeks. I expected this crowd to disperse, to give us a chance for a dash to the gate. Instead, they hung around, dancing and chanting. When one group wandered off, another appeared. Some of them had caught a Buddhist family and were torturing them to death near the gate.

"Now, how in the name of Mithras the bull-slayer," asked Otaspes, "are we to get through that gang without being torn to pieces? If we were naked holy men, they would not even notice us—"

"You've solved the problem!" I cried, clapping him on the back. "Come with me to the kitchen!"

"What do you mean to do?"

"We shall be naked holy men! Come on!"

"But, Eudoxos, I cannot run around with my private parts flapping in the breeze, like these folk! We Persians have a sense of decency—"

"Never mind what you can and can't do. Come on, or I'll drag you!"

A quarter-hour later, Otaspes and I stepped out of the inn into that deadly street. We were naked save for our money belts, which I hoped nobody would notice. We were smeared from head to foot with a mixture of soot and ashes, so that no one could tell what sort of skins we bore beneath this coating. Our hair and beards were disordered. We rolled our eyes, gnashed our teeth, and screamed:

"*Gao hamara mata hai!*"

Behind us, Gnouros followed, bent double under a big bundle. This consisted of our most important possessions, wrapped in my cloak. We had abandoned much of our gear, including all Otaspes' trade goods—even his prized bolt of silken cloth. But a reasonable man does not worry about such things when his life is at stake.

Down the road we capered, hopping and whirling and making the most idiotic gestures we could think of. As a result, the Indians paid us no attention whatever. We passed the dismembered bodies of the slain Buddhists, lying in huge, scarlet, fly-swarming pools. We danced out the South Gate and into the countryside. A heavy overcast hid the rising sun.

Half a league from Ozenê, we came upon the mountainous carcass of poor old Prasada, dead by the side of the road. Koka lay near him. The elephantarch had been pierced through and through by spear thrusts. From the elephant's side, just aft of his left foreleg, protruded the broken shaft of a long Arjunayana lance.

"Those abandoned temple thieves!" I said. "They must have heard that this pair had left the city before the rioting started and assumed that we were on the beast. When they caught up with the elephant, hoping to rob us, either they slew them in a rage at not finding us, or Koka failed to stop on command."

"Perhaps," said Otaspes. "I cannot feel too sorry for him, since after all he deserted us. But what is more important, I do not think it were wise for us to return to Mahismati. King Girixis is an affable monarch, but he might not take kindly the loss of his prize bull elephant."

"Right you are," I said. "I wonder where the Arjunayanas are now?" I began to don my garments.

"Looting the palace, I should think," said Otaspes, pulling on his Persian trousers. "If we head west across country, we shall come to the headwaters of the Mais. Following this river downstream, we come by a roundabout route to the sea, not far north of Barygaza—Oh, by the bronzen balls of Gou the demon king! Look!"

He pointed along the road to southward, on which a little cloud of dust now danced.

"Couldn't that be the Bactrio-Greeks on their way south?" I asked.

"Is not so," said Gnouros. "Are horseback riders. Not Sakas; the other kind, with turbans."

I glanced toward the Sipta. "We might get across the river. They might not want us badly enough to swim their horses after us."

Otaspes shook his head. "I cannot swim, and anyway I am foredone with all this running and capering. I am ready to die as a Persian gentleman should."

"Oh, come on! I'll drag you across. It's not deep here."

I had to bully the exhausted Persian back on his feet. We set out at a trot towards the river. At this place, however, a bend took the Sipta a couple of furlongs from the road. We were still far from the water when a hail and a drumming of hooves told us that the Arjunayanas were upon us.

We faced about and drew our swords, our bows having been left back at the elephant's corpse with the rest of our gear. A couple of the leading horsemen bore down upon us, lances couched and dyed beards fluttering in the air, with the obvious intention of running us through.

"Get ready to throw yourself to the side at the last instant," I gasped.

Then came the twang of a bowstring, and another, and a whole chorus of them. No musical tune ever sounded sweeter. One Arjunayana fell from his horse. The horse of another, hit in the rump, reared and threw its rider.

The Sakan troop galloped nigh, bows snapping and arrows whistling. In a trice the Arjunayanas had wheeled and galloped away. The foremost Saka, young Tymnes, cantered up with his green-and-russet cloak billowing.

"Now, sirs," he said, "you see that we lied not when we told you of the valor and ferocity of the noble Saulian clan."

"How did you happen along so timely?" I asked.

"We had to cut our way out of Ozenê and lost one of our brave lads doing it. When we came to the elephant's carcass, we saw those sand thieves chasing somebody towards the river. One of our men, whose sight is keen even for an eagle-eyed Saulian, said the fugitives looked like you and Master Otaspes. So, having broken bread with Master Otaspes, we did our duty as gentlemen. I have spoken."

The rest of the Sakas now arrived. Some led extra horses laden with baggage. A couple went after the riderless Arjunayana horses with lariats, while others dismounted to pick up spent arrows and to scalp the three fallen Arjunayanas. They hung the bloody scalps from their horse trappings and remounted.

I thanked Tymnes profusely and explained our situation.

"I had hoped," said he, "to enjoy the company of you and Master Otaspes from here to Vidisha, since I deem you persons of mettle suitable for a noble Saka like myself to befriend. But what must be, must be. Permit me, then, to present you with these three Indian horses. They are poor stuff compared with our noble steppe breed, but they will get you back to Barygaza. And I shall at least have the pleasure of your company to the next ford across the Sipta. Let us go!"

Book VI

ANANIAS THE JUDAEAN

As we beat our way westward, the country became more barren, until it bore a mere scattering of shrubs, like that on the hills in the drier lands about the Inner Sea. Otaspes assured me, however, that the true desert still lay far to the northwest.

Then I fell sick again. I asked Otaspes if it were not well to get me to some peasant's hut to recover.

"I think we shall do better camping out," he said. "The rains are over, and in such a hut you would probably pick up some even deadlier ailment."

So we camped. Otaspes killed an antelope with his bow, so that for a time we ate well. But I seemed to get no better.

"Go on and leave me to die alone," I said. "I'm weary of life, for I've failed in the main task I set myself."

"And what is that?" said Otaspes. "Learning the secrets of the universe from these so-called holy men?"

"Not quite." And at last I told the Persian of my real motive in coming to India.

"Oh," he said. "Well, your slave will not argue with you—one Hellene can out-talk three Persians any day—but I will certainly not leave you to perish. You saved me from the Arjunayanas when I was ready to give up, and I can do no less for you."

So, over my feeble protests, he and Gnouros nursed me back to health. With the return of health came the feeling that, while making love to a woman was certainly one of life's major pleasures, it was not the only one.

The moon was full, in the middle of Maimakterion, when we again took up our journey. The land became yet more desertlike. At night, instead of the snarl of the tiger and the trumpeting of the wild elephant, we were serenaded by the roar of the lion and the howl of the wolf.

Near the headwaters of the Mais, we passed through an area that the rains had missed the past season. Everywhere people were starving and dying. It was hard to find a place near the road to stop for lunch where a shriveled corpse or two did not lie in view. To keep from starving ourselves—since there was no food to be bought—we kidnaped one of those scrawny little cows that wander about, dragged her to a hidden ravine, and slaughtered her. If the Indians had found out, they would have torn us limb from limb. Any right-thinking Indian would as lief eat his own mother as one of these sacred beasts, even to save his life.

Once we passed a huge, stone-lined reservoir that some former king had built, with stone steps leading down from one side for religious ablutions. The reservoir was half full of water, which had been allowed to stand for a long time. The surface was covered with a green scum, under which we found the water clear and drinkable. When I wondered that the Indians did not use this water on their parched fields, Otaspes asked several until he got the story. Years before, it transpired, a man had fallen into the tank and drowned. This rendered the tank religiously polluted, so that they could not use its water again, a generation or more later, even to avert starvation.

This region was strongly Brachmanist. Having been warned of the Brachmanists' hatred of Hellenes, I bought a turban and learnt to wind it so as to be less conspicuous. I also kept my mouth shut around the Indians and let Otaspes do the talking.

Curiously, this land had no king. It was a kind of republic, ruled by an oligarchic senate of big landowners. Now and then we saw members of this aristocracy, going about their affairs and complacently ignoring the skeletal wretches expiring on all sides of them.

We reached the Mais and started down it. The land again became jungled. Progress was hard because many ravines, cut by the tributaries of the Mais, lay athwart our path. Furthermore, the land afforded good cover for tigers and for brigands. We were warned that it had plenty of both. But whatever gods there be must have decided that we had had enough adventures, for we saw neither tigers nor robbers.

And so, at the beginning of Poseidon, we reached Barygaza. I parted with Otaspes, rode to the *Ourania*'s dock, and dismounted. With a yell, Linos rushed ashore to greet me.

"Where's Hippalos?" I asked. "Still in that hut with the Indian girl?"

"No, sir …" Linos seemed at a loss.

"Out with it, man! What has he been up to?"

"You'll find Hippalos in the woods, Captain, living with that holy man."

"Sisonaga?"

"Aye."

"Hermes attend us! How did that come about?"

"Well, sir, I don't like to carry tales, but that Indian girl ran home to her father, complaining that Master Hippalos had mistreated her."

"How?"

"I don't rightly know. Beatings, I heard, and something about burning with hot coals. Anyway, her old man and two young kinsmen—sons or nephews, I suppose—came looking for Master Hippalos with spears. Hippalos fled to Sis-what's-his-name's hut, because the Indians won't do anything violent around a holy man.

"He's been there for nigh a month. When I go to him to ask about the ship, I find him standing on his head, and all he says is: 'See to it, Linos; I'm solving the secrets of the cosmos.'"

This was a side of Hippalos' character that I had not known of. Later that day, I went to Sisonaga's hut. Sure enough, there was my mate in one of the postures of yoga. He lay on his back, with his body raised in an arch so that only his head, shoulders, and feet touched the ground. Sisonaga, sitting in the sun, was droning philosophy.

When I arrived, Hippalos scrambled to his feet, crying: "Rejoice, dear Eudoxos! By Mother Earth, I didn't know you with that thing on your head. We had begun to fear that you had passed to your next incarnation. Did you get what you went for?"

"No. The man in Mahismati handed out the same kind of rubbish as our friend here." (Since we spoke Greek, Sisonaga could not understand us.) "He sent me to another man in Ozenê, who seemed to talk better sense; but he turned out to be a rascal who tried to rob and murder me."

"Then you've given up your quest?"

"That particular quest. But look here, I want that ship ready to sail in two days. You'll have to get to work right now."

"My dear fellow! The wisdom of the East is far more important. Linos can handle the details as well as I."

I glowered at him. "My good Hippalos, that ship will sail in two or three days, with or without you. If you would be aboard it, you shall obey orders. If you'd rather spend your life listening to this old faker's twaddle, I shall manage without you. I will count ten, while you make up your mind. One—two—three—"

"Oh, I'll come, I'll come, I'll come," cried Hippalos. He turned to Sisonaga, placed his palms together, and bowed over them, saying in Indian: "The world calls me back, reverend guru. I hope to pay you a last visit ere I depart."

As we walked back to the ship, I said: "Do you take all the old man's mystical nonsense seriously?"

"Why Eudoxos, what a way to talk about matters too profound for your limited, materialistic understanding! Of course I take it seriously. Don't you?"

"I think they're either fools or fakers, and often a bit of both."

"You're prejudiced because they couldn't help you to indulge your beastly sensual appetites. I suppose you think you know how the universe works better than men who have devoted a lifetime to thinking about it?"

"I have no idea how the universe works. As for your Indians, I suppose that one of them might hit upon some arcane truth now and then. But which one? Their doctrines differ widely among themselves, and they differ likewise from those of Hellenes who have thought just as long and hard on these matters. Obviously they can't all be right, and if even one of them is, all the others must be wrong. How can one tell?"

Hippalos: "By persevering study, I have thus gained my first glimpse of the true nature of things, and I know it is true because my inner consciousness tells me so. Perhaps it is my karma to bring the truths of yoga to the benighted West."

"If you ever get thrown out of the Ptolemaic court, it'll be useful to have some confidence game to fall back on."

"Incurably blind to the higher truths, that's all you are," said Hippalos. Although he had borne a solemn face, now the corners of his mouth twitched in the old satyrlike grin, and I could swear he gave a half-wink. One never knew whether Hippalos was being serious. Probably he took nothing much to heart, save as it bore upon his own self-interest.

"But tell me of your journey," he continued. "What's Farther India like?"

I told him some of my experiences. When I described conditions in Ozenê, I added: "We in the West may be blind to higher truths, but we have better sense than to fight over religious doctrines or to try to rule people's private lives and morals by law. Now, what's this about your mistreating that Indian girl?"

"Don't believe everything you hear. All I did was to scold the wench for not sweeping the scorpions out of the hut, and she went galloping off to her old man with all sorts of wild tales. I say, what's that thing around your neck?"

"This?" I held up the statue of Ganesha. "A gift from King Girixis of Mahismati." I repeated what the king had told me about the nature of this god and the properties of the amulet.

"Do you believe in these powers?"

"No. That is, I have no reason to believe them, but I would not flatly deny them, either."

"Sisonaga has theories about the action of minds at a distance, by means of some sort of cosmic radiation. He thinks the belief of people in amulets and idols endows these objects with such powers. Would you take a drachma for that little thing?"

"I don't want to sell it."

"Give you two drachmai."

"No," I said.

"Five!"

"I said, I don't want to sell. Don't pester me."

"It's nothing in you; you're a wicked Pyrronian skeptic who believes in nought. But I really want it. I'll pay any reasonable price."

"If you must have an amulet, why don't you buy one in a local shop? They have plenty of them on display."

"Because I feel a mystic affinity for that one. It must be that the stars were in the same positions when it was cast as when I was born, or something. Why won't you let me have it?"

"I mean to keep it until the end of this voyage, since you've convinced me that it might just possibly work. But I'll tell you. After the journey is over, if you come to see me in Kyzikos, I'll give you this gimcrack free. Now let's think of getting the ship ready. Have you had the bottom scraped?"

We discussed the inspection of ropes and sails, the loading of the cargo, and such professional matters. I spent my first evening with the crew, telling them my adventures. I did not minimize them; but then, sailors expect a yarn to grow in the telling. The following evening, I paid a farewell visit to Otaspes and his wife.

"This man," said Otaspes to Nakia, "is as stout a traveling companion as one could ask: strong, brave, resourceful, and good-humored. But Oramazdes save me from another journey with him!"

"Why, my dear lord?"

"Wherever he goes, troubles and violence spring up; he draws them as a lodestone draws nails. I have had enough narrow escapes to last me the rest of my days. And then I end the journey with a loss—not his fault, but there you are."

"Speaking of which," I said, "let me repay you for the loss of your trade goods in Ozenê."

"I would not think of it!" he cried. "It was your servant's risk; the loss might as well have been yours. …"

We had an hour-long, amiable wrangle, I pressing payment upon him and he refusing on his honor as a Persian gentleman. At last he let me give him the horses on which Gnouros and I had ridden home.

I also told him about the curious doings of Hippalos in my absence. Nakia said:

"Believe not that man's tale, Master Eudoxos. I saw the burns on the girl's body. The father brought her here, hoping that Otaspes could do something to get justice, for my lord has a good name in Barygaza."

On the fifth day after my return, we loaded our last supplies. Otaspes and Nakia came down to see me off; we embraced and parted. I never saw those dear people again; for, when I returned to India, they had left for their Karmanian home.

* * *

The return voyage was uneventful. As the six-month wind wafted us across the Arabian Sea towards the Southern Horn, Hippalos brought out a game set he had bought in Barygaza—at least, I suppose he bought it. This is a kind of war game called *chaturanga*. It is played on a square board divided into sixty-four small squares. Four players play as pairs of partners. Each player has an "army" of eight pieces: four foot soldiers, a horse, a ship, an elephant, and a king. Each piece has its own rules for moving, which makes the game far more complex than "robbers" or "sacred way." The pieces are beautifully carved from ivory—at least, those of Hippalos' set were. Each player sets up his army in one corner of the board, and throws of dice determine who shall move first.

The usual players were Hippalos, Linos, the cook, and I, although one or another of the sailors sometimes took part. We had to keep the stakes very low, for otherwise the crew could not have afforded to play at all. Hippalos urged me to stake my partner with some of my gems while he staked his with pearls. I tried this once; but, after Hippalos had won a good sardonyx from me, I saw through his maneuver. Since he had had the most practice, he was by far the most skilled player amongst us, and he hoped to use his skill to get my gems away from me. So we went back to playing for pence and chick-peas.

When we grew tired of *chaturanga*, I asked Hippalos:

"What were those tricks I saw you amusing the Indians with in Barygaza?"

He grinned. "Old boy, didn't you know I have mysterious powers, drawn from the nighted caverns of the underworld and the black gulfs of outer space? That, with a wave of my hand, I could make this ship and all aboard it vanish in a puff of smoke?"

"Ha! Let's have the truth for once. Where did you pick up these tricks?"

He was reluctant to discuss this skill at first; but at length his own boredom with the peacefulness of the voyage persuaded him to open up. "I learnt sleight-of-hand when I was a wandering entertainer," he said, "in the years after the fall of Corinth, when I was a stripling. The boss of our little band of showmen taught me, for his own fingers were getting too stiff with age for the tricks. Of course, it's easier to learn these things when one is young and limber, as I was. You, I fear, are much too old."

"Is that so! Suppose you try to teach me, and we shall see."

At last I won Hippalos' consent to make me his apprentice magician. As he had warned, I found my fingers exasperatingly clumsy; but, with hard work and incessant practice, I improved faster than he had thought possible.

He also taught me the patter and the tricks of misdirection. These presented no great difficulty, since a merchant's sales talk is basically the same sort of thing. Having, in my time, sold perfumes to stinking Scythian nomads and fur-trimmed mantles to sweltering Egyptians, I had no trouble with the verbal parts of Hippalos' lessons.

* * *

On the fourteenth of Anthesterion,[7] we moored the *Ourania* at the same rickety pier at Myos Hormos, whence we had set out seven months before. The port officials, who had never expected to see us again, were so astonished by our return that they never searched us and so did not discover the fortunes in pearls and gemstones that we bore, sewn into pockets on the insides of our belts. We had agreed that Hippalos should set out at once for Alexandria to report to the king, whilst I followed with our cargo. The day after we arrived, I saw him off, jouncing away on the desert road on a camel.

What with transferring my cargo from the *Ourania* to camels, and from camels to a barge at Kainepolis on the Nile, I did not reach Alexandria until the third of Elaphebolion. Spring was well advanced, although in those latitudes there is no real winter. I came out on the deck of the barge that morning to find us rowing gently through a predawn mist along the Alexandrine Canal, which follows

7 Approx. February 4.

the winding shore of Lake Mareotis. Now and then I glimpsed the surface of the lake through the immense beds of reeds that border it.

As the sky lightened, I was surprised to see, on the flats between the canal and the lake, what appeared to be a large, dark, shiny boulder. If there is any place where boulders are not to be found, it is the Delta, which is a great, flat, muddy plain cut up by the many serpentine arms of the Nile. As the mist thinned, the light waxed, and the barge came closer, I was startled to see the boulder move. At my exclamation, one of the Egyptian boatmen looked around, grunted "*Tebet!*" and went back to his rowing. It was a river horse, which had been grazing on some unlucky farmer's wheat. It trotted off towards the lake at our approach.

The sun was well up when we came to the south wall of Alexandria. The space between the wall and the canal was given over to flower gardens, now in a riot of color. After we had rowed along the south wall for ten or twelve furlongs, we pulled into the canal harbor and tied up. An inspector, followed by a couple of civilians and four soldiers, came aboard. The inspector said:

"Are you Eudoxos of Kyzikos?"

"Yes. This is—"

"Let's see your manifest."

"Here," said I. "This stuff belongs to His Divine Majesty."

The inspector ran his eye down the list and made a sign to the soldiers. Quick as a flash, two of them seized my arms and twisted them behind my back.

"*E!*" I cried. "What's this? I'm on a mission for the king—"

"You're under arrest," said the inspector. "Strip him."

In twenty winks, I was standing naked, while the civilians went through my clothing. One said:

"Here they are, Inspector."

He held up my belt, showing the little pockets on the inside. With a knife he slit the stitching of one pocket and squeezed out the emerald it contained. There was a gasp from the customs squad and the boatmen, for it was a fine stone.

The inspector looked again at the manifest. "As we thought, that stuff is not entered. Put his shirt back on but hold the belt for evidence."

"You stupid idiots!" I shouted with a fine show of indignation, "of course it's not entered! Do you think I want the king's jewels stolen by the first rascal who hears a rumor of this treasure? Those gauds are all to be presented to His Majesty in person. By the gods, you shall sweat when he learns of this outrage!"

"Shut up," said the inspector, and cuffed me across the mouth.

Rage gave me more than my usual strength, which even in middle age was considerable. With a mighty heave, I hurled one soldier away from me, so that he fell sprawling on the deck. I staggered the other with a blow from my free arm and then tried to tear loose to get at the inspector. Could I have reached him, I believe I should have broken his neck. But the rest of the boarding party sprang upon me and bore me to the deck in a kicking, clawing mass. Somebody whacked me on the head with the weighted pommel of a knife handle, so that I saw stars and the world spun dizzily.

When I got my senses back, I was standing with arms tied behind me and a noose around my neck. One soldier held the other end of the rope, so that if I tried to pull away I should merely strangle myself.

Soon I was being marched through the Canopic Quarter to the law courts. After half a day's wait, my case was called. The inspector showed the judge the belt and dug a double handful of gems from the secret pockets. I saw nothing of the emerald they had taken on the barge; no doubt the inspector had appropriated it for himself.

"This man," said the inspector, "has not only violated the law in regard to traffic in gemstones, but he also resisted arrest. Such a hardened criminal deserves a severe penalty."

The judge asked me if I had anything to say. I repeated in more detail the story I had told the inspector on the barge: how I had hidden the gemstones to protect them from thieves until I could present them to the king in person.

The judge listened without expression. With a faint smile, he picked up a roll of papyrus, saying:

"I have here the confession of the confederate of the accused, one Hippalos of Corinth, wherein he states: 'My captain, Eudoxos of Kyzikos, suggested that we try to get around His Divine Majesty's monopoly of all trade in gemstones in Alexandria and in Egypt, arguing that it was unfair for us to take all the risks of this voyage to unknown lands, while the king got all the profit. So we bought pearls and gems in India with our own money and had a native craftsman make us belts to hide these things in.'"

I was startled to hear that Hippalos had been caught, too, and then angry when I heard how he had put all the blame on me. I swore vengeance upon him if I should ever catch him.

"Such being the case," continued the judge, "I find you guilty and sentence you to hard labor in the mines for the rest of your life. Next case."

* * *

They hustled me away to a cell. A few days later, I found myself one of a gang of fifty-odd convicts on their way to the mines of Upper Egypt, with a squad of soldiers to guard us. We walked the whole two hundred-odd leagues. It took us a month and a half, into late Mounychion. At least, I think that was the time, albeit I lost track of the days.

Each convict had a fetter cold-forged around his right ankle. A chain was threaded through a large ring in each fetter and secured by a padlock through the last link. Since I was the largest man in the gang, I was given the last position on the chain, so that I could carry the padlock.

Up the Nile we trudged, past Memphis with its pyramids and its palm groves, and on into Upper Egypt. We had to march in step to avoid tripping over the chain. With each stride, fifty-odd right feet lifted the chain into the air and dropped it back into the dust with a clank. The soldiers and their officer did not treat us with any special brutality, but neither did they make any allowances. When a couple of elderly convicts collapsed and could go no further, the soldiers unshackled them, knocked them on the head, and threw the bodies into the Nile, where I suppose the crocodiles made short work of them.

At Koptos, we left the Nile for a road across the desert, between the Nile and the Red Sea. The heat was fearful. To keep us from collapse, the soldiers let us sleep in the shade of the boulders during the heat of the day and marched us most of the night.

At last we came to the rocky hills that sundered Egypt from Ethiopia. Here were heavily guarded stockades, which spread out for many furlongs. My gang clanked into one of these stockades. The gate slammed shut behind us, and I heard the heavy wooden bolt on the outside shot home.

People swarmed inside the stockade. They were mostly men, but there were also women and children, working the gold-bearing ore. Most were completely naked. All were filthy, and the men had long hair and beards. The women were such bedraggled creatures that, even in my lecherous youth, I do not think that the sight of them would have aroused my lusts. Supposing that Hippalos had received a sentence like mine, I kept looking for him but did not see him.

The officer in charge of us unlocked the padlock on the end of our chain, and we were unshackled and presented to a civilian official. This man asked each of us what language we spoke. I said:

"Greek."

"Any others?"

"Scythian, and a little Syrian and Indian."

"You shall go to Stockade Five, with these others. Next!"

In Stockade Five I was again lined up and looked over by an official, who said:

"You're too old and too tall for the galleries. We'll put you on the mortars. Next!"

I was taken to a large mortar and handed a sledge with a head of black basalt. Presently a naked boy of twelve approached with a basket of ore on his head. He dumped the ore into the mortar, and my overseer said:

"Now, you swine, pound that ore until it is crushed to fine gravel. Go ahead; I'll tell you when to stop."

I heaved up my sledge and brought it down on the ore. And again and again. The unfamiliar labor made my arms ache until I got the knack of it, but the instant I slowed up the overseer brought his whip down on my back.

When the ore was crushed finely enough, another boy appeared with a pail and a scoop. He scooped out the ore and took it in the pail to another part of the inclosure, where it was put into a large mill like a grist mill. Women and old men, with chains through their ankle rings, turned these mills by pushing capstan spokes round and round. The instant one of them faltered, he received a cut of the whip. Water boys trotted about with their buckets and dippers, not as a kindness, but because it was impossible in that heat to get much hard work out of men without a constant supply of water.

My overseer—unlike the officer who had marched me from Alexandria—was one of the nasty kind, who beat people for the fun of it. He was always seeking a pretext for inflicting insult or injury on his prisoners. But, even with his best efforts, he could not keep me busy all the time, because there were frequent delays between loads of ore. During these pauses, I looked about and learnt how the mining was organized.

The young, able-bodied men were sent into the underground galleries with lamps attached to their foreheads and picks and hammers in their hands, to follow the veins of gold-bearing quartz. Children gathered the ore in baskets and brought them out to the mortars. These were arranged in a long line, mine being in the middle. A score of hammers, pounding away at the same time, made a deafening racket.

The pounded ore was transferred to the mills, where it was ground to powder. Finally, this powder was taken to a large shed. There, I learned, skilled workmen separated the gold dust from the powdered rock by washing the ore down inclined wooden troughs with baffles across the bottom.

I got through the afternoon somehow. Black-skinned Nubian soldiers herded all of us in Stockade Five to a barrack, where we were lined up and served bowls of stew, big slabs of bread, and water laced with vinegar. While the food was a far cry from that served at Physkon's table in Alexandria, I have seldom tasted anything better. There is no sauce like a ravenous appetite.

After dinner we were taken in squads to the latrine and then back to barracks, where we were chained together by our ankle rings before being locked up for the night. The women were chained in a group at one end of the building. Only the children were not chained, it being assumed that each child would seek out its mother for the night.

When the guards had all gone out, leaving a hundred-odd naked convicts asprawl in their chains, I struck up acquaintance with my chain mates. The man on one side of me swore that he was no lawbreaker but had been put here by some envious kinsman, who had filed a false accusation. Perhaps; but he was a whiny sort of man whom I should not have believed no matter what he said.

My other neighbor was quite a different sort. He said he had been a burglar—"and the best mother-futtering burglar in Alexandria, too!"

"Why," I asked, "do they put all us Greek-speakers together?"

"To make it harder to escape. You see that our fornicating guards are Nubians? None knows a word of Greek, and I've never known a Hellene who spoke Nubian. Likewise you'll find the Egyptian convicts guarded by Celts, and the Judaeans by Illyrians, and so on. So there's no chance for collusion or bribery."

"Does nobody ever escape?"

"Not since I've been here. You work, and work, and work, and at last you die, and that's that. Most of these poor slobs are glad to die. Many kill themselves."

"But not you?"

The burglar spat. "Not I! By Poseidon's prick, I can stand it. Next year, who knows? Maybe that fat-arsed King Sausage will die, and his successor will celebrate by freeing us."

"Do you really think so?"

He gave me a gap-toothed grin in the dim moonlight that came through the small, barred windows. "Dip me in dung, man, but funnier things have happened; so why not hang on to what fornicating little hope we have? While you're alive, anything can happen; but once you're dead, you're gone for good."

I would have spoken more to him, but fatigue carried me off to dreamland in the middle of a sentence.

* * *

As things fell out, I did not have to put my cheerful, foul-mouthed burglars philosophy to the test. The second day after my arrival, I was whaling away at my mortar when I saw that a youngish man in a clean tunic and a broad-brimmed hat, with a close-cut black beard, had entered the stockade and was speaking to my overseer. Looking vaguely familiar, he was followed by a small group of men. Two were soldiers; the third was a stubby, familiar-looking shape. The overseer led the group to where I worked, saying:

"There he is."

"Gnouros!" I yelled.

"Master!" The little Scythian rushed forward to seize my hand and kiss it. Meanwhile, the man in the hat pulled out a roll of papyrus and handed it to the overseer. While the latter was reading, slowly and with much lip-moving effort, I asked Gnouros:

"How in the afterworld did you get here? And what's up? Have they condemned you to the mines, too?"

"No, sir. They held me with your other property. Was going to be auction to sell us, but then this man—this m-m-" A fit of stuttering overcame him until finally he said: "You see now."

The young man stepped in front of me, staring. At last he said:

"What is your name, my man?"

"Eudoxos of Kyzikos," I said, resting my sledge on the ground. "And you, sir?"

"Don't you know me?"

"Wait," I said. There was something familiar about that guttural Judaean accent. "By Bakchos' balls, aren't you Colonel Ananias?"

The man smiled. "The same. You I didn't know, either. The last time I saw you, you were decently dressed and clean shaven; now you're down to a wisp of rag and wear a great, gray beard. You're covered with dirt and burnt as black as an Ethiop."

"And the last time I saw you, you wore a suit of gilded parade armor. To what do I owe the honor of this visit?"

"Keep your voice down, Master Eudoxos. It was thought that my uniform would be too conspicuous. Besides, in this heat, inside a helmet your brains fry. My royal mistress has sent me to get you out of the country."

I whistled. "But what—"

"Details later. First we must make you look like a human being again."

They took me to the camp smith, who chiseled the fetter off my leg. This was a painful business, which left my ankle bruised and bleeding. They took me to the bathhouse used by the guards and officials. The camp barber trimmed my hair and whiskers. Ananias' men unloaded a couple of bags from a camel. The bags contained the personal possessions I had brought back from India. My Scythian bow and arrows were there; my scabbard was present but not the sword.

"I'm sorry about the sword," said Ananias. "Somebody must have stolen it. But then, you're lucky that I rescued your gear when I did;

a couple of days later it would have been auctioned, and never again would you have seen it."

The bags also contained my spare clothes and the little Indian statuette. When I was again decently clad, Ananias said:

"Almost again I can recognize you."

After a hasty meal, we set out on fast camels along the road to Koptos. I said to Ananias:

"Now let's have the news."

"What do you know about Hippalos' arrest?"

"Only what I heard in court. The judge read an alleged confession, in which Hippalos admitted trying to smuggle pearls and put the blame on me. I thought I should meet the temple thief at the mines, but I didn't see him."

"The scoundrel never got to the mines. He arrived in Alexandria about a ten-day before you did. But then he had to give a wild party for some of his cronies in a public tavern. He got drunk and hinted that he had worked some clever trick on the king. Then the perfume was in the soup. One of his so-called friends thought this a good chance to curry favor with the king, so back to the palace he bore the tale. His Majesty instantly sent police agents to pick up Hippalos. As soon as they searched him, they found that his belt was sewn full of pearls.

"He was convicted the next day and sentenced to the mines; and then, of course, he had to be tortured to reveal the names of his accomplices. The coward did not wait to suffer any actual pain. As soon as the executioner swished his scourge, Hippalos dictated that confession.

"He was put back into his cell to await the next draft of convicts for Upper Egypt. The following night, Her Majesty, Kleopatra the Sister, sent men to the prison with orders to smuggle the rascal out of the country. He was after all one of her faction, and doubtless she hoped to make further use of him. In strict confidence, the king has been unwell of late, and I think the Sister hopes to survive him and send Hippalos on another Indian voyage."

"I'm sorry for the poor jailer," I said, "getting contradictory orders from his different sovrans. Won't Physkon have his head when he finds out?"

Ananias shrugged. "Being confined to his bed, he will probably not find out. Besides, that jailer has survived these things before."

"Then how about me?"

"The judge who sentenced Hippalos passed a copy of his confession on to the customs department, and for you they were lying in wait. Agatharchides the tutor got wind of your fate. He rushed to my royal mistress, Kleopatra the Wife, pleading that it would be a crime against scholarship to bury you alive in the mines when you had just returned with all that first-hand knowledge of unknown lands. At least, that was the reason he gave for his intercession."

The Judaean shook his head, as if incredulous that any man connected with a royal court could act from such a disinterested motive. He continued: "It was Agatharchides' talk of the jewels of India that really interested Her Majesty. She hopes to put you to the same use as the Sister hoped to put Hippalos, after—ahem—a certain person is no longer with us."

The talk then turned to other matters, such as court gossip and my experiences in India. Ananias seemed to have a simple and fairly typical soldier's mind. He thought mainly of the brawls, carousals, and battles in his past and of promotion and pay in his future, and he cared not a whit for culture or intellect.

A few days later, however, as we were sailing down the Nile, he showed that he was not so simple after all. Like most courtiers, he had a sharp eye for the main chance. He said:

"O Eudoxos, if things change in Alexandria so that you can return hither safely, would you like to make another Indian voyage?"

"You mean under the patronage of your divine mistress?"

He made a face. "We Judaeans dislike to use the word 'divine' for anything but our God; but no matter. Have you such a plan in mind? I had rather it were you instead of that knave Hippalos, with whom I have a long score to settle."

"I might, if things fell out that way."

"You know that, but for me, you would still be sweating in the mines. I could have said I could not find you, or some such excuse made."

"What are you getting at?"

"That, as your go-between with the Wife, I expect a share of your profits on such a voyage."

"Go on," I said.

"You will naturally approach the queen through me. You also understand that, if you tried to cut me out of my share, I could easily spoil your deal through my brother, General Chelkias."

"I understand all that," said I, a bit nettled. "As I see it, considering the monopolies your sovrans claim, there won't be any profit to share. And India, while very interesting, is no place to visit for pleasure. If I ever went there again, it would only be to make a killing by trading on my own."

"The queens understand that, Eudoxos. When the time comes, you'll find them willing to make a reasonable agreement. I can help to bring them around, and I want to make sure I am not forgotten when the loot is divided."

"What had you in mind? Ten per cent?"

"Ha! Are you mad? I expect half, at least."

Knowing how courtiers made their living, I was not surprised. Nor was I affronted, since one Hellene should be worth two Syrians or three Judaeans in a bargaining session any day. We settled down to a real oriental haggle. For the next three days, while we drifted down the Pelusiac Branch of the Nile, we argued and threatened and chaffered. By the time we reached Pelousion, at the mouth of the river, we had agreed on twenty-five per cent of my net profits for Ananias and had roughed out the methods by which this should be calculated.

At Pelousion, I was surprised to find Agatharchides awaiting me. The old fellow had ridden one of the big, white Egyptian asses all the way from Alexandria to quiz me about India, while I waited for a coastal vessel to take me north. He also showed keen interest in my account of the gold mines of Upper Egypt and took voluminous notes.

Just before I boarded my ship, however, he showed that he had not made the journey solely in quest of geographical lore. Hesitantly, he said:

"Old boy, I don't like to press you when you have just suffered a financial shipwreck. But you did promise to underwrite publication of some of my writings if I got you that captaincy—"

"Have you the writings with you?"

"I have brought the main one, my *History of Europe*."

"Then give me the manuscript and I'll arrange to have it copied in Kyzikos."

"Hermes attend you, Eudoxos! If more men of means were like you ..." And he began to weep.

When he pulled himself together, he handed me a sack full of book rolls, comprising the only manuscript of this work. Then he embraced me affectionately, and I boarded the ship with a bag of Ptolemaic silver from Ananias to get me home. Luckily, no disaster befell the precious manuscript, and in due course it was published as I had promised.

* * *

When I reentered my home in Kyzikos, Astra looked at me as if I were a ghost. Then she gave a little shriek.

"Eudoxos! Darling!" she cried, and threw herself into my arms.

"I thought you dead," she said. "Then I didn't know you with another of those horrible beards. For Hera's sake, shave it off! It makes you look old enough to be my grandfather, and it's like kissing an ilex bush."

We had gone through this routine several times before, when I had returned bewhiskered from a voyage. "Now, dear one," I protested, "is that the way to greet a man who's been gone a year, who has escaped a score of deaths by a hairbreadth, and who has had all the profits of his voyage snatched from him by a greedy king? To carp at his beard? But to please you, the beard shall go. Here's a little something for you."

I pulled out a cheap silver bracelet, explaining: "I brought you some fine things from India, but Physkon got his fat paws on them, and I was lucky to get away with my head on my shoulders. I bought this in Tyre. I left Egypt with just enough money to get me home, and if I had spent more I should have starved. Where's Theon?"

"Out playing. Tell Gnouros to go fetch him."

Gnouros duly recovered my son. Then he made the rounds of my kinsmen, who came running. My middle brother wanted to give a feast at his house that evening, but I said:

"Tomorrow, please. I have an engagement tonight."

They hung around all afternoon, while I told them of the main events of my voyage. They in turn gave me bad news of the firm. One of our ships had been wrecked two months before on the Karian coast. The crew had survived, but the natives had stolen all the cargo.

Astra and I talked late that night. Next morning, when I awoke, I performed my husbandly duties like a lusty young man. I wondered if things had not changed permanently for the better.

But, as Herakleitos says, one cannot step twice into the same stream. As the days passed and I settled into the routine of the business, my marital relations soon sank back into their former frustrating state. I became moody. I spent hours pacing the shore, throwing stones at sea birds, shouting snatches from Euripides, defying the gods, and weeping.

* * *

During the rest of the season, I voyaged to Peiraieus, Delos, Rhodes, and Pantikapaion, to sniff out cargoes and to renew my contacts in those parts. Everywhere the word had gotten around of my Indian voyage. I was plied with free food and drink by other traders and shipmen, eager to learn what I could tell them. I held many a symposium spellbound with my tales of India.

For obvious reasons, however, I was not eager to start a stampede of voyages thither. Hence I stressed the tigers, the serpents, the deadly diseases, and the difficulties of dealing with India's peculiar people. I said nothing of the six-month seasonal wind, which furnished the key to direct voyages. News of the meteorological phenomenon, I thought, would leak out from Alexandria soon enough.

When shipping closed down for the winter, I oversaw the building of a new ship in my father-in-law Zoilos' shipyard, to take the place of the one lost off Knidos. Many an hour I spent at the slip, exposed to the cold winds and whirling snow out of Scythia, in furious argument with Zoilos over details of construction, until one would have expected us to come to blows. Each time, when it was over, we sought refuge from the weather in a tavern, where we got tipsy and roared old songs.

One day in spring, after our new *Ainetê* had been launched and shipping had started up again, I was at home reckoning my accounts. Gnouros announced a visitor.

"Is sailor," he said.

I went to the door, stared, and cried: "By the! Hippalos!"

"The same," he said with that old satyrlike grin. It was no wonder that it had taken us an instant to recognize each other. The last time he had seen me, I had worn a full, graying beard, which I had now taken off to please Astra. On the other hand, he, who had been clean-shaven throughout our Indian voyage, now flaunted a beard as red as his hair. He wore a sailor's little round cap.

"Come on in," I said after a slight hesitation.

I knew that Hippalos was a slippery character. I had left Egypt full of rancor towards him. Had I met him then, I should have had at him with my stick. But in the ensuing year my anger had died. He was always amusing company, and I was curious to hear what had befallen him.

"Get out a jug of that good Samian," I told Gnouros. I recounted my tale, and Hippalos told his. He apologized handsomely for his shortcomings.

"I'm truly sorry that I put the blame on you in the confession, old boy," he said. "But if I hadn't they'd have tortured me until I named somebody plausible anyway, and yours was the only plausible name I could think of."

"How did Physkon's men find out about your pearls in the first place?" said I, watching him narrowly.

"They saw me treating all my friends and reasoned: Here's Hippalos, who is always broke and cadging drinks, throwing his money around. He must have some clever scheme to cheat the king in mind."

"I heard that you boasted at that party that you did, in fact, have such a scheme."

"By the Dog of Egypt, that's absolutely untrue! I never said a word. They just looked at the feast I had ordered and drew their own conclusions."

"What happened after you were arrested?"

"The Sister sent an officer to get me out of jail. She told him to send me as far from Egypt as possible, so he put me on a grain ship for Rome.

"There I picked up a living in various ways—teaching Greek, for instance—but after a few months I got tired of Rome. It's a beastly, squalid sort of place. The ruling class are a haughty, stuffy lot, and the proletariat are a lot of thugs. Some upper-class Romans claim to be enthusiasts for Greek culture, but it hasn't had much effect. Besides, the Romans have some very odd laws. ..."

He paused, then went on without telling me which of these laws he had fallen foul of: "I shipped out to Massilia. I almost sold the Massiliot council a fine scheme for reorganizing their defense, but some envious detractor slandered me to them, and I had to leave. I shipped as a deck hand on a ship of Eldagon of Gades. Do you know that firm?"

"No," I said. "We never get Spanish ships here. Is that what you're doing now?"

"Yes. I've tried to find work worthier of my talents at some of the ports we've stopped at, but without success."

"And you're still sailing for this Gaditanian? How can that be? I've never seen a Spanish ship east of Athens. What in Zeus's name would bring such a craft to Kyzikos?"

"Oh, my ship is not here; it's at Naxos. The Roman governor at Gades insists on real Parian marble for his new palace. So we came east in silver, cinnabar, and salt fish and are returning in Parian marble, Athenian pots, and oriental carpets from Miletos. But our stupid captain ran into a pier at Naxos, and it'll take at least a month to repair us. So rather than idle around Naxos, I've worked my passage hither on a local craft, owned by Agathon and Pelias of Miletos."

"They're competitors of ours. I'm flattered that you should come all this way to see me," I said. "But I'm sure you have some more compelling reason than the wish to talk over old times."

He grinned. "To tell the truth, I have. Have you still that little bronze of the god Ganesha which you used to wear around your neck?"

"Yes."

"Well, you promised that, if I came to Kyzikos to ask for it, you'd give it to me."

I looked hard at him. I did not want to give up my grotesque little elephant-headed god, my only keepsake from the Indian voyage. On the other hand, a promise is a promise, even to a knave like Hippalos. Noting my hesitation, he said:

"I'm not asking for this for nothing, even though you promised it free. When they stripped and searched me, I managed to save a couple of Indian pearls by hiding them under my tongue. Since these are the entire profit from our voyage, it's only right that you should get half. Here it is.

Into my hand he put a big, handsome pearl. It looked too large for a man to hide a pair of them in his mouth. But then, this was only Hippalos' story; he might have obtained the pearl in some even less legitimate way. However, that was not my business. I thanked him for the pearl and got the statuette of Ganesha out of the chest where I kept such souvenirs. I said:

"You're welcome to the statue. But why should you go to such trouble and cost to get it? The pearl is worth a hundred times as much."

"Still suspicious, aren't you? But I need something to change my luck. Perhaps the statue's mystic powers will bring this to pass. I know you don't take much stock in such ideas. But who knows? The cosmos is full of unknown powers and forces. This amulet may be the focal point of some of them, as old Sisonaga preached.

"Besides, living by one's wits is all very exciting, but I'm nearly forty. It's time I settled down to some solid, respectable occupation. You wouldn't have an opening in your shipping firm, would you? You know I can do almost anything I set my hand to."

"Not just now, best one. Perhaps in a year or two, when a couple of our oldest employees die off ..."

Since Hippalos had come so far, it was only natural to invite him to dinner and to have my kinsmen in to meet him. Since he had not taken lodgings and we had plenty of room, it also seemed natural to put him up while his ship was loading. During these three days, although Astra kept to the women's quarters like a proper Greek housewife, it was inevitable that she should meet Hippalos. He was formal and respectful, exchanging bows with her and complimenting her on the efficient house she kept. She was polite but cool, confiding to me afterwards that she would be glad when Hippalos—of whose raffish character I had told her—had gone his way. He also played with my son Theon and quite won the lad's heart.

Just before he left, he said: "Old boy, keep your ears cocked to southward. I hear Physkon's health is failing."

"You mean there may soon be a chance for another Indian voyage?"

"That's as the stars shall decide. But bear it in mind. And don't be too surprised if you see me back here. Ask around among your friends in Kyzikos to see if any might have a good job for me. I'm serious about settling down."

And off he went, with the little Ganesha dangling from its chain around his neck.

Book VII

ELDAGON THE GADITANIAN

For the rest of the summer, to take my mind off my shameful infirmity, I threw myself into the work of the firm. Towards the end of the sailing season, Hippalos again appeared in Kyzikos, as the mate of a ship of our competitors, Ariston and Pytheas.

"It's that statue of Ganesha," said he with his satyrlike grin. "Didn't that Indian king say the possessor could convince anybody of anything? Naturally, my bosses couldn't refuse me promotion. By this time next year, I'll wager I shall be one of their captains."

"You had that gift before you had the statue, old boy," I said. I was pleased to see that the hostility that Astra had shown to Hippalos on his first visit was no longer evident. In fact, she seemed to have fallen under the spell of his charm like everyone else.

After a pleasant visit, Hippalos sailed off to his home port of Miletos, and winter closed down. One of our ships failed to return to Kyzikos on schedule. My kinsmen and I went around with knotted brows, fearing another wreck. Then, when snowflakes had already begun to fly, the missing ship appeared. We were ready to eat Captain Phaidon alive for taking such a risk, but his exceptional profits softened our wrath. He had seen a chance for a quick gain on a shipment of timber from Rhodes to Alexandria.

"Why did the Alexandrines need this timber so sorely?" I asked.

"They wanted scaffolding to build a grand tomb for the king," said Phaidon.

"What! Do you mean the old Sausage is dead?"

"Why, yes. He died a couple of months ago. Hadn't you heard?"

We had not, since news travels no faster than men can carry it. In winter, with the cessation of travel, the spread of news slows to a snail's pace.

"Zeus, Apollon, and Hera!" I said, my mind in a whirl. "That means another chance to make a killing from an Indian voyage, if I can reach Alexandria ahead of Hippalos. To go by sea now were out of the question; but I could go by land ..."

"Calm down, Eudoxos, calm down," said my brother-in-law. "It would take you over twice as long to get to Egypt by land. And suppose you did? When could you leave for India at the earliest?"

I thought. "If I remember rightly, the southwest wind begins to blow across the Arabian Sea five or six months from now."

"And when could you start back, at the earliest?"

"It's another six months before it begins to blow the other way."

"You see? There's no rush. You would only have to idle around Alexandria for months and then do the same in India. Besides, you'd have to cross the highlands of Bithynia and Pontus in the dead of winter. If robbers didn't get you, you'd probably freeze to death in a snowdrift."

"Oh, rubbish!" I said. "I've ridden the Scythian steppe in worse weather than that."

"Ah, but we were all a bit younger then."

"But Hippalos will have heard of Physkon's death, too, and he'll hasten thither to drum up royal backing for another voyage!"

"Let him. The winds won't blow any sooner for him than for you, and there's enough trade in India for both. If he gets the Sister to send him off in one ship, you can get the Wife to send you in another."

The other kinsmen—my two brothers and my cousin—joined in and talked me round. I was pleased that they seemed to value me as the head of the family and the firm, but a little hurt that they looked upon me as such a fragile oldster that I could no longer risk a strenuous overland journey.

* * *

It was early Skirophorion when I again saw the marble and gold of the palaces on Point Lochias. This time I came to Alexandria, not as a herald and ambassador, but as a mere sea captain in one of Theon's Sons' ships. So there was no special welcome.

Gnouros had complained of rheumatic pains, so I had left him at home to help with the house. Instead, for a personal attendant, I hired an orphaned cousin of fourteen, named Pronax, whom one of my brothers was bringing up.

When I asked at the palace for Ananias, the colonel himself came out to greet me. "I wondered how soon you would arrive, best one," he said. "Did that rascal Hippalos come with you?"

"No. I thought he might have gotten to Alexandria ahead of me."

"There has been no sign of him. Do you know aught about him?"

"The last I heard, he was an officer on a Milesian ship."

"Hm, hm. This may complicate matters."

"How so?"

"I cannot stop to explain now. Be here tomorrow after the siesta hour. A meeting I shall arrange to discuss these things."

When I arrived next day, an usher led me to a small chamber where sat the two queens—the fat old one, in a billowing purple gown, and the plump young one, loaded as usual with jewelry. With them were General Chelkias, Colonel Ananias, Agatharchides the tutor, the rotund little Prince Ptolemaios Philometor—the one we call Lathyros—and some official whose name I forget to assist the elder queen. When the bowing and the wishes for everyone's good health were over, and I had expressed insincere regrets for the death of the old monster, the Wife said:

"Master Eudoxos, Colonel Ananias tells me you are ready to undertake another Indian voyage."

"That is why I came to Alexandria, Your Divine Majesty."

"Then we are well met. I am sure—"

"You're not sure of anything!" snapped the Sister between wheezes. "Where is my dear Hippalos, Master Eudoxos?"

"The last I saw of him, my lady, was when he stopped at Kyzikos as mate of a Milesian ship."

"Why didn't you fetch him with you? Speak up, man; don't mumble." I raised my voice to compensate for her deafness. "Madam! How should I know where he is now? He might be anywhere from Karia to Carthage."

"Well, you could have waited at Miletos to intercept him."

"I didn't know Your Divine Majesty wanted him so badly."

"It's my business, whom I want."

"Oh, Mother!" said the Wife. "Stop fussing over every little detail. You shouldn't bully Captain Eudoxos—"

"Little detail? As if the choice of leaders weren't the most important—"

"You don't even know he'd want to go—"

The Sister smote the arm of her chair. "That's my business! You mind your—"

"It's my business, too! You're just being a stubborn old—"

"Shut up, Kleo!" shouted the Sister. "Anybody knows that, on such a mission, everybody should have somebody to watch him. You never had any sense about men, anyway."

"Better than you! I never let that red-haired trickster beguile me—"

"*Arrk!*" The old queen emitted a loud, angry squawk, like an enraged parrot. "Don't you dare call my man a trickster, you slut! He was more faithful to me than your tame Judaeans will ever be to you—in bed or out of it!"

"Don't you dare talk to me that way!" screeched the younger woman. "I'm a queen, too!"

"Ladies! Ladies!" bleated the official, trying to calm the storm. Chelkias and Ananias looked at the ceiling. The two queens went right on screaming and shaking fists, until I thought we should have a hair-pulling contest. "—you're still my daughter—" "—smearing the sacred name of the Ptolemies with dung—" "—foul-mouthed vixen—" "—fat, deaf old harridan—"

The guards around the walls traded nervous glances, evidently wondering where their duty would lie in case the twain came to blows. Being so old and fat, the Sister ran out of breath first. She took a gulp of wine, choked, sputtered, coughed, gasped for breath, and finally muttered:

"May the gods help the kingdom when you're sole queen! It's a mercy I shan't be here to see it. No matter what you say, I won't approve this voyage until I learn what has become of Hippalos."

"May I make a suggestion?" said Agatharchides.

"Go ahead," said the Wife.

"May it please Your Majesties, why not let Captain Eudoxos get his ship ready and collect a cargo, while you send a police agent to Miletos to find Hippalos and invite him hither?"

"Yes, yes, that's a good idea," said the Sister. She pressed a hand to her forehead, breathing hard. "Send for my maids. I am not feeling well."

Everybody was on his feet at once, assuring the old queen of his hopes for her quick recovery. The meeting broke up as that vast, wobbling mass of fat was helped out the door by her tiring women.

But the police agent was never sent. The next day, when I came to the palace, I learnt that the Sister had had a stroke the night before and was unconscious. She lingered for a ten-day and then died.

That ended all public business for many days, while funeral ceremonies took place. Then came a time of uncertainty, when the court was too busy settling the details of the new reign even to say good-day to me. I spent the time either in my room on the waterfront or in the Library.

Rumors of impending revolution ran wild in Alexandria. Men hurried furtively along the streets. Hellene, Judaean, and Egyptian glowered at one another, muttering threats and insults and fingering daggers. Several riots erupted and were put down by the garrison, with heads rolling in the gutters. At night, the deserted streets rang with the tramp and clatter of soldiers of the three armies, which remained united to control the city, but which might at any moment start fighting each other.

The gist of it was that the Hellenes and the Egyptians did not wish the Wife to reign alone. Their pretext was that it was indecent for a woman to play the part of a king. The real reason was that Kleopatra notoriously favored the Judaeans and relied on their support. The non-Judaeans wanted at least one co-ruler to redress the balance.

At last—luckily, without tearing the city apart first—the factions reached a compromise: that Kleopatra might keep her throne, but only as joint ruler with one of her sons. She chose the eldest, Philometor "Chick-pea." There was another monster parade, and the whole court went up the Nile to Memphis for a coronation according to the old Egyptian rites.

It was midsummer before Ananias could arrange a conference to set the final terms of my voyage. Luckily, the constant north wind off the Inner Sea keeps Alexandria pleasant even in summer.

At this final meeting, Queen Kleopatra said: "You must understand, Captain Eudoxos, that the laws governing trade in our kingdom, established by my divine husband, still stand."

"Does Your Majesty mean," quoth I, "that you don't want me to do any trading on my own?"

"That is right. Our royal monopoly must remain inviolate."

"Then perhaps Your Divine Majesty had better find another captain."

"Are you defying my commands, sirrah?"

"Not at all, madam. Correct me if I am wrong, but I do not believe that your writ runs in the free city of Kyzikos, whereof I am a citizen. If—"

"Now look here, Master Eudoxos, I am not accustomed to having mere mariners tell me what I shall and shan't—"

"Mother—" began the young king.

"Hold your tongue!" snapped the queen; then, turning to me: "As for you—"

"Please, my lady!" said Ananias. "Hear the man out."

General Chelkias leant near to the queen's chair and spoke in a low voice: "He's right, you know, Kleo dear. If you do not make this voyage worth the captain's while, he can do as he likes outside your jurisdiction, and there is nothing you can do to make him return to Alexandria. Let's not spoil a profitable project by a petty argument over royal prerogative."

The queen grumped and growled but finally gave in. I continued: "As I was saying, this voyage involves no small risk, and I expect a chance for gain in proportion to the risk."

"What had you in mind?"

"I do not mind trading the bulk cargo as part of my duties as your captain. But I want to be allowed to buy pearls and precious stones on my own."

"*Ei!*" cried the queen. "But that is just what I want for myself!"

I had expected this, so after a haggle we agreed to go equal shares on pearls and precious stones. Queen Kleopatra and I should each furnish half of the fund for buying these baubles, and we should divide the things equally when I returned. Distribution should be by letting me divide the loot into two parts and giving the queen her choice of the two.

Thus it came about that, almost three years to the day after my departure on my first Indian voyage, I weighed anchor in the *Ourania* at Myos Hormos for a second try. This time I knew better than to take olive oil to sell to the Indians. I loaded more copper ingots instead.

The second voyage was in most respects like the first, but less adventurous. With Linos as mate, I found Barygaza without difficulty. This time I did not seek out holy men for advice on stiffening my yard, having given that up as a bad job. Neither did I gallop all over India, getting involved with snake charmers, kings, robbers, and religious fanatics.

I stayed in Barygaza and did well enough. My friend Otaspes was no longer there, having left for his native Karmania. I partly disarmed the suspicions of the Arabs by buying some of my return cargo from them. I also bought some of the rare woods that India supplies, being sure that the skilled Egyptian cabinetmakers would find good use for them. The only event of any moment was that poor young Pronax fell sick with a flux so severe that I thought I should lose him; but he recovered.

I bought a statuette of Ganesha, like the one King Girixis had given me on the first voyage. It had irked me to have to give my first one to Hippalos, even though I had promised it to him. After hunting all over Barygaza, I found another, the same size as the first but carved from ivory instead of cast in bronze. Moreover, it showed the elephant-headed god riding on a mouse instead of sitting on a flower. Either the divinity must be a very small godlet, or his mouse must grow to even more gigantic size than do the real mice of India, which are as large as kittens or puppies.

To replace my fine Persian sword, which had been stolen, I also bought a sword of the marvelous Indian steel, with a rippling pattern on the blade and edges sharp enough to shave with. I had to have it fitted with a new hilt, however, to fit my big hands.

* * *

On the way home, we met a storm. The stout old *Ourania* rode it out well enough, but it threw us off our course, so that we raised the African coast far south of the Southern Horn. The shore was more heavily wooded than that around the Southern Horn, but the woods were of a scrubby, thorny sort. The coast ran nearly straight for many leagues, with no sign of a decent harbor. A heavy surf beat against terrifying offshore rocks. Altogether, a coast less inviting to mariners were hard to find.

To aggravate matters, we found ourselves struggling into the teeth of the seasonal wind, and the *Ourania* was one of those ships with little ability to beat to windward. For one thing, her mainsail was too baggy; despite my vigilance, Physkon's officials had managed to pass off an inferior piece of sailcloth on me. Up the wretched coast we plodded, zigzagging in and out from the coast and gaining only a few furlongs with each tack. Our food and water ran lower and lower—especially the water. We kept watching for the mouths of rivers, but there seemed to be none. More than ever I wished there were some sort of sail by which one could sail closer to the wind.

At last, when we were nearly dead from thirst, the lookout called that he saw the mouth of a river. Since there were no rocks in sight at this point, we felt our way in, sounding continuously, as close to shore as we dared and anchored. Then we put over the skiff. A sailor named Aristomenes rowed me ashore.

Our disappointment was great when we found that the river was only a small stream—and, moreover, that it was now completely dry. Swells from the sea washed in and out of its mouth, but this water was salt as far up as it went.

"We're out of luck, Captain," said the sailor. He sat down wearily on a piece of driftwood. "We might as well eat before we die." He began to open up the lunch we had brought ashore.

"Don't give up," I said. "There might be a pool up the bed of this stream."

He looked gloomily at the tangle of thorn bushes and long grass. "If we could ever get up there to find out. A man could get lost in that stuff and walk in circles for days until—"

The sailor broke off, staring towards the bush. I whirled to look, too.

"Company," I said. "Whatever you do, don't show fear or excitement."

A black face peered out of the dry vegetation. Behind it, I caught glimpses of the shiny black skins of other men moving about. I got to my feet with a leisureliness I did not feel.

"Rejoice!" I said with a forced smile. "Come on out! Won't you join us for lunch?"

The owner of the face could not, of course, understand my Greek, but I hoped that he could interpret the tone. Presently he pushed through the leaves and stood on the sand of the beach. He was a tall, well-built man of middle age. He was very black and quite naked save for a string around his waist, into which he had thrust a few small belongings. He trailed a spear with an iron head. His hair and beard formed a circle of frizzy gray wool around his head, and on his body were decorative lines and circles of little scars.

The black smiled a nervous little smile, as if uncertain whether to bolt, attack, or accept my invitation. I dug into the food bag and brought out two loaves of bread. I bit into one and held the other out to the black.

He came a little nearer, poised for flight, and at last nerved himself to snatch the bread from my hand. He stared at it and at me for a long time before working up the courage to take a bite. He chewed for a while with a puzzled expression, as if he could not make up his mind whether or not he liked this strange food. I sat down again and went on with my repast. At last the black squatted with us in the sand. His companions formed a line along the shoreward edge of the beach, staring and muttering. Two of them had an antelope slung by its feet from a pole.

I got out a small wineskin and poured a cup for myself and one for our visitor. He drank and burst into speech, none of which I could understand, but he looked pleased. At last I pointed to myself and said: "Eudoxos!" Then I pointed to the sailor and said: "Aristomenes!" Lastly I pointed to the black with a questioning expression.

"Bakapha," he said. When he had relished a dried fig, he spoke to the men who carried the antelope. Soon they had built a fire, which they started by rubbing sticks together, hacked off a haunch, and were roasting it. When it was done, Aristomenes and I were each given a slab.

Bakapha proved a man of some intelligence; for, when I pointed at various objects, he at once gave the names for them in his own tongue. Thus I soon worked up a vocabulary of a score of words, wishing the while that my memory were as keen as it had been thirty years before. With my few words and much sign language, I also made him realize that we needed fresh water.

Bakapha smiled and pointed up the dry stream bed, saying something that I took to mean: "Come, I will show you."

"Be careful, Captain," said Aristomenes. "They may want to get you off into the bush to kill and eat you."

"Perhaps," I said, "but we must take that chance. If they kill me, Linos can get you back to Myos Hormos."

I followed Bakapha upstream, winding through the bush on game trails that I should never have noticed alone, but which afforded passage with the least damage to garments and skin. Sure enough, a furlong or so upstream, we came to a sandy pool in the stream bed.

When I got back to the beach, I found Aristomenes standing amongst the blacks, who—chattering and laughing uproariously—felt his skin and fingered his ragged tunic. He looked unhappy but cheered up when I told him about the water. He said:

"Captain, here's something you ought to see."

He indicated the piece of wood on which he had sat. We pulled it out and knocked the damp sand off it.

"That," I said, "looks like the stem post of a small vessel, with a figurehead in the form of a horse's head. Let's take it aboard. Row out with it, while I fraternize with Bakapha here. Bring a couple of jars back with you, and a tablet and stylus from my cabin."

He rowed off, whilst I amused the Ethiopians with some of the conjuring tricks I had learnt from Hippalos. The rest of the day, the sailors spent in laboriously ferrying jars to shore in the skiff, carrying them upstream to the pool, filling them, and taking them back to the ship. Meanwhile I conversed with Bakapha, noting new words on the tablet as they came up. The tablet fascinated his men, who crowded around me, looking over my shoulders six at a time, until their pungent odor almost overcame me. I suppose they thought it was big magic.

I learnt that Bakapha was a chief from a village to the northwest. Their women were home cultivating their crops. We ended the day with a grand feast on the beach, pooling the meat of the antelope and the ship's provisions.

The next day, the Ethiopians were still there. When I came ashore, Bakapha indicated that he wanted to visit the *Ourania*. This was done, while I remained with his men to assure them that their chief should come to no harm. I should like to have warned him against other shipmasters who, if a naked native came trustingly aboard, would seize the man for a slave and sail off with him. But I knew too little of the language to express so complex an idea. Bakapha assured us that several other streams emptied into the sea to the north, where we could replenish our water as we had done here.

When we had refilled our water tank, we took our leave of Bakapha and his band. We last saw them waving to us from the beach. They were the nicest savages I have met.

* * *

At last, with much sweat, we rounded the towering cliffs of the Southern Horn. I got back to Alexandria in the middle of winter. When I reported to Ananias at the palace, I said:

"I got what I went for. Could you get me a room in the palace, where I can lay out my pretties in two lots for Her Majesty to choose from?"

"I think I can," said the colonel. "Don't forget that a quarter of your share I get."

"You mean, a quarter of my share after deducting what it cost me!"

"I suppose so. I'm no merchant, nor am I good at figures. I'll have a clerk from the Treasury in to check your calculations."

As it turned out, the queen could see me that afternoon. She arrived in the chamber that I had been given, with the usual guardsmen, ladies in waiting, her two Judaean officers, and a couple of other officials. Pronax and I had spread out the pearls and stones on a linen-covered table in two lots, as much alike as we could make them. One lot, for instance, had a hundred and forty-six pearls, the other a hundred and forty-seven; but the largest pearl of all was in the first lot.

The queen stared at the table for a long time, as if unable to make up her mind. Then she turned to me with a frown.

"Captain Eudoxos," she said, "I wish it understood that I do not suspect you of chicanery. Nevertheless, to make sure that no question shall remain of our complete honesty with each other, you will not, I am sure, mind if I have you searched."

I did mind, but queens are queens. "All right, I suppose so," I growled.

She stiffened at my tone. "Strip him!" she commanded the guards.

"Madam!" I said. "I have my dignity, too—"

But two hulking Celts grabbed me and began peeling off my clothes. In a trice, I stood naked before the queen. She looked me up and down with an appraising eye.

"I daresay," she said, "that when you were young, you could stroke the girls many a mighty stroke. What is that thing around your neck?"

I had tucked my statuette of Ganesha inside my tunic. I explained what the amulet was and how I had come by it.

"Why," asked Queen Kleopatra, "did you not include it in the two piles on yonder table?"

"It's not a pearl, nor yet a precious stone."

"It is still a small and valuable ornament and should therefore have been included. The fact that you tried to hide it shows that you had a guilty mind."

"I did not try to hide it, Your Majesty! I tucked this thing inside my shirt because a Hellene does not ordinarily wear such a foreign bauble, and I did not wish to be conspicuous in Alexandria."

"I don't believe you, but you can earn my forgiveness by giving it to me."

"*What?*"

"Don't roar at me, graybeard! If you are saucy, by Pan's prick, I'll apply the old law and strip you of everything on that table. Now, will you give me that statue?"

"I will not!" I could have bitten my tongue as soon as I said it. By groveling, I suppose I could have saved my jewels even yet. But I had taken enough injury from the Ptolemies, and at this latest extortion I was furious enough to have thrown this pudgy little Macedonian queen, with her longshoreman's vocabulary, out the palace window, bangles and all.

"You will not, eh?" she screeched, the little green eyes blazing out of her round kitten's face. "We'll see about that, you dung-eating old sodomite!" She motioned to one of the officials. "Gather all that stuff up and deposit it in the Treasury. Take Captain Eudoxos' statuette, too. As for you, you mannerless old peasant, you had better be out of my kingdom tomorrow, unless you crave another lesson in gold mining!"

While I put my clothes back on, the officials hastened to assure Her Divine Majesty that she had done exactly right. "That is the way to treat these lying men of the sea," said one. "Give them a digit and they take a furlong."

He gathered up the corners of the linen tablecloth and slung the resulting sack, containing all my loot from India, over his shoulder. The queen swept out—if a dumpy little woman can be described as "sweeping"—with all her bracelets jingling. Everybody but Ananias followed her. The Judaean remained behind, glowering.

"Why in the name of the Unspoken Name did you have to bungle it?" he growled. "I thought a man of your age and experience knew enough not to sauce royalty."

"By Bakchos' balls, Colonel," I replied, "I have had all I can take from your divine mistress, and you had better not start berating me, too. I'm sorry there are no profits to give you a quarter of, but it's harder on me than on you. Besides, my beard is no grayer than your brother's, and he seems to do all right."

Although a rather humorless man, Ananias smiled a little. "I thought she had touched a sore spot. But one cannot tell off a queen, regardless of the provocation."

"I don't think anything I could have said would have made any difference."

"How so?" he said.

"I think she was lying in wait for me, determined to find some pretext to confiscate my stock. If one thing hadn't worked, she would have tried another. The old Sausage said she was mad—literally crazy—about gems."

Ananias looked at me with some sympathy, but he only shrugged. As a practical courtier, he was not going to voice any criticism of his sovran in the palace, where somebody might be listening from a secret passage.

"What's done is done," he said at last. "But what next?"

"Well, how in Tartaros shall I get out of Egypt tomorrow? The shipping is closed down, save for a few fishermen who won't go out of sight of their home port."

"Let me think," said Ananias. "Is that boy going back to Kyzikos with you?"

"Yes. He's a cousin."

"I can lend you a couple of horses from my stable. They're not the noblest steeds in the world, but home they should get you. One can carry you; the other, the boy and your baggage."

"That's good of you. But how shall I ever return the animals to you?"

Ananias waved a hand. "The next time one of your ships sails to Alexandria, tell the captain to pay me for the beasts. They cost about two hundred drachmai for the pair; that's close enough."

"That is extremely kind and generous of you."

He shrugged again. "As your go-between, I feel somewhat responsible for you."

* * *

Since it was too late in the day to set out upon our journey, I went to the waterfront with Pronax, carrying that stem post with the horse's head. There I struck up a conversation with some ships' officers, who knew my name from the first Indian voyage. I asked them if they had ever seen anything like this stem post. At last one old skipper, who spoke Greek with a Spanish accent, said:

"Aye, I know that. The fishermen in Gades put those things on their boats."

"Horse-figureheads?" I said.

"Aye. But that's not just a horse; that's a *sea* horse."

"What's the difference, since the carving shows the head only, not the fishy tail?"

"There *be* no difference!" roared the salt, slapping me on the back and doubling over with laughter. "But don't call one of them things a plain horse's head to a Gaditanian fisherman, or you'll have a fight on your hands. How'd you come by that thing?"

I told him of finding the figurehead beyond the Southern Horn.

"Oh, hah!" said the Spaniard. "Sometimes they sail their little cockleshells down the Moorish coast as far as the river Lixus. One of 'em must have sailed too far and been blown clear around Africa."

* * *

Spring had come again to Kyzikos, and the hills were bright with poppy and hyacinth and cyclamen, when Pronax and I, shaggy and worn, rode up to the Miletopolis Gate of Kyzikos. If I had come ashore at the docks as usual, every longshoreman and waterfront loafer would have known me and spread the news of my return. As it was, we arrived before my house unheralded.

Leaving Pronax to hold the horses, I banged on the door and shouted "*Pai!*" But all remained quiet, as if the house were deserted.

"Uncle!" said Pronax. "If you'll hold the horses, I'll run to your brothers' houses and tell of your return."

"Do so," I said.

Soon my kinsmen appeared, hastening towards me. There were my middle brother and my brother-in-law and my cousin; my younger brother was away on a voyage. They embraced and kissed me and showered me with questions about my voyage.

"Later, later," I said. "First, where is my family?"

They hesitated. I was stricken with dread that my wife and child had been carried off by some mishap. Any traveling man knows this fear, which often strikes when one has nearly reached home.

"Well, out with it!" I said. "Are they alive or dead?"

"They're alive," said my brother. "But—ah—"

"I'll tell him," said my cousin. "Eudoxos, your wife eloped with another man and has not been heard of since. Theon is all right; he's living with Korimos and Phylo." (These were my brother-in-law and my sister.)

I leant against the house. I suppose I turned pale, for my brother muttered: "Get ready to catch him!"

"It's all right," I said. "I shan't faint. When did this happen? Do you know the man?"

My brother-in-law said: "It was your old comrade-in-arms, Hippalos the Corinthian, who arrived as captain of a Milesian ship last summer, soon after you left for Alexandria. The whipworthy rogue gave us a party, explaining that he had come to join you in another Indian voyage. He would have arrived sooner, he said; but he had been laid up in Syracuse for the winter and so had not heard about Physkon's death until long after it had happened.

"He stayed in town for a ten-day, waiting for cargo. We had no idea he was calling daily, unchaperoned, on Astra. Then little Theon came to my house with a letter from Astra, saying that she was going away with Hippalos and asking us to take care of the boy until your return. We all grabbed our swords and rushed to the waterfront, but Hippalos' ship had left."

"Didn't anybody try to follow him, to avenge the family's honor?"

"I was coming to that. Tryphon—" that was my younger brother—"went to Miletos, since Hippalos had told our harbormaster that he meant to return to his home port. Tryphon stormed into the office of Ariston and Pytheas, demanding to know where the depraved one was.

"Hippalos, they told him, had already departed for Peiraieus. Yes, they said, he had brought a woman, whom he introduced as his wife, from Kyzikos. She had shipped with him to Peiraieus. This was somewhat unusual; but, as newlywed captains sometimes take their brides on their first voyage after the event, they thought nothing of it.

"Tryphon thought of sailing to Peiraieus; but then he might arrive after Hippalos had left that port, the gods knew whither. He thought he'd have a better chance of catching the scoundrel by waiting for him in Miletos.

"Then Hippalos' ship returned to Miletos without its captain. The mate told his employers that at Peiraieus, Hippalos had unloaded his cargo, loaded the new one, and announced that he was quitting to take another berth. He turned the ship over to the first officer and disappeared, and the woman with him. That is the last that anybody knows about him."

"Death take him!" I said. "And to think I could have so easily let my mutinous sailors cut his throat! Has anybody a key to my house?"

Inside, I looked around for some note that she might have left me, but there was nothing. I threw myself on a couch to weep, beat the wall with my fists until they were bloody, and cry out Astra's name, while my kinsmen stood around uneasily, making awkward attempts to console me. When I had finished, I asked:

"Where's Gnouros?"

"He went with Astra," said my brother-in-law. "Gnouros told Theon that you had charged him to take especial care of your wife, and this was the best way he could think of to do so."

"He'd have done better to have killed that temple thief," I growled.

"Oh, come now! The poor fellow was only a slave. Besides, Hippalos was much the younger and the larger of the two."

"What became of Dirka?"

"Gone back to her village. She said she'd come back to Kyzikos to work if you wanted her."

My brother entertained me and our kin that night. A somber homecoming feast it was; I could not even report a commercial success to lighten the gloom. I said:

"I hope I shall have better sense than ever to trust a Ptolemy again. To let myself be robbed once was bad enough, but twice!"

"There's still wealth in the Indian trade, though," said my brother. "Isn't there some other route by which we could come to that land?"

"There's the route through Syria, down the Euphrates to Babylon and Apologos and out the Persian Gulf. But the Parthians control that route. I doubt if an outsider would be allowed to keep much profit; Mithradates would skin him as the Ptolemies did me. And anything that he missed, the Seleucids would get."

"Of course," said Korimos, "the geographers tell us that the earth is round, and that one could reach India by sailing westward from Gades, straight out into the Atlantic."

"Let us not seek to wed Aphrodite," I said. "Nobody knows how far one must sail to raise land in that direction, nor how the prevailing winds blow. At the least, India must be thousands of leagues across the water from Spain, and your crew would be as dead as Darius the Great before they reached it. Gades, Gades … It reminds me of something. Ah, yes. The first time Hippalos came here, he'd shipped for some Gaditanian firm—Eldagon, I think the name was."

"It sounds Phoenician," said my cousin.

"It probably is. Now, if you were running away with a friend's wife, like Paris with Helen, and wanted to put the greatest possible distance between him and yourself, whither would you go?"

"To the farther end of the Inner Sea," said my brother-in-law.

"Just so. Eldagon's ships trade as far east as the Aegean. So what more natural than that Hippalos, finding one of them at Peiraieus, took a berth on it to get to Gades? He's probably captaining one of Eldagon's vessels in the western seas right now."

"Are you thinking of going after him?" asked my brother.

"Yes, I am. I'll load up the *Ainetê*—"

All my kinsmen shouted objections, and a noisy argument raged. But I beat them down, one by one. For one thing, I cited the advantages of cooperation with a shipping firm whose home port was too far away to compete directly with us. By joining forces with this Eldagon—provided I liked the cut of his artemon—we could make ourselves leaders in long-distance shipping in the entire Inner Sea.

As I spoke, another thought struck me. I said nothing, because my kinsmen would have tried to make me give it up. I recalled the arguments of Agatharchides and Artemidoros about the shape of Africa, and Herodotos' tale of the Phoenician fleet that sailed around Africa, and the Gaditanian fisherman whose horse-head stem post I had found. If they could do it, why not I?

I should have to time my arrival on the East African coast to take advantage of the six-monthly southwest wind. Then, I should leave this coast at the Southern Horn and head northeast over the open sea to India. Thus I could exploit the Indian trade without coming in reach of the Ptolemies' greedy grasp, and it was surely no riskier than searching for India by sailing west into the unknown Atlantic.

I knew the danger. Beyond the deserts, Africa was said to swarm with wild beasts and wilder men, some of whom would give a dinner for foreign visitors with the visitors as the main course. None knew how long the African coast was. It had taken King Necho's Phoenicians over two years to make the circuit, with two stops of five or six months each to grow a crop of wheat, so their actual time in transit was more than a year. Even if, with a large, modern ship, I could better their time, the Indian Ocean was still a vast, unexplored sea.

Who knew when a storm might hurl me ashore on some unknown, monster-haunted continent in the midst of it?

But then, what had I to lose? I had spent two years on those Indian journeys, and all I had to show for them was the name of an intrepid voyager with interesting tales to tell. But I had had that repute before I ever went to India. I had lost the only true love of my life. Among my fellow men, a cuckold is a figure of fun, and I had no doubt that many Kyzikenes laughed at me behind my back. So I did not foresee a serene and pleasant old age in my native city.

Therefore I resolved, while I was still active enough, to try the most daring voyage that man had ever essayed. If I succeeded, wealth and fame beyond that of kings should be mine. If I failed, I should at least go out in a blaze of glory.

One who would not sneer at my misfortunes was old Glaukos the physician. While the *Ainetê* was being readied, I spent an afternoon with him. I discussed my problems and plans, except the circumnavigation of Africa.

"Yes, I met your Hippalos," he said. "A charming fellow, who would be none the worse for hanging. Tell me, suppose you catch up with him and your wife, what then?"

"I'll kill him, first."

"If you can. He's a big, powerful fellow, and you are not exactly a youth."

"I can still throw men half my age in the gymnasium. Anyway, I'll take my chances."

"How about the law? Revenge is sweet, but having your own head chopped off afterwards is bound to take some of the pleasure out of it."

"That's not likely," I said. "He's a homeless wanderer. There would be no kinsmen to prosecute me, not even a Corinthian consul to bring an action on his behalf."

"Don't be too sure. Gades is under Roman rule, and Roman law differs from ours in many ways."

"I'll ask about it when I get there."

"All right, suppose you slay Hippalos. What will you do with Astra?"

"Bring her back, of course."

"Will you beat her?"

"I suppose I ought, but I—I don't think I could. I love her too much."

"When you get her back, how will you satisfy the lusts that led her to run off in the first place?"

"Oh," I said. "I hadn't thought that far ahead. But a wife's duty—"

"To the afterworld with her wifely duty!" said Glaukos. "When I was younger, I took those catchwords seriously, also. We men like to think of our women as passive vessels, satisfied to keep our houses and bear our brats. Nice girls are not supposed to enjoy being futtered, but to submit as a wifely duty. The fact is that they like it just as well as we do, and they get just as cranky and skittish when they don't have it."

"You sound like one of those Egyptians, who give their women almost as many rights as men."

"Hmp. Tell me, how often have you and Astra had a really successful bed-scrimmage in the last—how long since you got back from India the first time?"

"Nearly three years."

"Well, how often during the two years between your Indian voyages? I mean, where she quaked at the climax like a fish on the hook."

I thought. "Oh, perhaps four or five times."

"There you are. A healthy woman of her age ought to be well plumbed at least once or twice a ten-day. Another of my patients has similar trouble; in her case the cause is that her husband loves another man. Howsomever, perhaps you had better leave bad enough alone."

"You mean to ignore this adulterous pair? Let them go scot-free?"

"Just so—unless Astra has repented her bargain and really wishes to return to you."

"I couldn't do that! The honor of the family demands—"

"Honor, *phy!* Another catchword. Don't try to make up your mind right away, but think over my advice."

* * *

A month later, I set sail in the *Ainetê* with a cargo of Scythian wheat, Bithynian timber, and Mysian silver and wool. I stopped at Peiraieus to sell it and loaded up with Attic goods; then on to Dikaiarchia in the bay of Neapolis, in the shadow of Mount Vesuvius;

then to Massilia, and so on until I threaded the Pillars of Herakles and so came to Gades.

At each stop, besides selling my cargo and buying a new one, I had talked to the shipping people of my grand project. I had no trouble in getting an audience, for my fame as the man who had twice sailed to India had run ahead of me. This reputation enabled me to profit most gratifyingly from this voyage. Many merchants, I think, bid on my goods more for the sake of questioning me about the Indian trade than because they needed the goods.

I also got offers to go shares on the journey, and some to go with me. I chose a few of these, such as the Athenian physician Mentor and his apprentice, and several shipwrights. I meant to be as well prepared for disaster as foresight could render me. As a result of these additions, the *Ainetê* was badly crowded by the time we reached the Bay of Gades, at the mouth of the Cilbus.

Gades is a small city, at the northern end of a long, narrow island, called Kolinoussa, across the mouth of the bay. We tied up at a quay on the eastern side of the island, next to the temenos of the temple of Herakles, among the massive, high-sided ships used in the Atlantic trade. I also saw several small fishing vessels with horse-head stem posts; but I must admit that these did not look much like the one I had found on the African coast.

Aside from this temple and one to Kronos on the west or seaward side, there was little to see in Gades. Inside the wall, the city consisted mainly of warehouses and facilities—taverns and lodginghouses—for sailors. The houses of the merchants, landowners, and officials were villas scattered around the periphery of the bay and on the smaller island of Erytheia, in the midst of the bay.

The streets of Gades swarmed with sailors, dock workers, and merchants. They were a mixture of Hellenes, Phoenicians, Moors, native Iberians, and now (since the Roman domination) Italians as well. The various peoples did not inhabit separate districts, as in Alexandria. The crowded quarters and the shifting population, over half of which was at sea at any one time, made such segregation impractical.

The different races had been mixing and intermarrying for many years, so that one met people with names like Titus Perikles ben-Hanno. They looked like any other nondescript seaport crowd. With modern transportation, all the port cities in the Inner Sea are coming to look more and more alike.

I submitted with the best grace I could muster to the insolence of an arrogant Roman harbor master, put my cargo under guard, and gave the mate the job of finding lodgings for my people. Then I set out with Pronax, now a gangling youth, to find Eldagon. At his warehouse, they told me that the boss was not in that day and gave me directions for finding his villa.

I hired a boat to take me across the bay and found Eldagon's villa. The house was a normal upper-class dwelling of the courtyard type, large but not palatial. Around it, however, stretched a remarkable landscape of parks and gardens, like those of a Persian grandee. Here grew trees and shrubs of many exotic kinds. Around the corner of the house I glimpsed a kind of stockade, whence came some curious noises—grunts, whines, and other animal sounds.

The doorman led Pronax and me into the courtyard and bade us be seated while he went to find the master. Eldagon, he said, was "with his beasts." Presently Eldagon himself came in.

Eldagon the son of Balatar was a man of medium height and muscular, broad-shouldered build, with heavy, black brows and a big, hooked beak of a nose. Unlike most Punics in these days, when everybody from Karia to Carthage affects Hellenic dress and manners and shaves his face in imitation of the divine Alexander, Eldagon retained the old-fashioned Punic dress and full beard, beginning to turn from black to gray. He wore an ankle-length gown and a tall felt hat with a low turban wound around it. He clasped his hands together and bowed over them.

"Rejoice, sirs!" he said. "To whom am I indebted for this visit?"

"I am Eudoxos Theonos, a Kyzikene shipmaster," I said. "You may have heard of me, sir."

"Not the one who sailed to India?"

"Yes, sir."

"By Milkarth's iron yard!" cried Eldagon. "This is indeed an honor. Sit down and tell me all about it. Miknasa! Fetch wine! Our best Campanian!"

A half-chous of wine and an hour later, I got down to business. "Have you a sailor named Hippalos the Corinthian in your employ?"

Eldagon stared. "How strange that you should ask!"

"Well, have you?"

"Yes; at least, I did have. A few years ago, he signed up as a deck hand. Then he quit to work somewhere in the East. A few months back, he reappeared as a mate on one of my ships. The mate of that ship had fallen off a pier at Peiraieus while drunk and drowned, and Hippalos—who was then the skipper of a merchantman in those parts—persuaded my captain to ship him in the dead man's place. He was so eager to get back to the West, he said, that he would give up a step in rank. My captain had always liked him and knew him for an able mariner."

"Where is he now?"

Eldagon shrugged. "He sailed as first officer on two short coastal voyages from Gades, and then he disappeared again. Why or whither, I know not."

"Did he say anything about having sailed with me to India?"

"Not a word. Do you mean this man had actually been to India with you?"

"On my first voyage."

"But why—why should he be silent about so thrilling an adventure? You Hellenes—no offense meant—are the most garrulous folk on earth, and I cannot imagine a Hellene's keeping mum when he had such a tale to tell."

"I think he had his reasons. Tell me: when he put in here from Peiraieus, had he a woman with him?"

"Now that I think, I believe he did, albeit I never met her. He also had a slave—an elderly little barbarian of some sort. But, Master Eudoxos, you arouse my curiosity to the fever pitch. What is this all about?"

"I have a little matter to settle with Master Hippalos," said I grimly. "Might I speak to some of your officers, to learn if he gave any hint of whither he was going?"

"Thrice evil to evildoers! I have no objection." Eldagon looked closely at me. "Was this woman your daughter?"

"No, but you're close." To change the subject, I asked: "What is that stockade behind your house, whence come those strange bestial noises?"

"Oh, my dear sir!" cried Eldagon. "I must show you my beasts! Come, we shall have plenty of time to see them before dinner. They are my main interest in life. Ships and cargoes and contracts are all very fine, but I chiefly value them because they let me indulge my hobby. Come, and bring the youth, too."

We went out to the stockade. This was actually a number of adjacent inclosures housing various beasts. Pronax gave a little shriek and shrank back as an elephant thrust its trunk between the bars to beg for dainties. Eldagon dug a handful of nuts out of a pocket in his robe and gave one to the huge beast.

"The trouble with such a creature," said Eldagon, "is that it never stops eating. Malik, here, consumes three talents of hay and greens every day, and he is not yet full grown. Tell me: is it true, as many aver, that the elephants of India are larger than those of Africa?"

"That's hard to say," I replied. "I rode on one monster in India, seven or eight cubits tall; but the late King Ptolemaios Evergetes of Egypt had one in his menagerie, from Ethiopia, that was at least as large."

"This one comes from Mauretania," said Eldagon. "King Bocchus got him for me. They seem to be a smaller race, seldom exceeding five cubits. Now, here in this next cage is my most dangerous single beast, a wild bull from the Idubedian Mountains of Spain. This next is the common European lynx. And now, here is one that, I am sure, would like to make your acquaintance. Will you step into the cage with me?"

I followed Eldagon into the cage, with Pronax behind me. At first I saw nothing. A big oak grew in the cage, and something lay in the shade on the far side. The something got up and came towards us, and I saw that it was a lion, not quite full-grown. It trotted over to Eldagon and rubbed its head against his knees, making throaty noises. Eldagon scratched the roots of its scanty young mane as if it were a dog. Then the lion looked me up and down with its big, yellow eyes. I stood my ground. But Pronax backed against the bars, and the lion made for him, stopping a foot from him and looking up at him with a deep, rumbling growl.

Frightened half to death, the poor lad pressed himself against the bars with his eyes goggling. Eldagon pulled the lion back by its mane and spoke sharply to it. The animal let me nervously pat it and wandered back to its patch of shade.

"Hiram loves to frighten people who shrink from him," said Eldagon. "But he has never hurt anyone. In this next cage, I have a pair of gazelles from the African desert ..."

And so it went. Eldagon was still talking about his animals when lengthening shadows reminded him of dinner time. He pressed me to stay, which I did without reluctance.

"You must remain the night, too, best one!" he exclaimed. "Why, I have not even begun to tell you about my rare plants and trees!"

Here, evidently, was a man with a real enthusiasm—or obsession, depending on the point of view. In fact, if given a chance he would talk about his collection of plants and animals until the hearer became deaf or fell asleep. I said:

"This park and its beasts must cost you a pretty obolos to keep up."

"It does that. My wife scolds me for not saving the money to spend on her jewels, or to give to the poor, or anything but a lot of 'ungrateful beasts' as she calls them. But then, what does one live for? My children are all grown and doing well, so why should I not indulge this harmless passion?"

"No reason at all, sir. Do you show your menagerie to many people?"

"A great many. Twice a year I invite all of Gades to file through and take a look. My main worry is that our dear governor may take it into his head to seize my animals and ship them off to Rome, there to be butchered in those bloody public games. I make handsome gifts to the Roman to keep on his good side."

I kept hoping that he would bring the talk around to the shipping business, so that I could introduce my own proposal. But all he wished to discuss were exotic animals and plants. At last, as dinner was brought on, I said:

"I saw some remarkable animals in India, you know. There was a rhinoceros ..."

Now I had his attention. He listened eagerly, asking searching questions, as I described the beasts of the East. "Would that I could go thither," he said. "But I fear my health would not withstand the journey. How about you? Do you ever expect to return to India?"

"Not unless I can get around the Ptolemaic blockade." I told him of my difficulties with that grasping dynasty. He shook his head.

"We have a saying," he said, "never trust a river, a woman, or a king. But what is your plan for the future?"

This was the opening for which I had been waiting. "I do have a scheme for reaching India," I said, "although it is one that some would consider mad. ..." And I told him of my project for sailing around Africa. "I see, however, that I shall need another ship. My *Ainetê* is too small for the size of the crew I mean to ship. Besides, I shall need a longboat or two for exploring the shoreline."

"Perhaps I can help you," said Eldagon. "My brother Tubal is a shipbuilder; we work together. He makes them; I sail them."

"Would you be interested in a partnership for this voyage? You furnish the ship; I sail it."

Eldagon frowned. "I do not know. Your voyage sounds exciting but terribly risky. We have lost two ships in the last two years, so it behooves us to be cautious until that loss can be made up."

"Even if I could fetch you strange animals and plants from India?"

"Well, ah—I do not—" I could see him weaken. "I admit," he said, "that if anybody could do it, you could. I liked the way you stood up to that lion. For such a journey, all your courage and self-control would be needed. What sort of agreement had you in mind?"

Well, nobody—not even a Phoenician—has ever yet gotten the better of me on a dicker of that sort. We chaffered all through dinner—which we ate sitting in chairs, in the Punic manner—and for hours afterwards. Before we went to bed, we had our agreement roughed out.

* * *

Tubal ben-Balatar was a contrast to his brother Eldagon. There was nothing visibly Punic about him save a slight guttural accent. A younger man than Eldagon, whom he otherwise resembled, he wore a Greek tunic and cloak. His face was clean-shaven, and his hair was cut short in the Roman fashion. He even gave me the Roman salute, by shooting his right arm forward and up, like a schoolboy asking his teacher for leave to speak. He examined the *Ainetê* at her quay and said:

"You are right in wanting a larger ship for this voyage, Master Eudoxos. Howsomever, you will need a ship different not only in size but also in kind."

"How so?"

"See you that big fellow in the next dock? That's the kind of ship one needs in the Western Ocean. Notice the high freeboard and wide beam. They are required by the great swells one meets during a blow."

"The Inner Sea has some pretty lively storms."

"Yes, but you avoid most of them by lying up in winter. In the Atlantic, one meets storms at any time of year. Therefore one must either have a ship built to withstand them or do without shipping. Such a ship requires extra-heavy bracing to keep the long swells from racking her to pieces."

"Do you propose to build such a ship from the keel up, or has your brother one already in service?"

"Better than either; we have a new ship on the ways, almost ready to launch. Let's go look at her."

We climbed over the side of the *Ainetê* by our rope ladder into Tubal's boat, a six-oared harbor tug. We rowed to the mainland, where his shipway stood. Here on the slip sat the new ship, called the *Tyria*. She was a huge craft, even bigger than the *Ourania*, and somewhat differently proportioned. I could see from her massive construction and tubby form that she would prove slow; but then, Tubal knew more about shipbuilding for the Atlantic trade than I did.

It was evening by the time I had finished inspecting the *Tyria*, and Tubal wanted to show me some of Gades' famous night life. Eldagon begged off.

"That sort of thing began to bore me years ago," he said. "Besides, I must look to my animals. The male ibex has been ailing."

Tubal indicated young Pronax. "Are you sure that you wish your cousin to attend? The girls put on a fairly bawdy performance."

"After India, I don't think anything in Gades would shock him."

And indeed the floor show, in Gades' largest tavern, was tame enough. True, the dancing girls wore tunics of transparent, filmy stuff; but none showed her naked teats and cleft as they do in India. A comedian cracked jokes that must have been funny, to judge by the roars of mirth they elicited. But *oimoi!* he used such a strong local dialect of Greek, sprinkled with Punic and Iberian words, that I missed the point of half of them.

I suppose the reason for the repute of Gades as a center of wicked night life is that it is virtually the only city west of Neapolis where there is any night life at all. There is little or none in the Punic cities, like Panormos and Utica, because Phoenicians are a strait-laced, sober lot. The Massiliots, although Greeks with a reputation as gourmets, have much the same outlook. So, to those who like a bit of rowdy fun, Gades seems like an oasis in a vast desert of rigid morality.

Watching the girls sing, dance, and tweetle their flutes gave me an idea. I asked Tubal:

"Who owns those girls?"

"The proprietor. There he is, over there." He pointed to a burly, sweaty man talking to some sailors at a table.

"May I speak to him?"

Tubal caught the man's eye and beckoned him over. "Our genial host, Marcus Edeco," he said.

After the amenities, I asked Edeco: "Would you be interested in selling any of those girls?"

"I don't know. At a price, maybe," said Edeco. "What have you in mind?"

"I'm planning a long voyage, and at the end of it are some Hellenes stuck in a far land, who want Greek wives. It's a risky voyage, so I won't take any girls who don't want to go."

"Stay around until closing time and I'll let you talk to the girls."

I had quite a time staying awake until then, since some of the customers seemed determined to make an all-night revel of it. A couple of hours before dawn, Edeco got the last of them out and lined up his girls in front of me. There were seven of them.

"Would any of you girls like husbands?" I asked. "Real, legally wedded spouses?"

All seven let out a simultaneous shriek and threw themselves upon me, kissing my hands and face and chirping: "When? Where? Who? Are they young? Are they handsome? Are they rich?"

"There's your answer," said Tubal with a grin.

"Easy, girls," I said. "It's not quite so simple as that." And I told them of the Bactrio-Greek soldiers who had asked me to fetch

Hellenic brides for them. Since I did not make light of the length and hazards of the journey, the girls sobered up. In the end, four said they wanted to go. The remaining three—two of whom had children—preferred to stay in Gades. It took a ten-day of haggling, off and on, to beat down Marcus Edeco to a reasonable price. I also bought two more girls at another tavern.

Most of the crew of the *Ainetê* declined to sail on the *Tyria*. So I put my mate in command of the *Ainetê*, hired a few extra sailors, bought a new cargo, and sent the *Ainetê* off for Kyzikos.

I hired more local men to fill out the crew of the *Tyria*. Several had sailed down the Mauretanian coast as far as the mouth of the Lixus, albeit none had even been so far as half-legendary Kernê. Remembering the story of King Necho's Phoenician circumnavigators, I put aboard plenty of seed wheat, with hoes, sickles, and other tools for light farming. I had hired several sailors with farming experience.

And so, on the twenty-fourth of Metageitnion, in the third year of the 166th Olympiad, when Nausias was archon of Athens, the *Tyria*, with two longboats in tow, stood out from the harbor of Gades into the windy, tide-tossed Atlantic, on her way to India.

Book VIII

MANDONIUS THE IBERIAN

My mate was a Spaniard named Mandonius, who wore the tight breeches, black cloak, and little, round black bonnet of the Iberian peoples. He had sailed the Mauretanian coast and seemed able. When we set out, I had the sailors rig a tent forward of the deckhouse, which I assigned to our six music girls. I told Mandonius:

"Pass the word that I will have no intrigues with those girls. The men shall keep hands off."

Mandonius' black, drooping Spanish eyebrows rose. "You cannot mean that, Captain!"

"Of course I mean it! What do *you* mean?"

"But—but my Captain! What are women for, anyway?"

"Whatever they're for, these girls are not for the pleasure of the crew. That includes you."

"Is it that you want them all for yourself, Captain? At your age, I should think—"

"Never mind my age!"

"A thousand pardons, sir. But it is not as if these women were virgins—"

"Look, little man," said I with an effort to keep calm. "I'm taking the wenches to India to sell to Greek soldiers, who want to free and wed them. Now, everybody knows that a virginal dancing girl is like a fish with feathers. But I don't intend to spoil the deal by having them arrive in India with babes in their arms."

"You can always drop unwanted infants over the side—"

"Plague! Eight months pregnant, then."

Mandonius cocked his head, with a flicker of amusement on his usually dignified countenance. "Captain, do you really hope to have six pretty girls on a crowded ship with thirty-odd healthy men for a year, and not have even one tiny little bit of belly-bumping?"

"By Bakchos' balls, I certainly do expect it! Now run along and pass the order."

"Aye aye, sir. But *you* are feeling your years, Captain," he murmured, and then was gone before I could retort.

We sailed south from Gades, across the western horn of the Strait of the Pillars. Aft lay the pale-yellow sand hills of Belon, conspicuous against the dark olive-brown Iberian mountains. To port, barely visible in the distance, rose the vast rock of Calpe, soon hidden behind the other Pillar. This is the long Elephant Ridge, culminating in Mount Abila, which is really much larger and higher than Calpe albeit not so precipitous. We steered to starboard and headed down the Moorish coast, pushed by a fresh, mild northeaster.

The sun set as we passed Tingis. While taking a turn on deck after dinner, I observed Mandonius at the rail with one of the girls. They were laughing their heads off, and the mate was buzzing about the girl in a way that left no doubt of his intentions. He poked her ribs, pulled her hair, tickled her, and fondled her, while she shrieked and giggled. I nudged the mate and jerked my head towards the cabin, which he and I shared.

When we were seated inside, I said: "I told you, hands off those girls! Don't you understand plain Greek?"

"But I had no harm in mind, Captain—"

"Oh, yes? I suppose all that fingering was just a challenge to a game of sacred way? When I give an order, I expect it to be obeyed, without any ifs or buts! Do I make myself plain?"

Mandonius gave a snarl of anger. "Captain Eudoxos! I will have you know that I am a real man. And when a real man sees a woman, what does he do? I will tell you—he futters her, that is what he does!" He smote the table. "You Greeks can do without women, because you amuse yourselves with sodomy and other beastliness. But we Spaniards are real men. When there is a woman on board, I do what my nature tells me—"

"Shut up!" I shouted. "I don't care what kind of man you are. Either you keep those wandering hands—and other organs—to yourself, or by all the gods and goddesses, I'll put you off at Zelis!"

"You insult my honor!" he yelled, jumping to his feet.

Although Mandonius was shorter than I, the overhead of the cabin was still too low for him to stand upright. As a result, he hit his head a terrific blow against a beam and fell to the deck, between the table and his bunk.

Stooping carefully, I rose and went to him. He was crouched on the floor, holding his head in his hands and groaning. I helped him to bed and fetched the physician Mentor, who dosed him with drugged wine. Although, the next day, Mandonius had a headache and a great lump on his scalp, nothing seemed to be cracked. He was very apologetic, and for some days a more respectful and conscientious first officer could not have been found.

On our port, the distant, olive-colored peaks of the Atlas slid away, becoming lower as the days passed. The *Tyria* stood well out from shore, a good league from land, so that the actual shoreline could not be seen from the deck. The breeze freshened as we got farther south, and a current helped us along.

My passengers—the music girls, the doctor and his apprentice, and the shipwrights—pestered me with silly questions, like: "Are we halfway to India yet?" or "When shall we see a sea monster?" As the hills sank below the horizon, they became nervous and urged me to sail closer to shore.

"By Zeus the Savior, I assure you I know where the land is!" I told them. "I send a man up the mast every few hours to make certain."

"But it makes us fearful that we cannot see the coast," said one of them. "Please, Captain, do us a favor by sailing closer in!"

"No! And I'll tell you why. This is a dangerous coast, with sandy shoals extending far out under water. You think you're safely offshore, and *plêgê!* you're aground."

"But, Captain—"

"Besides, out here in the Atlantic you have those beastly flows and ebbs of the sea called tides, which pick the sand up from one shoal and dump it on another, so that they are always changing position. It seems to have something to do with the moon. No, thank you, I'll stay out here where it's safe."

This nonsense continued for three days. Then came a night when I went to sleep at midnight, giving Mandonius the watch until dawn.

The next thing I knew, the cabin lurched violently, spilling me off my pallet. There was a frightful racket of snapping timbers, shrieks and screams, the roar of breakers, and the sound of water rushing into the hull.

In no time I was out on deck. A lantern, hung from the mast, shed a faint, yellow light into the darkness. A mist hid the stars, and the moon had not yet risen. It took no yogin's wisdom, however, to tell that we had gone aground.

The sailors reported several feet of water in the hold. Others ascertained that we were on a sandy beach, but that with the moderate surf we were not likely to break up. There was nothing to do but wait until dawn. When I had the screaming women calmed, I took Mandonius aside.

"Now then," I said, "what happened?"

He sighed and drew his dagger. Thinking that he meant to stab me, I leaped back and grabbed for my own; but he only extended his to me hilt first. With his other hand, he pulled his tunic aside to expose his chest.

"Kill me, Captain Eudoxos," he said.

"Later, perhaps. Right now, I merely wish to know how this occurred."

"It is all my fault."

"I have guessed that already. But how?"

"Well, sir, you know those girls?"

"Yes."

"As I have told you, a real man who sees such a filly thinks of only one thing; and we Spaniards—"

"By Herakles, will you get to the point, you stupid ox?"

"Well, as you know, they have wanted to sail closer to shore, because the sight of so much water terrifies them. And yesterday they came to me and promised that, if I would take the ship in closer, I might lie with any or all of them as my reward. So I steered a *little* nearer the coast, and then that polluted mist came up, and I lost my way."

"Why in the name of the Dog didn't you take soundings and anchor when you found it was shoaling?"

"Because I was futtering one of the girls, sir, and a man does not think of such things at such a time. Now will you please slay me?"

I drew a long breath. "By the Mouse God, you deserve it! But I shall have to deny myself that pleasure. We must either repair the ship and sail on; or, if that prove impossible, we must get back to Gades. In any case, I shall need every able man. Now take some hands below to see what can be done about hauling cargo out of the water in the hold."

Dawn showed us beached on an offshore island—actually, a big sand bar, several stadia long and separated by a narrow channel from the Moorish coast. This coast was low and level here, with a row of hills rising a few furlongs inland. We had evidently struck at high tide, for the entire hull was now out of water.

Since there was no chance that the ship would float away with the rising tide, we all climbed down the ladder and stood on the sand. I called the shipwrights and made a circuit of the ship to inspect the damage. I was puzzled by the speed with which we had filled, since so stoutly built a ship should have been able to withstand grounding with no worse effect than springing a few seams.

"Here you are, Captain," said my head shipwright, a Gaditanian named Spurius Kalba. "That's what holed her."

The *Tyria* had run, not merely upon a sandy beach, but also upon a ledge of rock that protruded from the sand like a boulder. There was not another such rock in sight in either direction along this beach. With leagues of soft sand to choose from, Mandonius had to put my ship upon the one real rock in the entire region. The rock had split several garboard strakes to kindling and had cracked the keel right through.

"What are our chances of repairing her?" I asked Spurius Kalba.

"None, Captain," he replied. "If this were the Bay of Gades, and we had plenty of men and an Archimedean winch to haul her out on a shipway, we could cut out all that broken wood and mortise in new timbers. But here we have no shipway, no winch, and no spare timbers."

"Let's try the longboats," I said. "Could we get everybody into them to row back to Zelis?"

We unhitched the boats and shoved them into deeper water. We found that we could crowd our nearly forty persons into them. But then they were heavily laden, with little freeboard, and so would fill and sink at the first real blow. Moreover, we could not carry food and water enough for the journey.

We unloaded the longboats and hauled them up on the beach. The hysterical excitement of the first few hours after the grounding had died down. Sailors and passengers stood or sat, watching me with expressions of doglike expectancy, as if I were a god who could solve our problem with a snap of my fingers. While the cook got breakfast, I discussed schemes with Kalba. Others joined in from time to time.

"I say we should walk it," said Mentor. "Each of us can carry enough food and water to get him to the nearest town—"

"Ha!" barked Mandonius. "Do you know where we are, Doctor?"

"No. Where?"

"Near the mouth of the Lixus. The Lixites are the world's worst robbers. If we tried to walk the coast, a horde of them would swoop upon us the first day out and cut all our throats for the sake of our possessions."

"But if we had no possessions except food and water—"

"They'd slaughter us first and ask questions afterwards. Believe me, sir, I know these knaves." The mate turned to me. "If I may suggest it, Captain, you had better serve out arms and post watches right now, before they get wind of our presence."

I took Mandonius' advice about reorganizing the party. Some brought supplies ashore whilst others put up a camp. Setting up the camp and digging a ditch around it for a fortification took the rest of the day.

I also sent sailors off in the longboats to explore. Late in the day they returned. One reported a dry stream bed, a league to the northeast, which would probably run water with the first autumnal rain. The other announced the mouth of a big river—undoubtedly the Lixus—three leagues to the southwest.

Over dinner, I resumed my discussion with Spurius Kalba but seemed to get no nearer to finding a way out of our predicament. "At least," said I, "we have plenty of time to make up our minds. There's food for months."

"And plenty of firewood to cook it with," said Kalba, jerking a thumb towards the bulk of the *Tyria* looming above us.

"You're thinking of breaking her up?"

"Not exactly, sir; but those broken timbers in the bottom, at least, will never be good for anything else."

"You give me an idea," I said. "Suppose we did break up the ship. Could you build a shipway from some of the timbers, and a smaller ship from the rest?"

He stared at me popeyed. "Why, Captain, if that isn't the damnedest—begging your pardon, sir—the damnedest idea anybody ever—well, I suppose we could, now that I think. Let's see. If we planned a seventy-footer ..."

He jumped up and strode off into the dusk, muttering numbers. I followed him. He paced off a rectangle, thirty by eighty feet, on the sand, and marked its outline with a piece of driftwood.

"Now," he said, "we should need wood for a frame of this size, good and solid, and wood for props to brace the hull. We shouldn't need to prop up the shoreward end of the frame, because the natural slope of the beach takes care of that. ..."

The next ten-day, Kalba and I spent in designing the new ship while the rest of the crew plowed up a plot of the sand bar and planted our wheat. About the third day after our stranding, a party of Lixites—lean, brown men in goatskins—appeared on the mainland opposite our island. Although they bore spears and had quivers full of light javelins slung on their backs, they did not look like a war party. They had their families, their asses, and their flocks of sheep and goats with them.

"If we were few, they might attack," said Mandonius. "As it is, they may decide to make friends."

The Lixites approached the channel sundering the island from the mainland. After long hesitation, one man, smiling nervously, laid aside his arms and splashed through the shallows to the island. Nobody could understand him until I awoke a sleeping sailor who spoke Moorish. After listening to the Lixite, he said, "He speaks Moorish, Captain, but a dialect. I can understand about half of it."

We bought three sheep and a jarful of goat's milk in return for some of my trade goods. I said, "Ask him whence the Lixus River comes."

"He says," translated the sailor, "that it flows from the southeast, then from the northeast, and finally rises in the Dyris Mountains. That's what the Moors call the Atlas."

* * *

When we had drawn and erased a hundred sketches of the new ship on my waxed tablets and argued every little point from a hundred angles, I gave the word to the shipwrights. I told my people that, until we were at sea again, Spurius Kalba was their boss, under me, and anybody who did not wish to turn a hand to shipbuilding was welcome to start for Tingis afoot. Despite some grumbling, nobody challenged my order.

Luckily, we had shipped plenty of tools. Extra tools were given to the handier sailors, while those who showed less skill were reserved for simpler tasks, such as lowering timbers from the deck of the *Tyria* and dragging them to the shipway.

All day, the camp rang with the sound of saw and hammer, as the men knocked out pegs and pulled out nails. The music girls, who were a little light for such rough work, I put to cleaning up the camp, carrying water, and entertaining us in the evening with their musical specialties.

As I prowled the camp one evening, I saw, in the dying light, two pairs of bare feet protruding from the door of a tent: a male pair together with toes painting downwards, and a female pair flanking these and pointing upwards. Enraged at this flouting of my orders, I had a mind for an instant to drag the guilty pair forth by their telltale feet and give them a good drubbing with my fists. But then I thought: relax, Eudoxos. You will not reach India on this try anyway, so why not let them have their fun?

I planned to call the new ship the *Mikrotyria* ("*Little Tyria*"). She could not be started until the *Tyria* was almost completely broken up, since we needed the keel timbers of the old ship to build the keel of the new. The curved members of the new ship required adzing to make them fit the smaller plan; but then the *Mikrotyria*, being smaller, did not need such massive timbering.

When the *Mikrotyria* was under way, with keel and garboard strakes in place, I took one of the longboats to explore. We rowed up the Lixus a few leagues and then drifted down again. Whereas most of the country was near-desert, with occasional patches of dry grass or thorny shrubs, the vale of the Lixus was well wooded, with hundreds of date palms and acacias.

At the mouth of the river, as we descended, another party of Lixites called out to us. "They say," said the Moorish-speaking sailor, "that if we will come ashore, they will give us a feast."

"They outnumber us," I said. "We'd better stay where we are. Ask them ..."

With the help of the sailor, I conversed with the leader of this band. Among other things, he told me that there was a large island out of sight in the ocean. By sailing due west for a day and a night, I should come within sight of it. Then he renewed his importunities to get us ashore, holding out a handful of dates as bait. When they saw that, despite their solicitations, we were heading out to sea, they gave a yell of disappointment and hurled a volley of javelins at us. These missiles fell into the water all around us, and one struck the side of the boat and stuck quivering in the wood.

"You guessed right that time, Captain," said a sailor.

"Let's have a look at that island," I said. "If we don't find it, we'll cut across the wind back to the African shore."

We put up our little sail and followed the setting sun westward, while the African coast sank out of sight on our port. Sure enough, by the middle of the following morning, the top of a mountain appeared out of the waves ahead of us, and soon after noon we reached the island. It was mountainous and looked at least thirty leagues in length.

We coasted along the southeastern shore for a few leagues, noting landing places and streams that entered the ocean. At one small, sheltered beach, we rowed in, beached our boat, and ate our lunch on the sand. We saw no signs of men or of large beasts, although the scrub was full of small, bright-yellow birds, singing melodiously. Then we reembarked, pointed our bow southeast, and sailed with the wind abeam back to the African coast.

* * *

It was the beginning of Anthesterion, five months after our grounding, that the *Mikrotyria* was completed. The weather was comfortably cool, with occasional showers. To the east, the barren mainland turned green. The northeaster blew day and night. We had never been in danger of starvation, for several times during the five-month stay, parties of Lixites had come past and sold us food. Now our wheat was harvested, so that we did not lack for bread. The six girls took turns at the querns.

Looking at the *Mikrotyria*, anyone could see that she was a rough job, without the finish that a real shipyard gives its craft. We cared nothing for that, however, so long as she floated, sailed, took us whither we would go, and did not leak faster than we could pump her out.

At high tide one day, therefore, we launched her, with my entire company, including the girls, hauling on the ropes to make sure that she did not bound out to sea and blow away for good. We anchored her just beyond the grounding line at low tide, rigged her, and loaded her with the gear we had taken out of the *Tyria*. We had to abandon some of our bulkier pieces of cargo.

I should like to have made a couple of practice cruises before taking the company on board. Such a proposal would have caused trouble, however, because those left ashore would fear that I was about to sail off and abandon them. So, a ten-day after the launch, we hoisted the anchors and stood out to sea.

Now began our troubles. For we wanted to sail directly into the teeth of the prevailing northeaster, and the *Mikrotyria* had other ideas. Some ships can sail a fair angle to windward; others cannot. The *Mikrotyria* proved one of the latter, besides responding erratically to the steering oars. We spent the day sailing out from shore and back again, trying to beat to windward. Between the ship's bad steering and the current—which flowed the same way as the wind—we ended each shoreward reach exactly where we had started, offshore from our abandoned camp.

At the end of the day, much cast down, we anchored and came ashore again. The next day we tried towing into the wind, without any sail. The sailors sweated and strained at the oars of the longboats and gained a few score furlongs. Then, when they tired, wind and current swept us right back to our island again.

Ashore that night, I told Spurius Kalba: "I have long wished there were some kind of sail whereby one could sail closer to the wind."

"What other kind of sail *could* there be, Captain? Sure, the oblong sail is the only land of sail there is or ever has been, and it's used the world over."

"Well, you've seen for yourself that it is not good enough. Why won't an oblong sail permit one to sail closer to the wind?"

"Because that's the nature of things, sir, and the nature of things can't be changed."

"Oh, rubbish! You're like most people: you think because you were brought up on one way of doing things, it's the only method possible."

"Well, you clever Greeks do make some wonderful inventions; but I'd rather stick to what I know works."

"To get back: what interferes with the use of the oblong sail against the wind?"

"How should I know, Captain?"

"Use your eyes, man! The wind catches the weather edge of the sail and flutters it. That spills the air out of the sail, so that it no longer presses against its yard."

"I suppose so," mumbled Kalba.

"So the big weakness of this sail is that it has a loose weather edge, not stiffened by any yard. What we must do is to devise a sail with some sort of stiffening on its weather edge."

"But, Captain, the weather edge on one tack becomes the lee edge on the other! Are you going to stiffen both?"

"I might. What I need is a model; it's easier than experimenting with a full-sized ship. Let you and the boys make me a model of the *Mikrotyria*, about *so* long." I held my hands a cubit apart. "The cabin and such need not be accurate, but the mast and the rigging must be carefully made to scale."

Three days later, my company sat watching me and trying not to laugh as I waded the channel between the island and the mainland, sailing my model boat. After each day's experiments, I gave the shipwrights orders for another model sail, and they had it ready for me the next day.

I tried all sorts of weird rigs, such as a rectangular sail with yards that ran completely around the rectangle. I had to knock down one sailor whom I caught describing circles with his forefinger next to his head to show what he thought of my ideas.

At last some god—if gods there be—whispered in my ear: why must a sail be rectangular? Why not three-sided? With a yard carried at a slant, so that one edge of the triangle skimmed the deck …

It worked fine on one tack but not on the other, since to wear ship in the usual manner brought the lee edge of the sail upwind. I puzzled over this difficulty for hours.

Then I thought: who says the normal position of the yard must be athwartships? Why not mount it parallel to the keel and let it swing to port or starboard, depending upon which side the wind is on? Then the yard would be the weather edge on both tacks. To change tacks, put the helm down instead of up, until the wind fills the sail from the other side.

"I've got it!" I yelled. "Kalba, come here …"

"Begging your pardon, Captain, but nobody in his right mind would sail under such a crazy rig."

"Well, some people in their wrong minds are going to sail with it. Cut and sew me a full-sized sail like this."

"But, Captain Eudoxos! You won't be able to tack like you say, because the forward end of the spar will foul the forestay!"

"*Oi!*" said I, frowning. "You're right, curse it." I pondered some more and said: "We'll cut off the forward point of the triangle, so. Then the spar will clear the forestay. Also, the sail will look a little more like a conventional sail and so frighten the sailors less. There will still be a short unstiffened weather edge, but I hope that won't matter."

Spurius Kalba still looked upon my new sail design with something like horror. Then began a tug of wills, which no doubt a god looking down from Heaven would have found very funny, between Kalba and me. He did everything he could think of, short of open mutiny, to prevent the construction of the new rig. He made transparent excuses; he invented delays; he sulked and grumbled. But I stood over him and drove him on until the sail was made to my directions.

The sail was no longer a true triangle, but a figure that the geometers call a rhomboid. I still call it a triangular sail, though, since nearly everybody knows what a triangle is, while the term "rhomboid" only brings a blank look to the faces of most people.

When the *Mikrotyria* was rerigged, the sailors all put on long faces. One said: "Begging your pardon, sir, but I'd rather stay here to be speared by the Lixites than go to sea in that thing."

The rest wagged their heads in agreement. I could see that force would only push them into open mutiny, and I did not care to have to fight them at odds of twenty to one.

"I'm going, anyway," I said. "I wouldn't ask you to sail until the rig has been tried out, but the ship is too big for one man to handle. I must have five or six men. You've taken chances already; who'll take one more to get us home?"

They avoided my eye until Mandonius said: "Captain, I will sail with you. It takes a real man to sail with a crazy rig like that, but we Spaniards are real men. Now, which of you dung-eating dogs will prove that he has more courage than a mouse, by sailing with us?"

We rounded up four more volunteers, who went aboard with the look of men going to their doom. When we weighed anchor and stood out to sea, though, their expressions changed. For the *Mikrotyria* headed north, diagonally against the wind, as if the sea nymphs were pushing her along. When we were half a league out to sea, I put the helm down and swung the bow to starboard. The wind filled the sail on the other side, and soon we were slanting in towards the coast at a point well to windward of that we had left.

The new rig did not work quite so well on the port tack as on the starboard, because the slanting yard was hung on the port side of the mast. Therefore, on the port tack, the wind blew the sail against the mast. But it worked well enough to enable us to gain on wind and current, so that we returned to the coast several furlongs upwind from where we left it. I made two more tacks to prove that this had not been accidental, then put the helm up and ran free back to our island.

The next few days were spent in modifying the new rig in the light of experience, and then we sailed for home. "I always knew that sail would work," quoth Spurius Kalba.

* * *

Despite the success of my new sail, the *Mikrotyria* soon showed the effects of her hasty construction. She leaked, and every day she leaked faster. Everyone was kept busy with pumps and buckets, and I put in at Zelis to beach her at high tide for hasty caulking and tarring. Then we went on to Tingis.

I had hoped to sail her back to Gades, but to attempt this in winter in the ship's present condition had been foolhardy. So I put in at Tingis, a bustling port through which passes nearly all the foreign trade of Mauretania. To tell the truth, I was also ashamed, after all my big talk, to face Eldagon and Tubal and admit that I had run the *Tyria* aground during the first ten-day of our voyage.

At Tingis, the harbor was practically closed down, because it was still winter, and snow could be seen on the peaks of the Atlas. The only ships that went out were fishermen, and they only for brief cruises on fair days. The *Mikrotyria*'s arrival was a startling event. Her bizarre rig advertised her coming. Within an hour of arrival, every seaman, shipbuilder, longshoreman, and waterfront loafer was swarming around and asking questions. Were we from the fabled land of the Antipodes? From the moon?

Then came the merchants, sniffing out a chance to buy new stock ahead of their competitors. Not having received any cargoes for months, they were hungry. I took my time, selling the cargo bit by bit. Thus I got quite a decent price on most items.

I paid off the crew, adding fares to take them back to Gades. The Athenian shipwrights I sent home to Peiraieus. Learning that there was not a single Greek physician in Tingis, Mentor and his apprentice resolved to stay, set up practice, and write to Athens for their families to join them. The six music girls I gave their freedom. Some had formed attachments to members of the crew, and I think they all found one way or another of making a living.

I rehired four sailors, including the one who spoke Moorish. They were grateful, since winter is a lean time for seamen. Although, like all ports in the Inner Sea, Tingis had a few Hellenes, most of the folk were Moors who spoke little or no Greek. Therefore I determined to learn the rudiments of that tongue, which I did with the help of the Moorish-speaking sailor. I also needed a few men to help me demonstrate the *Mikrotyria*, which I meant to sell. Between chaffering with the merchants and taking the *Mikrotyria* out to show off her paces, the ten-days slipped by. When I hinted that the ship could be had, there were remarks about her crazy rig. But a syndicate of merchants and shipbuilders came secretly to offer to buy the ship. Although doubtful about the strange sail, they would try it out. If it did not work, they could change it for a more conventional rig.

When the ship and the longboats had been sold and I added up my total gains, I was astonished to discover how well I had done. I had a total of around three talents of silver. Little by little, I changed nearly all of this into gold. That weight of silver could not be carried on the person, and to travel about with a two-hundred-pound chest of money was asking for trouble. The equivalent in gold was a mere eighteen pounds, which I divided between Pronax and myself. Each of us wore a money belt under his clothing.

By the middle of Elaphebolion, the weather showed signs of spring, and the shipmen began caulking, tarring, and painting their craft. Pronax and I visited the local sights. One was the alleged tomb of Antaios, which some clever fellow had put a fence around and charged admission to see. The grave was half open, exposing the huge bones of the giant. They said he must have been as big as the Colossus of Rhodes. To me, the bones looked suspiciously like those of an elephant.

I also meant to call on King Bocchus, who ruled the land from a castle high up on Mount Abila. Perhaps I could get him to back another attempt at circumnavigating Africa. With reasonable luck this time, I ought to clear enough profit to pay back the investments both of the king and of my Gaditanian backers, with a profit for each as well as myself.

* * *

While I was mulling this plan, Tingis staged a spring fair in honor of some moon goddess. Pronax and I enjoyed the storytellers, the musicians, the games, and the sports. One fellow asked people to guess which of three walnut shells a chick-pea was under. I discomfited him by guessing right three times running, having learnt that trick from Hippalos.

I also astounded all of Tingis by winning the archery contest. I had learnt to shoot among the Scythians, and the Moors are even worse archers than my fellow Hellenes. I let them put a wreath on my head and made a little speech of thanks, first in Greek and then in bad Moorish, which mightily pleased the Moors. I also had to listen to a long-winded ballad improvised in my honor by the local bard, who twanged his lyre and sang about the tall, gray-bearded stranger who came from far, unknown lands to carry off the prize, as Odysseus had done at the court of King Alkinoös.

Afterwards, when Pronax and I were wandering the grounds, we stopped before a tent with several people lined up in front of it. Over the entrance, a pair of posts upheld a wooden board on which was written, in Greek letters:

SRI HARI
THE GREAT INDIAN YOGIN
SEES ALL—KNOWS ALL
SPEAKS WITH GODS AND SPIRITS
CASTS HOROSCOPES

I said: "Let's have a look at this fellow. I'll speak to him in *prakrita*, and if he's a fake I shall know it."

After a wait, the people in front of me had taken their turns and departed. The flap of the tent was drawn back, and a voice said: "Come in!"

I entered, with Pronax behind. A small man was holding back the tent flap, but in the sudden gloom I could not tell much about him.

The tent was lit by a pair of huge, black Etruscan candles in candlesticks at the ends of a low, narrow table placed athwart the tent. At the rear rose a piece of canvas, about four feet wide and seven high, on which was painted the elephant-headed god Ganesha sitting on a flower.

Behind the table and before the painting, on a pile of cushions, Sri Hari sat cross-legged. He was a tall man with a graying red beard and a huge red turban on his head. He spoke:

"Welcome, my beloved son. How can I serve—"

"Hippalos!" I roared, and hurled myself across the low table with my hands clutching for his throat.

My eye caught a metallic flash in the candlelight as Hippalos snatched up a short sword, which lay on the floor in front of him, hidden by the table top. As I threw myself upon him, he whirled the sword up for a slash at my head. The blow would have split my skull like a melon had it not been too hasty to have much force, and had it not been stopped by my wreath.

Then we were grappling on the floor, tearing and kicking. One candle and then the other fell over and went out. I got a hand on the wrist that held his sword arm. When he persisted in trying to stab me, I sank my teeth into his arm until I tasted blood. Then he dazed me with a blow on the side of the head and a kick in the belly and tore himself loose.

I grabbed the sword, which he dropped. As he bolted out the rear of the tent, I plunged after him, tripping and stumbling in the dark. By the time I found the back door to the tent, Hippalos had vanished.

I turned back into the tent, where there was now some light, since the doorkeeper had tied back the flap of the front door. Hippalos' next clients were peering in.

"That's all for today," I said. "A demon invoked by Master Hari got out of control and carried him off. You had better go away, lest the demon return for more victims."

They went, fast. I turned to the doorman and cried: "Gnouros!"

"Master! Is good to see you!" We threw ourselves into each other's arms, kissing and babbling.

"Let's light the candles and close the door," I said, "and you shall tell me everything. Where is Astra?"

"Is dead, master."

"Oh," I said.

"You bleed!"

"Just a little scalp cut."

I sat down on Hippalos' cushions and wept while Gnouros lit the candles and bandaged my head. He and Pronax tidied up the tent, which looked as if a whirlwind had been through it.

A dull gleam from the floor caught my eye. I picked up the little bronze statuette of Ganesha, which I had given to Hippalos. It had served as a model for the painting at the back of the tent. I must have grasped it during our struggle in the dark and broken the chain by which it hung from Hippalos' neck.

When the tears stopped flowing, I asked: "How did she die? Did he kill her?"

"Nay, master. She kill herself."

"Oh?"

He told me the story. Astra had fallen madly in love with Hippalos, for reasons that were plain to me now after old Glaukos' talk on the needs of women. For the first month or two of their elopement, all was love and kisses. They settled in an apartment in Gades.

Then Hippalos' cruel side, of which I had had a glimpse in India, reappeared. He began by tormenting Astra in petty ways, playfully threatening to abandon her, to sell her, or to feed her to the fishes. From this he passed to physical torment, poking, pinching, and finally beating. When she wept and pleaded, he told her: "You're only a burden to me. If you really loved me, you would slay yourself."

So, when he was away on a voyage, she hanged herself.

"By Herakles, why didn't she come back to me?" I asked. "Why didn't you urge her to?"

"I did. I said you would do no worse than beat her little. But she said she could not face you, because she had done you so big wrong. She was ashamed. And when he acted like he hated her, she had nothing to live for."

I now have cursed little to live for myself, I thought. "Death take him! Why did he quit his job with Eldagon ben-Balatar? How did he come to be here?"

"When we were sailing from Peiraieus to Gades, he bribed harbor masters to write him if they saw you sailing west after him. One day he got letter, and away we went. We fled to Balearic Islands, and then Master Hippalos had idea of dressing up as Indian wise man. So now he is King Bocchus' big wizard. We came down to Tingis for fair, to make money from stupid people."

"I suppose he's bolted back to his royal master's castle, eh?"

Gnouros shrugged. "Maybe so. We go kill him, yes?"

I could have reproached Gnouros for not having avenged his mistress by slaying Hippalos himself, but I forebore. He was a dear little man but no fighter—one of those natural-born slaves of whom Aristoteles wrote. In any case, a slave who attacks a free man, whatever the reason, has little chance of living when the other free men get their hands on him. Perhaps there is something to this idea of some radical philosophers, that slavery is inherently wrong.

Book IX

BOCCHUS THE MAURETANIAN

Next morning, through a drizzle, I climbed the winding road to King Bocchus' castle. Behind me marched Pronax and Gnouros. At the gate, a squad of wild-looking Moorish soldiers, in vermilion-dyed goatskin mantles and spotted catskin turbans, surrounded me. The instant I said who I was, they swarmed all over me, grabbing my arms and legs and taking away my Indian sword.

"*Ê!*" I cried. "How now?"

"You are fain to see the king, yes?" said the most ruffianly-looking of the lot, whom I took to be the duty officer.

"Yes, but—"

"Then you shall see him. His audience starts any time."

"But why this rough treatment?"

"We hear you are a dangerous man, so we take no chances. Come, now."

Hippalos' work, I thought. They hustled me into the courtyard. After a wait, they took me into the throne room. This was tiny compared to that of the Ptolemies, but a larger room than one finds in most Moorish houses, which are mere hovels. A fire crackled on a hearth in the middle of the floor. The smoke was supposed to go out a hole in the roof but did not.

When my eyes got used to the gloom, not much relieved by smoking, sputtering torches thrust into holes in the wall, I saw the king seated at the far end amid a small crowd of royal kinsmen, officials, and hangers-on. Bocchus of Mauretania (or Maurusia, as some call it) was a man of medium size, somewhat younger than I, wearing a bulky hooded coat against the chill. The hood was pushed back, so that his bald head gleamed in the torchlight. He was clean-shaven and not ill-looking, being no swarthier than the average Spaniard.

"Give me your name and rank," said the usher, another Moor bundled up against the weather. Coughing on the smoke, I told him:

"I am Eudoxos Theonos, of Kyzikos: former polemarch, former military treasurer, and former trierarch of the city of Kyzikos; head of the shipping firm of Theon's sons, of Kyzikos; explorer of the Borysthenes, the Tanaïs, and other Scythian rivers; author of *Description of the Euxine Sea*; and inventor of the triangular mainsail. Can you remember all that?"

The usher stumbled but finally got it all out. The king said: "You might have added that you are the only Hellene I ever heard of who spoke Moorish."

"Badly, sire."

"You will doubtless improve with practice. I knew not that I should receive so eminent a visitor. You need not hold him so tightly, men; methinks he will attempt no desperate deed. Let him go."

"But, sire!" said a soldier, "the Indian holy man warned us—"

"I said, let him go!" said Bocchus sharply. "Now, sir, what brings you hither?"

"Two things, O King. First, may it please Your Majesty, I have a tale to tell about the golden wind to India. ..."

I told about the seasonal winds that sweep across the Arabian Sea and my two voyages, omitting my troubles with the Ptolemies. I did, however, say that it was a shame that this dynasty of fat, degenerate schemers should have a monopoly of this trade, and I told of my plan to sail around Africa to India.

"I have just returned from a voyage down the coast," I said, and told of the island I had found off the mouth of the Lixus. "Now, sire, the main limiting factor in these voyages is the amount of supplies one can carry. To improve one's chances of completing so long a voyage, it were wise to set up depots of stores as far along the route as possible. I have discovered two places where such depots can be set up to advantage. One is at the mouth of the Lixus, which, I have ascertained, rises in the Atlas not far south of here. It should not be difficult to open up a regular trade route along the Lixus, to the advantage of Your Majesty's kingdom. The other is that island whereof I have told you, west of the mouth of the Lixus."

I proposed that Bocchus outfit an expedition, on terms like those that Balatar's sons had given me. When I had finished, he said:

"That is very interesting. But what is the other matter, Master Eudoxos?"

"Your Majesty has at his court, I believe, a man who passes himself off as Sri Hari, the Indian holy man."

"What mean you, sir, 'passes himself off as'? Have you reason to doubt he is what he says he is?"

"I have excellent reason, sire. I have known the man for years. He is Hippalos of Corinth, a wandering entertainer, sailor, and adventurer, who sailed with me on my first Indian voyage."

"Assuming that you speak sooth, what would you of him?"

"Know, O King, that he stole my wife and then drove her to her death. I would have justice upon him. To put it shortly, I want his head."

"Indeed?" said King Bocchus. "I think you are he of whom Master Hari has already complained." He spoke to the usher: "Fetch the Indian."

While we waited, I told the king about my Indian project. Then the usher returned with Hippalos, with a bandage on his right wrist and wearing another turban to replace the one he had lost in our fight. He stared down his nose at me with no sign of recognition.

"This man," said the king to Hippalos, "avers that you are no Indian at all, but a Hellene named Hippalos, who has done him wrong. What say you?"

"That is ridiculous, sire," said Hippalos, speaking with a nasal Indian accent. "I have never seen this man before in my life—well, not quite. He it was who yesterday assaulted me in my tent at the Tingite fair. May I beg Your Majesty to requite his attack on your servant as it deserves?"

"So, Master Eudoxos," said the king, "Sri Hari denies your charge. Can you prove what you say? Can you, for instance, produce witnesses who also knew this Hippalos in former days and can identify Hari as the same man?"

"I could, sire; but to bring witnesses hither from other parts of the Inner Sea would require much time and expense. To obviate this delay, may I make another suggestion to Your Majesty? That Master Hippalos and I have it out with swords and shields, to the death."

Bocchus looked pleased. "Now that sounds amusing! How say you, Master Hari?"

Hippalos put his palms together and bowed over them in a perfect imitation of the Indian salute. "O King, live forever. Your Majesty knows that a man who has devoted his life to the search for higher wisdom and cosmic truths could not possibly have spared the time to acquire skill in arms. So any such contest would be a simple execution of your servant."

"He is a coward, that is all," I said. "I am nearly sixty, and he twenty years younger; but he dares not face me."

"The fact is as I have stated," said Hippalos. "I fear Master—what is the name again?—Master Eudoxos has been deceived by a chance resemblance between your servant and this man whom he seeks. Or else his years have robbed him of his wits."

Bocchus scratched his bald head. "You are both plausible wights, gentlemen, and I cannot decide between your claims without further thought. You may withdraw. And, oh, Master Eudoxos! Tomorrow I expect my colleague, King Jugurtha of Numidia, to arrive to wed my daughter. There will be a grand feast, to which you are bidden. I cannot ask you to stay at the palace, because the Numidians will occupy all the sleeping space; but you are welcome to the festivities—provided that you make no move against Master Hari. I will not have the occasion spoilt by brawls. Do you promise?"

"I promise, sire," I said.

* * *

The Numidians are a branch of the Moorish race, wearing similar garb and speaking a dialect of the same language. They arrived in a cloud of light horse, galloping recklessly about, tossing javelins up and catching them, and whooping and yelling like the fiends of Tartaros. In the midst of them came King Jugurtha in a gilded chariot, lashing his horses to a gallop up the winding road to Bocchus' castle and skidding in the mud on the turns until I was sure he would go over the edge.

Mikipsa, who had been king of Numidia at the start of my tale, had divided his kingdom amongst three heirs: his own two sons, Hiempsal and Adherbal, and his nephew Jugurtha, who was older than either. Despite his illegitimate birth, Jugurtha had elbowed his way into the succession by the skill and valor he had shown in war and by his personal charm and craft. He was a tall, lean man in his thirties, brown-skinned, bearded, and singularly handsome. He arrived in barbaric finery, with a huge golden ring in one ear and a necklace of lion's claws around his neck. I have heard that, when the occasion demanded, he could don Greek or Roman garb and manners and quote Homer with the best of them.

After Mikipsa died, Jugurtha seized the first chance to murder his cousin Hiempsal and attack his other cousin Adherbal, in hopes of seizing all Numidia. The Romans, who ruled the African lands of the old Carthaginian confederation, compelled Jugurtha to leave Adherbal alone with his fragment of the kingdom, the easternmost third. Jugurtha, however, was not one to leave anything alone if he could help it. He was now harassing Adherbal's territory by raids and seeking to strengthen his position by a marital alliance with his other neighbor, King Bocchus of Mauretania.

The proceedings took several days. On one, the two kings went hunting. At the end of the ceremonies, there were dancers and singers and speeches. The bride and groom were presented to the people and cheered with a deafening uproar. The fact that Jugurtha already had a few wives bothered none.

The feast comprised whole roast oxen, rivers of wine and beer, and a few sober Moorish guards to squelch any fights. Quarrels easily occur when soldiers of two nations get drunk together and start boasting. The Moors are generally a sober, abstemious folk, but on such occasions they make up for lost time.

I saw nothing of Hippalos. Despite the king's protection, the ready-for-aught was taking no chances of coming within my reach.

I was gorging and guzzling with the rest when a brown hand fell on my shoulder. I looked up to see a tall, hawk-faced Numidian standing over me.

"Are you not Eudoxos the Kyzikene?" he asked in barbarously accented Greek.

"Why, yes! And you're—ah—Varsako! I remember you from Alexandria. How did you know me, with this bush on my face?"

"I heard you were in Mauretania," he said, sitting down on the bench beside me, "so I was looking for you. I could not forget the man who saved my life!"

"Oh, that," I said, remembering our scuffle with the robbers. "It was nothing. But tell me ..."

And we were off on reminiscences of our respective adventures during the last five years. Varsako, I learnt, was a provincial judge in Jugurtha's kingdom. We ended the evening staggering about with arms about each other's shoulders, singing tipsily until others threatened to drown us in the beer tub if we did not shut up and let them go to sleep.

Pronax I had sent home early, and Gnouros had feasted with the palace servants and slaves. I fetched him from the slave quarters to walk back to Tingis with me. Many other guests were straggling homeward, too, down the winding road from the castle. The sky was clear and the moon, just past full. It lit up the hillside, showing the recumbent forms of dozens of copulating couples. The Moors practice sexual licence on such occasions, and all the younger women of the vicinity, save those of the royal family, seemed to have turned out to give the Numidian visitors a pleasant memory of their stay.

When the crowd had thinned out, so that nobody was near us, Gnouros said:

"Master! You in danger. King means to kill you."

"What's this, old man?"

"Aye! I hear all the talk in servants' quarters. Servants know everything their masters do, and one who talks Greek got drunk and told me."

"Just what did he tell you?"

"You remember first day we come to castle?"

"Yes."

"Well, after we go back to Tingis, Master Hippalos made king believe he really was Indian seer, like he said. Also, he warned the king that, if you spread story of how Lixus River rises in Atlas Mountains, some enemy—Romans, maybe—might land at mouth of the Lixus, march up it, and take kingdom by surprise, through back door. King's kinsmen and courtiers joined in denouncing you, because they fear that if you make kingdom rich like you say, you will rise in king's favor and they will go down.

"Now, if you only ordinary man, king would have your head off right away, *tsk!*" He struck his own neck with the side of his palm. "But you are too important and famous."

"I wish I thought so," I said. "Go on."

"King does not want to be blamed for killing a so big man like you. So, Hippalos said to him he should pretend to agree to your plan for voyage. One of his ships will take you down the coast to look for landing places. When they find some little island with nothing but sand, they put you ashore and leave you. Then the king tell people you fell overboard and drowned."

"Well, I suppose I shall have to bribe some fisherman to run us across to Belon," I said.

"Oh, no! The king has sent word to watch ports and roads, in case you try to escape."

"This *is* a fix!" I said. "By Bakchos' balls, how are we to get out of this damned kingdom?"

Gnouros spread his hands. "How I know? Master has mighty mind; he will think of a way."

"Your confidence touches me, but I wish I could share it. Let me think. When do the Numidians leave for home?"

"Day after tomorrow. Tomorrow, everybody have too big hangover to start journey."

* * *

Next day, hangover or no, I went again to Bocchus' castle and asked for Varsako. When he came, I murmured:

"Come out for a stroll with me, Varsako. I want to discuss something I don't wish overheard, so we'll talk loudly about something else until we're out of earshot." Then I raised my voice: "By the gods of the underworld, that was some party! I haven't been so drunk since that time we were on the town in Alexandria. ..."

He played up to me with noisy anecdotes of his own allegedly bibulous past. When we were well away from the castle wall, I told him of my troubles with King Bocchus.

"You once met this Hippalos," I said. "Do you remember? The night I met you in the Ptolemies' banquet hall, he was the choragus who directed the entertainments, and I think he got you a girl for the night. Have you met him here in his disguise as Sri Hari?"

"Now that you tell me, this Indian did look somehow familiar."

"Well, could you identify him as Hippalos to the king?"

"Perhaps, but I do not advise it."

"Why not?"

"First, from what gossip I heard, the alleged wise man has Bocchus under his thumb. If we accused him, he would merely think up some plausible counteraccusation, and the king would believe him rather than us. Second, Jugurtha warned all of us Numidians to keep aloof from Mauretanian affairs during our visit, and if I took your part he might have my head for it. And third, Bocchus is a king who notoriously hates to admit he is wrong. You prove to his face that he has erred at your peril."

Altogether, Mauretania began to look like a most unhealthy place for me to linger. We discussed the situation at length, Varsako and I, without finding any practical solution but flight. I finally said:

"You're leaving for home tomorrow with the rest of the Numidians, aren't you?"

"Aye."

"Would anybody notice if you had added a couple of servants to your train?"

"I suppose not—if they did not look like anyone the Moors were seeking."

"That will be taken care of."

Next day, when the Numidians set out, nobody observed that Judge Varsako, who had arrived with two servants, departed with five. The new additions were a singularly unkempt, unprepossessing lot, too. Gnouros and I had shaved off our beards, and Pronax, who was a fair-haired, blue-eyed, pimpled youth, we had stained brown all over. We rode mules and led others, which carried our lord's gear and our own.

From Tingis to Tunis is a hard ride of about three hundred leagues, over roads that are mostly mere tracks, without a pretence of grading or paving. By secret communications with friends in Adherbal's part of Numidia, Varsako arranged for us to be passed through this kingdom without trouble. At the frontier of Roman Africa, the guards asked a few questions and waved us through. We reached Tunis a month after leaving Tingis.

At Tunis, I wrote a long letter to my kinsmen in Kyzikos, telling my tale and revealing my plans. Since Gnouros' rheumatism was worse and I did not wish to inflict upon him the pains of another long voyage, I sent him off with the letter on a ship for Peiraieus.

Then I spent a ten-day on the waterfront, looking for ships. I finally bought one aged, leaky coaster, whose owner's new ship had just come off the ways. I had the oldster hauled out, scraped, caulked, tarred, and painted, and then I set out with Pronax and a cargo of African goods.

Two months later, in Skirophorion, I sailed into the Bay of Gades. When I stepped into Eldagon's warehouse and Eldagon saw me, he dropped and broke an antique Athenian painted pot.

"Hammon!" he cried. "I never expected to see *you* again! Thrice welcome! Come into the office and talk. I thought King Bocchus had done you in."

"Oh, you have heard about my troubles there?"

"Your former mate, Mandonius, came here to ask for a job. He told us about your journey, albeit he was so vague about the stranding that I suspected him of being to blame."

"He was," I said. "But he did a good job in other respects."

"I don't care how good a ship's officer is in other respects; if he wrecks my ships I don't want him. But tell me all."

"First, I have a little indebtedness to settle. Pronax, bring out your money belt and your wallet."

We counted out the gold we had been carrying, together with the gold and silver I had gained by trading on my way to Gades.

"Now," I said, "this pile represents the value we put on the *Tyria*. The rest represents the cargo, as nearly as I could come to it by selling the *Mikrotyria* and her cargo, and the profits I made from Tunis hither. I think you'll find that I'm still a few thousand drachmai in your debt, but I can pay that off with another voyage or two."

He sat with his mouth open, then said: "By the gods of Tyre, you are a wonder! I have lost ships before, but never has the captain made a new ship out of the wreckage of the old, salvaged and sold most of the cargo at a profit, made extra profit by trading, and then come home to pile the whole thing in my lap! And without losing a single member of your crew, too. Truly, some god must watch over you."

I shrugged. "I've had my share of good and bad luck. Bad when Mandonius ran us aground, and with King Bocchus; and good in getting the crew back to civilization, and escaping from Bocchus, and trading from Tunis hither."

"Do you plan another try at circumnavigation?"

"I'm thinking of it. Would you and Tubal back me again?"

"Since you can apparently make a profit even out of shipwreck, we might."

"Shall I have to wait whilst you build a ship?"

"I think not. The *Jezebel* is due from Neapolis soon, and she needs refitting anyway."

"Fine. How are your beasts?"

Eldagon became animated. "I have a pair of new bear cubs, born during the winter while the she-bear was in her den. You must see them. ..."

* * *

Without trying to skin a flayed dog, I made a new agreement with Eldagon and Tubal. The *Jezebel* (named for Eldagon's wife) duly arrived and was refitted for the voyage.

For an auxiliary, I had decided that longboats were inadequate. For inshore exploration, I needed a galley big enough to take care of herself if a blow parted her from her mother ship. So I had Tubal rebuild an old eighty-foot-dispatch bireme to my requirements. By permanently closing the lower oar ports, cutting down topweight, and removing the ram, I got a more seaworthy ship than most galleys of any size. With only twenty-four rowers, she was slower than with her full complement of forty-eight but still fast enough for my purposes. The larger crew would have put too much strain on the food supply.

I should like to have rigged both ships with my triangular sail. But I gave up the idea when I saw that, if I did, no sailors would sail with me, since they mortally feared anything new. Nevertheless, I had a fore-and-aft sail (as I like to call them) and a spar for it secretly stowed in *Jezebel*'s hold, in case we had to buck a prevailing wind and current as had happened before.

By late Boedromion, I was ready to go. Again I shipped shipwrights, carpenters, and plenty of tools; also the means for growing a crop of wheat. Hearing of my plans, Doctor Mentor and his assistant came over from Tingis and signed on for another try. Mandonius also asked for his old job, but I regretfully turned him down. Although a likable fellow, he was too volatile and irresponsible for my first officer. I hired a Gaditanian Hellene named Hagnon instead.

I did not ship any more dancing girls; once was enough. I did, however, do something that I ought to have thought of the first time.

There were a number of black slaves in Gades. I tracked them down, one by one, and asked them where they came from. Most had originated in eastern Africa, whence they had been kidnaped and brought to the Inner Sea by way of the Nile and Alexandria. A few, however, came from the West, having been caught by Moorish slavers. Although the great African desert is a formidable barrier, it is not quite impassable. There are routes by which daring traders or raiders can cross it, and some of the hardiest desert tribes make a practice of this.

When I learnt that some of these Africans came from the parts I meant to visit, I tried to buy them. Some owners would not sell, and I obtained only three. Although they bore the usual Greek slaves' names, for my purposes I preferred to call them by their original African appellations: Mori, Dia, and Sumbo. I told these three that, when we reached their homelands, I wanted them as interpreters. If their work was good, I should free them and either put them ashore or sign them on as sailors, whichever they liked. Two seemed pleased by the prospect; the other man, Mori, was apprehensive.

"My tribe all eaten up," he said. "No have tribe any more. You go there, they eat you, too."

"Who will eat us?"

"Mong. Man-eating tribe."

Although I am less superstitious than most men, the idea of ending up in a tribesman's stomach instead of in a proper grave made me wince. I commanded my blacks to say nothing of this quaint habit to the crew. Many men, brave enough ordinarily, would turn pale and flee at the thought of such a fate.

All three blacks agreed that, if one continued southward down the west coast of Africa for hundreds of leagues, one passed the desert and came to forested lands. The desert belt, in other words, extends right across Africa from east to west, and a forested belt stretches parallel to it to southward.

And so, on the twelfth of Pyanepsion, the *Jezebel* and her companion, the galley *Astra*, sailed from Gades for a final try at the wealth of India.

* * *

For the first two ten-days of our voyage, everything went like a dream. We stopped at the island I had found on my previous voyage to top off our water. As the skiff pulled away from shore, a group of men rushed out of the scrub and down to the shore. They were lean, brown men of the Moorish type but seemed more primitive than even the Lixites. Some wore goatskin mantles, while others were altogether naked. They danced and capered on the beach, shaking wooden spears and clubs and shouting across the water. I was wrong in reporting this island as uninhabited.

We coasted the island to the southwest and discovered that it was really two, divided by a narrow strait. Beyond the second island we sighted other islands of the group, further out to sea.

For many days there was nought but the heaving blue sea to starboard, the long, low, buff-colored coast to port, the blinding sun overhead, and the eternal northeast wind behind us. Once, indeed, the wind changed. A hot blast swept over us from the southeast, bringing such masses of dust and sand that we could no longer see to navigate. We felt our way in to shallow water, put down anchors, covered the hatches, wrapped our faces in cloth as the desert folk do, and waited out the storm. Presently there came a crackle of thunder and a spatter of rain—just enough to turn the soil that now cumbered our decks into slimy mud. When the storm ceased, we had a terrible task getting our ships clean again.

As Pyanepsion ended and Maimakterion began, signs of greenery appeared. The *Astra*, nosing in towards shore, reported that the land was now well covered with grass and herbs. The men also said they had sighted wild animals. Later they saw a group of huts, but too far away to discern the people.

Now the coast trended more to the south. The shores became covered with masses of a peculiar tree that grows in mud banks covered by shallow water in those parts. Whereas in most trees the roots join to form the trunk below ground, in this plant they join to form the trunk above the water. The tree thus stands on long, stiltlike roots, which spread out and down into the water like the legs of a spider. Behind these trees we caught glimpses of wooded plains.

The climate, too, changed. The strong northeaster, which had brought us so far so fast, dwindled away to light, variable airs. The sky was often overcast. Sometimes a flat calm prevailed, and the *Astra* towed the *Jezebel*. The men found rowing hard in the humid heat; sweat ran off them in rivers. Hence our drinking water dwindled fast, and what was left became scummy and foul. At night we durst not anchor too close to shore, because swarms of mosquitoes murdered our sleep.

Since the coast was now more variable, we proceeded more slowly to give the *Astra* time to explore. Thus we presently found an immense bay, surrounded by reedy marshes. Crocodiles sprawled by the scores on sand bars, while river horses snorted and splashed in the shallows.

A long bar blocked the entrance to this bay, but the *Astra* found a channel through it. We landed on a small island, about six stadia in length. While we were exploring, Hagnon the mate rushed up to me, crying:

"Come, Captain! Here's something you'll want to see!"

He had found a cluster of ruins—the lower walls of small, square houses of mud brick. They were so overgrown and so destroyed by time and weather that little more than their ground plans could be discerned. But I recalled my readings in Alexandria.

"I think," I said, "that we have found the last outpost of Hanno the Carthaginian. This isle must be his Kernê."

"Who was he?" asked Hagnon.

I told him: "Two or three hundred years ago, Carthage sent an expedition down this coast, over the route we have been following, under an admiral named Hanno. They halted at a place they called Kernê, on an island in a bay, and set up a trading post. They also explored the neighborhood before returning home."

"What became of the people left to man the post?"

"I don't know, but my guess is that this place is so far from civilization, and it's so difficult to beat one's way back to the Pillars against wind and current, that the outpost was soon abandoned."

The *Astra* explored the bay and found the mouth of a great river coming down from the interior. But the water was too brackish for our use, and I did not want to take the time to send the *Astra* upstream far enough to find sweet water. Since, save for the Phoenician ruins, there seemed to be no men hereabouts, we proceeded on our way.

Further down the coast, however, we saw signs of human life: a blue thread of smoke ascending from the forest; a point of light or a sound of drumming at night; a small boat drawn up on the shore. Between the heavy surf and the wall of stilt trees, though, the coast afforded few good landing places.

Now the coast trended more and more to the east. Optimists among the crew speculated that we had already reached the southernmost extremity of Africa. Having studied Herodotos' account of the voyage of Necho's Phoenicians, I was sure that the continent extended much further south than this. The Phoenicians had gone well south of the equator, which we had not even reached as yet.

* * *

A few days after leaving Kernê, we met two fishing boats, each made from a hollowed-out tree trunk. They fled and vanished into the wall of stilt trees. Since our need for fresh water was acute, I ordered Hagnon to follow them with the galley. When the *Astra* pursued the boats, she found a channel big enough for the *Jezebel*. Beyond lay a bay and the mouth of another river.

We filed into the bay under oars. On the far shore stood a cluster of small round huts, with fishing boats drawn up nearby. The two boats that we followed were paddled frantically up to this landing.

The paddlers leaped out, splashed ashore, and ran shouting up the slope to the village. In a few heartbeats, the villagers boiled out of their huts and fled into the forest.

Ahead of the *Jezebel*, the *Astra* gave a lurch. Hagnon rushed to the poop deck and shouted back at me:

"Beware! There's a rock or something there!"

The roundship crept ahead slowly, sounding with a pole, and thus avoided the obstacle that the *Astra* had brushed. We anchored near the deserted village. Hagnon, voluble with excuses, came aboard looking crestfallen. "... I'll swear I was taking soundings every fathom. That stupid Spaniard must have skipped one. ..."

"You mean, you were all so busy watching the blacks running into the bush that you forgot about rocks and shoals," I said. "Well, it's time the bottoms were inspected anyway. Is the *Astra* leaking?"

"I don't think so. Maybe it was only a log."

"If the natives are friendly and we can find a decent beach, we'll ground the ships at high tide," I said. "Tell the boys to lower the dinghy."

"Hadn't you better send someone else ashore first, Captain? We can't risk losing you—"

"Oh, to the crows with that! I want to see this village at first hand."

I went ashore with a couple of sailors. We found nobody in the village; even the dogs had run away with their owners. I left several strings of beads and returned to the *Jezebel.*

"Now," I told my people, "we shall wait and see."

As I had expected, curiosity at last overcame the fears of the villagers. They came out of hiding, found the beads, and began to quarrel over them. Two men paddled out to where my ships rode at anchor and shouted up to us.

"Sumbo! Mori! Dia!" I cried. "Can any of you understand them?"

Mori, the black whose tribe had been destroyed by cannibals, said that he could make out some of it. "They say, will you give more beads, so every man have one string?"

"What will they give us in return?" I replied. After more talk, Mori reported:

"Can give a little food. Fish ..." and he added a string of native names.

"That will be fine," I said.

A trade was arranged. The villagers depended heavily on fish, but they also hunted and raised a few simple crops, such as a kind of grain that made a fairly horrid porridge and an underground tuber with a yellow inside and a sweet taste. These blacks were a clan of the Baga tribe, which was spread along this coast. They were of medium size and powerful build. Both sexes went completely naked. They were very primitive, using sharpened stones for spearheads and making their fishhooks from fishbones.

Once their initial fears were overcome, they proved an amiable lot, much given to joking and laughter. They were clean in their persons, bathing at least once a day in the bay despite the danger of crocodiles. But their village, called Gombli, was filthy, with dung and garbage all over.

I feared lest the lusts of my sailors for the Baga women give trouble, but I need not have worried. For a small present, a Baga husband was glad to lend his wife for the night; nor did the wives seem to mind. It would not surprise me if the next generation of Gomblians had lighter skins than their fellow tribesmen.

With Mori as interpreter, I had a long talk one evening with Teita, the headman. Teita wanted to know if we had come down from Heaven. No, I said, but from a place about as distant. We were not, he persisted, the ghosts of his ancestors, come back to haunt him? We were certainly pale enough for ghosts. No, I said, we were men like himself. Doubtless I could have exploited these poor fishermen by claiming that we were gods. But, having seen in India what unchecked superstition can do, I thought it better to avoid the supernatural.

Then Teita asked if we were connected with the Gbaru. These, Mori explained, were a powerful tribe further inland. Teita suspected a connection because we, like the Gbaru, had the strange habit of covering our bodies with cloth. The Baga feared the Gbaru, who raided them.

Now the greatest menace of this part of Africa—sickness—began to visit us. Four of my sailors and my young cousin Pronax came down with fevers and fluxes. I made them as comfortable on the *Jezebel* as I could. Doctor Mentor puttered around the patients and looked wise, but I do not think he knew any more about African ills than I did.

When we examined the *Astra*, we found that the rock had done more damage than we thought. One of the strakes was cracked and leaking. We patched the ship's bottom with tarred wool, sheet lead, and some boards which we shaved down to fit snugly over the site of the damage. With reasonable luck, that patch should have held throughout the journey.

All this took over a ten-day. About two days after my conversation with Teita, we were ready to launch the ships at the next high tide. Around noon, while we were still awaiting the tide, a Baga rushed screaming into the village. Instantly, all the other Baga dropped what they were doing to scamper off, as they had done when my ships sailed into the bay. I looked for Mori to ask the cause of this commotion, but he had fled with the rest.

A thunder of drums echoed across the bay, and a swarm of armed blacks burst out of the forest and rushed upon us, yelling like furies. One Baga, who had been slow in starting, ran towards the river. When they saw he was gaining on them, one of them shot an arrow at him. African bows are puny little things, and the arrows are not even feathered. Nonetheless, the shaft struck the fleeing Baga in the back of the shoulder. Although it did not look like a serious wound, after a few more steps the fugitive began to stagger. Soon he sank to the ground, twitching in his death throes. The arrow had been poisoned. Meanwhile, the newcomers swarmed down from the village to where my ships lay.

Only a few of my crew were armed. Life among the peaceful, friendly Baga had made us careless. I drew my sword and shouted to the others to arm themselves, but it was no use. A half dozen spears and swords could do nothing against a hundred native warriors, many of whom bore spears with heads of iron or bronze.

The newcomers wore kilts and loincloths, either of fur or of coarse, striped cloth. They bore headdresses of feathers and monkey fur and jingled with necklaces, bracelets, and other ornaments of shell, ivory, and metal. Besides their bows and spears, they bore large, oval shields of the hide of Africa's thick-skinned beasts. Their faces were painted in patterns of red and white. They were, I soon learnt, the Gbaru of whom Teita had spoken.

An older man, clad in a kind of toga, seemed to direct them. At a barked command, they drew up in a semicircle around us, spears poised and bows nocked. We stood in a clump with our backs against the *Astra*.

The man in the toga shouted something at us. When we looked blank, he stepped forward, tapped the blade of my sword with his spear, and pointed to the ground. I dropped the weapon, and the other armed men in my party did likewise.

As soon as we were disarmed, a group of Gbaru sprang upon us, pulling us out of our own crowd one by one. They stripped us of everything but our shoes. My bronze statuette of Ganesha was taken from me with my clothes. I suppose that to this day it hangs from the neck of some Gbaru warrior as a *grigri* or talisman, half a world away from its Indian home.

The Gbaru then bound our wrists with rawhide thongs, of which they had brought an ample supply. Other thongs linked each man with the next, until we formed a human chain, like that in which I had marched to the gold mines of Upper Egypt.

Other Gbaru climbed aboard the ships and fell upon the loot they found there. There was a perfect shower of glassware, purple garments, and other trade goods falling from the deck of the *Jezebel* as the whooping, laughing Gbaru threw them over the side. Much of the stuff they broke or ruined in their haste and ignorance. My five sick men, including young Pronax, they hauled out and killed by smashing their skulls with clubs. Had Lady Luck spared him, that boy would have grown into a fine man.

One of my three blacks, Sumbo, had been caught with the rest of us. He was, in fact, only four men from me in the human chain. I called:

"Sumbo! Do you understand these people?"

"Who, me?" he said. "What?"

"I said, do you understand these people?"

Sumbo thought awhile and said: "I understand a little only. I am Bulende; my tribe live far off that way." He pointed to the southeast. "But every man speak a little Gbaru."

In fact, since the Gbaru were the strongest tribe in this part of Africa, their language had become an intertribal tongue, like Greek in the Inner Sea. I said:

"What do you think they'll do with us?"

"Do with us?"

"Yes, you idiot! Eat us?"

Again the long pause. "Not know. Make slaves, maybe. Gbaru not maneaters, but they kill many men for sacrifice to gods."

"Then you shall teach me Gbaru," I said.

"Me? Teach you?"

It went on like this for the rest of our journey. While docile and willing, Sumbo was as stupid as a Cyprian ox—certainly the last man anybody would choose to teach a strange and difficult language. These African tongues, I was surprised to find, had very complex grammars. Moreover, the tone of a word affected its meaning, so that one had to sing one's sentences. It gave the language a musical sound but made it even harder to learn.

Still, by the time we reached Klimoko, I had mastered the words for such elementary things as food, drink, parts of the body, and material objects like houses, rivers, and trees. I could even put together a few simple sentences. The Gbaru made no attempt to silence us; they were usually chattering away loudly themselves. Africans are a noisy folk, always talking, laughing, arguing, shouting, and singing, save when actually hunting or laying an ambush.

Book X

NKOA THE AFRICAN

Our captors loaded us with the loot from the *Jezebel* and marched us off on a jungle trail. Near the coast, the forest is scrubby, with many openings. In these open spaces grew huge flowers of every hue—scarlet, azure, gold, and purple.

As we marched inland, however, the trees grew taller and taller until they reached a size I had never seen before. We found ourselves inclosed between towering walls of monotonous dark green. Vines hung down from gigantic trees in loops and strands, as tangled as the web of a hedge spider. The ground beside the trail was covered with ferns and palms in riotous profusion.

Birds and monkeys chattered in the trees. We seldom saw large beasts, although we heard them often enough—the trumpeting of the elephant, the snarl of the leopard, the grunt of the wild pig, the scream of the giant man-ape.

The trail was fairly passable, since this was the dry season. Now and then we had to wade through a patch of swamp, where huge white lilies stood up like ghosts. The biting flies and mosquitoes tormented us to distraction, the more so since we were now naked. Some men were frightfully bitten by venomous ants when they carelessly trod upon a procession of the creatures.

We came to a place where the jungle had been cleared for farms. Amid the wide, deforested plain stood Klimoko, the capital of the Gbaru. Klimoko proved much larger than Gombli; practically a real city. I guessed that it sheltered five to ten thousand people. A stockade, the points of which were decorated with human skulls, surrounded it.

As we neared the town, our column halted. A violent altercation had broken out among the leaders of our plumed and befurred captors. Sumbo told me:

"They angry because sacrifices are all over for this year. Each chief blame the other for making us late."

"Do you mean that we were to have been sacrificed, but now it's too late for that?"

"Yes, sir."

"How do they know the sacrifices are finished?"

"You see soon."

And see we did, as we got closer to the skull-decked stockade. The first sight was a headless black body lying by the path. Then more and more bodies appeared. Some were headless like the first. Others had been hung from trees by their wrists and used as targets for missiles, or had been done to death in other ingenious ways. While most of the bodies were of men, some were of women. The number of corpses must have been in the hundreds. The stench was appalling.

Despite having seen much slaughter and rapine, I was a little shaken. This, I thought, was worse than the Roman gladiatorial games, or the mass burnings of children in which the Phoenicians used to engage.

The entrance to the town was a small wooden door in the stockade, so low that one had to bend double to get through it, thus affording a defender inside a fine chance to dash one's brains out. We filed in, one by one, while around us drums thundered and the Gbaru pranced in a victory dance.

They marched us to a central square, in the middle of which rose a man-high, conical pile of human heads. At one side of the square stood the palace, like the other houses of Klimoko but twice as large, with a walled compound behind it containing separate huts for the king's many wives. A pile of elephants' tusks lay beside his front door.

The fat old king of the Gbaru, gaudy in fur, feathers, and golden ornaments, sat before his thatched palace on a big wooden stool, elaborately carved and inlaid with shell and ivory. The chiefs who had commanded the war party prostrated themselves before him while the drums roared. Everybody talked at once at the top of his voice. Children screamed, dogs barked, and speckled fowl ran around amongst the feet of the crowd.

After a discussion that dragged on for hours, the king gave his decision. Sumbo explained that, since it was too late for this year's sacrifices, we should be worked as slaves and saved for the big event next year.

I thought, in that time I shall surely devise an escape, or my name is not Eudoxos Theonos. Prospects for an escape looked good. The Gbaru divided us into squads of five to ten men, each with an overseer. At night the squads were brought together in an inclosure, where we slept, guarded by several warriors. The watch was lax, however, and the watchmen often slept at their posts. The Gbaru seemed unconcerned about our trying to escape. As Sumbo explained it, if we did escape, we should soon lose ourselves in the surrounding forest and perish of starvation, snakebite, or some other misfortune.

The overseers varied like other men. Some were harsh, some mild; some were exacting, others lax. Our man was a stout black named Mabion, an easygoing and, most of the time, not unkindly fellow. He was, however, unpredictable. One day when we were cleaning the street of Klimoko, one of my sailors did something to offend him. Thereupon Mabion seemed to go mad. Screaming and foaming with rage, he plunged his spear into the unfortunate mariner and then stood over the body, stabbing it again and again. But next day Mabion was his usual sleepy, good-natured self again.

* * *

As the days passed, my efforts to organize an escape plot were repeatedly thwarted by sickness among my men. Man after man fell ill, and few recovered. Some like poor Hagnon were knocked on the head by impatient overseers when they could no longer drag themselves to work. Some were allowed to lie around the sleeping inclosure until they gave up their ghosts on their own.

With so many men sick, I began to recognize the symptoms of the principal ailments. One was an ague that gave the victim chills and fever and turned his urine the color of dark red wine. Another tinged his skin and eyeballs yellow. Still another caused a bloody flux and, usually, death in a few days. Doctor Mentor was one of the first thus carried off. Some men succumbed to an overpowering desire to sleep; they drifted off into a coma and never awoke. Others developed sores that would not heal, or parasitic worms and insects burrowed into their flesh and drove them mad with itching.

The blacks sometimes came down with similar ailments but usually recovered. The African jungle is an even sicklier place for outsiders, without immunity to its plagues and poxes, than the coast of India.

Once I caught an ague, with chills and fever. When the worst of it had passed, it left me so weak that I could barely stagger for days. However, my rugged constitution pulled me through. For years thereafter I had recurrent attacks, but the attacks weakened until now I hardly notice them.

About the time I had recovered from this ague, the overseers herded us together—the mere eighteen or twenty still alive and active—and began marching us in a single chain out the north gate. I asked Mabion what this portended.

"You will not be here any more," he said. "You palefaces are dying off so fast that the king has decided to sell you to the Mong, since there would not be enough of you left alive for the Great Sending."

This Great Sending was the annual mass human sacrifice. The victims were brought to the king, one by one. The king gave each a message to one of his dead ancestors or other kinsmen. Then the victim was slain, and his spirit was supposed to deliver the message in the afterworld. Since the king had a long pedigree with many deceased relatives, and since the victim's ghost could not be trusted to remember more than one message, there had to be one sacrifice for each message. This custom had grown until the capture of slaves from neighboring tribes for sacrifice had become the main business of the Gbaru. For, if the supply of slaves, prisoners, and convicted malefactors gave out before all the messages had been sent, the king designated some of his subjects for the honor. He found this a convenient way to get rid of malcontents.

"What do the Mong want of us?" I asked.

Mabion grinned and slapped me heartily on the back. "*Niama!*" he said, this being the word for "eat" in several African tongues. He then laughed uproariously at my expression.

I recovered my self-control and said, "I do not see my friend Sumbo. Is he being traded, too?"

"Nay. Sumbo is a human being, even if he is not a Gbaru. So he will be kept for the Sending."

Evidently we palefaces were not deemed human; but I was too weary to argue, even though I was now fairly fluent in Gbaru. I shambled off into the jungle with the rest.

A day's march from Klimoko, we came to a clearing in the jungle—actually, the site of an abandoned village, not yet completely overgrown. Here we met a party of Mong. These were tall, lean blacks, completely naked like the Baga. When they smiled, they showed front teeth that had been filed to points.

On the ground lay a pile of the goods for which we were being traded: iron implements—mostly heads for spears and hoes—and some of the egg-shaped sea shells used as money hereabouts, similar to those used in India for small change. Although the Gbaru were far ahead of the primitive Baga in the arts and crafts—making their own pots and weaving their own cloth—they did not know how to mine, smelt, and work metals. So they got their iron, copper, and bronze from more northerly tribes, who in turn got them by trade from Moors, Garamantes, and other denizens of the great desert.

Here is an opportunity for some enterprising trader, to open up a regular sea route between these lands and Gades. He would have to use my triangular sail to get back to the Pillars against wind and current. He would also have to enlist a black crew, to withstand the diseases of this coast. The Baga, being skilled boatmen, should be easy to train as sailors. Were I but younger …

The Mong counted and poked and pinched us as if we had been so many hogs at market. Then they haggled with the head overseer. At last they were persuaded to add a few more shells to the pile. The Gbaru gathered up the spoil and marched back the way they had come, while the Mong herded us off on another trail.

The main village of the Mong, called Dinale, was between Gombli and Klimoko in size; but it was the cleanest African town I had seen. It was also the best laid out, with the huts in regular rows, like the tents in a Roman camp.

Again we were lined up and looked over by the chief men. At least I suppose they were such, although it is hard to distinguish ranks and offices where everyone goes as nude as a frog. Then another man appeared—a small, lean man with his face painted like a skull, anklets of monkey fur, and other adornments. He came towards us in a kind of shuffling dance, crooning a chant. I asked a guard in Gbaru:

"Who is this?"

"Nkoa, the wizard," replied the man.

"What is he doing?"

"He is smelling for witches."

"What if he finds one?"

"Then that one will be burnt at once, instead of being kept to eat."

Nkoa danced up and down the line, peering into our eyes and smelling our breasts. He pointed to one man and spoke in Mong, whereupon that one was dragged away. I heard the sound of a heavy blow and a shriek. This was repeated with several others.

Nkoa looked at the man next to me and said something else. This man was dragged away and tied to a post. While the wizard continued his inspection, firewood was piled around the last man and ignited. The screams of this man mingled with the shrieks and moans of the previous victims, who, I later learnt, had had their legs broken to prevent escape.

Nkoa came to me last of all. My tired old brain had been working at extra speed. Before the wizard reached me, I had picked up a couple of pebbles. When the skull-faced one danced up to me, I said in Gbaru:

"O Nkoa, I am a wizard in my land, too. I can show you some useful tricks, like this—what is that in your ear?"

I took one of the stones out of his ear, as Hippalos had taught me to do. "And what is this in your nose?" I produced the other pebble.

Nkoa started back. "What is this?" he snapped.

"Of course," I said, "I cannot be useful to you if I have been burnt or eaten. Do you understand?"

He looked at me narrowly. "Are you a member of the Poro in your land?"

I assumed that the Poro was some wizards' society. "We call it by another name, but it is the same thing."

"We cannot waste a good Poro man," said Nkoa. He spoke to the other Mong, who cut my thongs.

I followed Nkoa back to his hut. Inside, sitting on a reed mat on the floor facing him, I showed him my little repertory of sleight-of-hand, handicapped as I was by having no clothes to hide things in. When I showed him how the tricks worked, he gave a dry little chuckle.

"Now that I know your tricks, I could turn you over to the warriors to break your legs like the others," he said. "But you interest me, man. I have heard of this land of the palefaces but never believed it until now, when I have seen some of these creatures with my own eyes. Can you tell me all about this land of yours?"

"I can tell you a good deal. I have lived long and traveled far among the lands beyond the great desert."

"Very well, then. So long as you keep me entertained by such tales, you shall live."

"Perhaps I could be your assistant?"

"If you were younger, perhaps. I need an apprentice, and there is none among the young men of Dinale who suits me." He spat. "Stupid oafs, caring for nought but filling their bellies and futtering their women. But alas! you are too old. You must be well past forty."

I did not mention that I had just turned sixty. Nkoa judged me by the standards of his own folk, whose primitive, disease-ridden lives aged them fast. He was, I think, about my age, which made him practically an immortal among the Mong.

"Besides," he continued, "when I die, my apprentice would take my place, and the people would never accept a man so strange as yourself, with your ghostly color and all. Nevertheless, you shall be useful to me."

"How so, master?"

"When your companions have been eaten, the people will clamor for more meat. I must prepare a spell to assure the success of their next foray. You shall help me."

Thus I became Nkoa's assistant in fact if not in name. The next day, he and I built a small hut outside Dinale. We retired to this hut for two days, while Nkoa consulted his spirits. Sitting cross-legged on the floor, he went into a trance, moaning and muttering. When he came out of it, he told me the spirits had given him instructions for the spell.

I am sure he honestly believed in these spirits. If he sometimes played tricks on the tribesmen, he reasoned that spirits are flighty creatures on whom one cannot rely. One must therefore have a few tricks ready to save one's credit with the tribe when one's spirits let one down. The priests of Alexandria, I understand, justify their fakeries by similar reasoning.

We moved back into Nkoa's regular hut, and the wizard assembled the warriors of the village. He sent one into the forest to get the seed pod of a certain tree. Another he sent to dig up a curious two-pronged spear, which had been buried outside the village in a secret place.

Then, on the night of the new moon, Nkoa and I went into the forest, with me carrying a basket. Far from Dinale, Nkoa found another tree. He chewed the seeds from the pod and spat them against the tree, chanting: *"Phaa!"* Let no arrow strike me! Let no spear pierce me! Let no club smite me!"

Then he climbed the tree, with agility surprising in such a withered oldster. At the first main branches, he picked off pieces of bark with his nails and fluttered them down to me. I caught them in the basket, not being allowed to pick one up from the ground if I missed it. Nkoa climbed down, and we repeated the whole process with a tree of another kind.

Back at Dinale, Nkoa commanded the warriors to fetch a large clay pot. The men laid a fire in front of his hut, with stones around it and the pot resting on the stones. The following night, Nkoa took me to a fresh grave, which we opened. We dug out the corpse, that of a middle-aged Mong. Nkoa cut off the corpse's head with a knife. While I held the two-pronged spear, he jammed the head down upon it, saying:

"O corpse! Let no man hear what I say! And harm me not for thus entreating you!"

He brought the head back to his hut on the points of the spear. There we twisted off the head of a speckled fowl and let the blood drip on a large leaf. Nkoa also dripped some of the blood into the big pot. Then he put into the pot the corpse's head—still on the points of the spear, whose shaft stuck up out of the pot—some arrows, and water.

Again he summoned the warriors and lit the fire. When the water boiled, he dipped the skin of some beast of the cat tribe into the pot and sprinkled the warriors, saying:

"Let no man go in unto his woman for the rest of this month!"

For the next month, the warriors practiced war songs and dances in the village, while their wives worked on their farm plots as usual. Nkoa quizzed me about the land of the palefaces. One by one my unfortunate sailors, whose sufferings with their broken legs must have been terrible, were slain, broiled, and devoured. I racked my brains for some scheme to save them, without success. Nkoa bristled at the mere suggestion, and I was in no position to coerce him.

With the coming of the next new moon, Nkoa performed more magical operations. He mixed some powdered wood with the fowl's blood that he had caught on the leaf, tied up the mixture with the corpse's head in the skin of another animal, and hung the stinking bundle in his hut. Next day he again gathered the men. They tore apart a fowl and some plantains, put the pieces in the pot, cooked them, and ate the stew. Nkoa opened the bundle, mixed the mess inside with the bark of another tree, and smeared the stuff on the men's chests, crying:

"Let no shaft strike here! Let no spear pierce here! Let no club smite here!"

Then he led them in procession through the town, calling upon the people to shoot him to prove his invulnerability. At the right time, I shot a headless arrow at his chest. When it bounced off, he cried out that it was a real arrow, whose head his magic had destroyed at the last instant. The Mong shouted yes, they had seen the real head on it, too. The ceremony closed with an orgy of drumming, singing, and dancing, during which Nkoa anointed the rest of the townsfolk with his foul ointment. The next day, the warriors marched off, leaving Nkoa and me safely behind in Dinale to watch the magical bundle and to pray to the spirits for success.

* * *

During this time I came to know Nkoa quite well. I think he even developed a small affection for me—as much as these wizardly types ever do for anyone but themselves. By our standards I suppose he was a heartless, bloody, tricky old scoundrel. But in intellect he was far above his fellow tribesmen. With a little formal education, he could have held his own in the company of any Athenian philosophers.

He was full of interesting ideas and loved to argue, reason, and speculate. Theology fascinated him, and he loved to hear my tales of the gods of Hellas. I thought it wiser not to admit my own skeptical viewpoint. He knew that different tribes had different tales of how the creator-god made the universe, and that these stories could not be reconciled. This puzzled and disturbed him, but he never came to any conclusion about it. When he was a little drunk on plantain wine, he taught me some of his sleight-of-hand tricks.

While I told him about the lands and peoples of the Inner Sea, I also extracted from him information about the countries between the Mong and the great desert. I had not given up hope of escape, although my efforts were more lethargic than usual. Age, disease, and the unaccustomed diet seemed to have stolen away my energy. I was no longer able to plan so readily, nor yet to carry out my plans so promptly and resolutely, as in former years. Thus, for instance, I never did learn to speak Mong well. Somehow I could no longer compel myself to grasp the new grammar and memorize the new words.

Ever since my arrival on the African coast, I had wondered at the lack of domestic animals, other than the dog and the speckled fowl. Such beasts would have done much to relieve the blacks' constant danger of starvation, and there was no lack of greenery for the beasts to feed on. Nkoa knew about domestic hoofed animals; he told me of a tribe to the north that had asses and cattle. But it seemed there was something about the dense jungle that caused all such beasts to sicken and die whenever they entered it.

As the months passed, the folk of Dinale got used to me. I even took part in some of their cannibal feasts, when an expedition brought back a few trembling captives for their larder. Human flesh, I found, tastes much like veal. Some savages, I have heard, eat their fallen foes for magical reasons, for example in hope of ingesting the courage of the deceased. But the Mong ate people simply to fill their bellies. Lacking cattle, sheep, and swine, they had no other ready source of meat.

Their dietary habits aside, I found the Mong in many ways admirable savages—at least, in their dealings with one another. They were brave, honest, dignified, and courteous—in one word, gentlemen. Outsiders, however, they viewed as fair game, against whom any cruelty or treachery was legitimate.

Shortly after the first spell in which I had assisted Nkoa, I came upon a group of Mong loafing in the shade of a big tree and laughing loudly. Approaching, I found that they were tormenting a young monkey, which one of them held on a leash. They poked the creature, pulled its stumpy tail, turned it upside down, and rubbed its face in the dirt. It screamed at them and tried to bite, meanwhile rolling bloodshot eyes in a vain quest for escape.

I was not overly softhearted about animals, but this made me indignant. Like Pythagoras, I thought it wrong to inflict pain wantonly upon them. I knew better than to upbraid these young killers, however. I strolled back to Nkoa's hut and asked the wizard:

"Will you lend me a few cowries, Nkoa?"

"What for?" he snapped.

"I have seen something I wanted, that is all."

"Oh, well, take them," he said, pushing a handful of the shells at me.

I walked back to the scene I had witnessed. The Mong had begun to be bored by their game. Two had fallen asleep, and the rest were tormenting the monkey in a halfhearted, lackadaisical manner. When I offered the man with the leash a couple of cowries for his beast, he was glad to hand it over.

I tried to lead the monkey back to the hut, but it sat down and had to be dragged. I did not care to pick it up for fear of being bitten. Back at the hut, I tied it to one of the wall slats. I fed it, and in a few days it had become quite tame as far as I was concerned, although it still hated blacks and screamed and bared its teeth when one came near. It had olive-brown fur, a black face, and a long, piglike snout. Nkoa told me it was the young of the big baboon of these parts—a fiendish-looking creature the size of a large dog, with a startling red-and-blue face and an equally disconcerting red-and-blue arse.

With familiarity, Nkoa and his people came to trust me more, even though I could never be truly one of them. I went on a couple of their foraging expeditions for human meat, to utter spells to make the Mong invulnerable and invincible and to fill the hearts of their foes with terror. If the raid failed, Nkoa could always aver that some warrior had violated his injunction against copulation. Men being what they are, one or another was sure to have broken this rule, thus giving the wizard an infallible excuse for failure. My own purpose was to familiarize myself with the country roundabout, in case a chance of escape was offered.

One day, a Mong ran excitedly into Dinale to say that an elephant had fallen into one of their covered pitfalls. The warriors boiled out of the town and rushed to the site. The beast was already nearly dead from the piercing of its vitals by the stake at the bottom of the pit. A few spear thrusts finished it off.

Then the whole town turned out to cut up the beast, salvage its hide, and gorge on its meat. I have never seen people eat so much at once. They invited the folk of the other Mong villages to the feast, and for a ten-day the carcass seethed with black humanity, like a swarm of ants attacking a piece of garbage. They kept at it after the stench became too strong for me to endure.

The chief saw to it that the tusks were removed to Dinale. Then he called a council of elders. These decided that, when the two new tusks were added to those already in the village, there would be enough to justify a trading venture to the Lakopi country, in the north, to sell the tusks for metal.

Among barbarians, an affair of this sort is set in motion only after an enormous amount of talk. Everything must be discussed: who should go on the expedition, what route they should follow, who should command the party, and so on. The chief's power to order his men around is not very great, since, if he tries to enforce too many unpopular commands, his people simply walk out on him and go to dwell in other villages. So night after night, the warriors squatted in the square, talking and talking until they arrived at a common policy.

They would carry the tusks on their own shoulders, since they did not keep slaves in the usual manner. The captives they took in their raids had their legs broken to prevent escape and were eaten soon after their capture. At this time there were only a few such unfortunates awaiting consumption. If the Mong obtained a good cargo of metal, they would try to capture a few victims on their return journey. When these had served their purpose of bearing the cargo to Dinale, they would be devoured in their turn.

Many were doubtful about the project, because the route to the Lakopi country took them close to the land of the Jalang. This tribe bore enmity to the Mong, because the latter had often carried off and eaten their people. Therefore, the doubters said, they did not wish to take part in the expedition unless Nkoa went with them to cast protective spells over them.

I discussed the matter with Nkoa in our hut. Nkoa grumbled: "I do not wish to go on this journey, either. These days, my breath comes too short and my joints ache too much for long journeys. But what should I do, Evok?" (This was the nearest the Mong could come to my name.) "If I tell Dinale of this, some young oaf will say: Nkoa grows too old and feeble to be a good wizard. Let us knock him on the head and get another one from some nearby village."

This was the first time he had ever asked my advice. Cautiously I replied: "Well, you might send me in your place."

His bright little eyes sought mine. "I know what you have in your mind, Evok. When you get to the Lakopi country, you will give our warriors the slip and set out for your own land."

"Why, master!" I exclaimed. "Whatever gave you such an idea? No such thought—"

"Never mind the lies," he said. "A good wizard knows what others are thinking, even though they say not a word. But I have enjoyed our talks about far lands and strange gods, these past months, and I would do something for you in return. Besides, we men of intelligence must stand together and help one another against the unthinking masses. So I will send you to Lakopiland with the traders, and whether you return or not is your affair."

* * *

On this journey, I bore a spear and a small bundle of belongings and food. Satyros, as I called my monkey, trotted along with me. Since I often let him off his leash, he could easily have escaped, but he had become so attached to me that he never tried to do so. He had grown a lot since I had bought him and had begun to show the fantastic red-and-blue markings of the adult male. He now weighed at least thirty pounds and was armed with formidable dogteeth. The Mong let him severely alone.

We had no trouble with the Jalang, since the rainy season had begun and most of the inhabitants of the great forest stayed close to their villages. But even under these conditions, travel was most unpleasant. Terrific tempests lashed the jungle, day after day, with such lightning and thunder that one would have thought the end of the world was at hand. Now and then the wind would overturn some gigantic old tree, bringing it down with a roar louder than the thunder and an impact that shook the earth.

Along the trails, we waded in water ankle to knee deep. Betimes the leading man would step into a hole and go in up to his chin or over his head. Every so often, we had to climb out of the water to pull off the huge leeches that fastened upon our legs. I got a parasitic worm under my skin, which itched me half crazy until one of the cannibals showed me how to pull it out by reeling it around a twig. A spell of ague assailed me on the third day out, so that I reeled along with chattering teeth. I could keep up only by virtue of my length of leg and the fact that I was not expected to carry a tusk.

The Mong were not very efficient marchers. There were always a few lazy fellows who did not want to start with the rest in the morning, and much time was lost in argument to get them going. Then they wanted to stop early in the afternoon, and this led to more discussion. If they had put the energy into walking that they did in disputation, they could have reached Lakopiland in half the time. As it was, between the flooded trails, the storms, and the incessant delays, we seldom did more than two leagues a day.

After the first ten-day, however, travel became easier, because the great forest began to thin out. At first it became scrubby, like that along the coast. Then it turned into a mixture of scattered trees, thickets of brush, and open stretches of grass. Rain still fell, but not so hard and incessantly. We even had some sunny days.

Animal life became commoner, or at least we could see it more readily. The Mong often brought down an antelope with their poisoned arrows, so that we had fresh meat.

After a journey of perhaps twenty days—I cannot give an accurate count of time during this period—we came to Bakalenda, the Lakopi capital. This was a big town, comparable to Klimoko. It was surrounded, not by a wooden stockade, but by a crude dry wall of fieldstone.

We filed into the city, under a row of heads set on spikes over the gate, and proceeded to the marketplace. The square was crowded with Africans, showing their wares and chaffering in a score of tongues. There were cattle and goats and asses, for we had now reached the lands where such beasts could thrive. Some of the traders were naked like my own Mong; others wore every sort of garb from mere codpieces to full-length robes.

Heavily armed Lakopi warriors leant on their spears, watching to make sure that men from hostile tribes did not disrupt commerce by fighting. Like the Gbaru, the Lakopi wore clothes of a sort. Their city was a trading center for tribes from all over the great forest and the coast.

My Mong consulted with a Lakopi official, who guided them to a place where they could set out their tusks. He collected one tusk as the market tax and departed, a slave carrying the tusk behind him.

Then came a long wait. Some of the Mong wandered about, accosting traders with metal to sell and trying to interest them in their ivory. Other traders came to our display and made a few tentative offers. In time I got bored with the lack of action and explored the town. I struck up conversations with several Gbaru-speaking traders and sounded out market conditions. By evening I had some idea of local supply and demand.

By evening, however, the Mong had not yet sold a single tusk. Getao, the leader of our party, said:

"You do not understand trade, Evok; but then, of course, you are only a poor, ignorant foreigner. One must never show eagerness, either to buy or sell, lest one be worsted in the deal."

So, I thought, I'm just a poor, ignorant foreigner who does not understand trade? Next morning, when the trading started, I said:

"Getao, lend me one of those tusks."

"Why?" said the Mong suspiciously. "What do you want it for?"

"I will show you. You shall have it back tonight, undamaged."

I picked up the tusk and walked off with it before he could think of further arguments. I strolled over to the stall of one of the merchants to whom I had spoken the day before. ...

When the trading stopped at sunset, I returned to the Mong plot with the same tusk over my shoulder. I led an ass, whose paniers were stuffed with spearheads, hoes, knives, beads, copper wire, and other trade goods.

"How did you do that?" said Getao.

"Oh, I sold the tusk for some cloth, and the cloth for some leather goods, and so on until I had enough to buy the tusk back."

"You must have cast one of your spells on the other traders," he growled. "Is that beast yours, too?"

"Yes."

"The more fool you; it will die on the road back to Dinale."

"I know that, so I will sell it before we leave Bakalenda." Ignorant foreigner, forsooth! Some of these Africans were pretty sharp traders, but none had ever been up against a Greek sea captain.

Since the Mong had sold only four of their tusks, they were likely to stay in Bakalenda for several days. Early next morning, I slipped out of town with a party of Mbutaran tribesmen returning to their home. This, I understood, lay near the mouth of a great river, north of the Lakopi country. I led the ass, while Satyros perched on its back. The Mbutaran looked nervously at the baboon. I explained that, since every great wizard required a familiar spirit, Satyros was mine. He could, I assured them, read their thoughts, and he would infallibly warn me if any evil persons thought to murder me in my sleep for my trade goods. A few sleight-of-hand tricks convinced the Mbutaran that I was all I claimed to be, so I had no trouble with them.

In the Mbutaran town, I used my trade goods in preparing the next step in my homeward journey. I bought another ass, and a piece of cloth from which I could make a tent and a tunic, and a wooden shovel. I bought fishhooks and line, waterskins, hay for the asses, and all the durable foods—dates, smoked meat, and a kind of coarse flour—that the beasts could bear. Then I set out.

In return for my casting a protective spell on their herds and fields, the Mbutaran ferried me across the great river. I then followed the river to its mouth, skirting the marshes around its estuary. I do believe that this river was the one in whose bay we had seen the ruins of Hanno's Kernê. Then I reached the coast and struck out to the north.

* * *

North of this river, vegetation thinned out until I was marching along the edge of the great African desert. I soon learnt that the best way was to sleep through the hottest part of the day and do most of my marching at night, as I had marched through Nubia on my way to the Egyptian gold mines. Day after day I plodded ahead, along sandy beaches against which the Atlantic surf forever thundered, over rocky outcrops, and around salt marshes. Sometimes I shared my food with Satyros. For the most part, though, the baboon fed himself, turning over flat stones and snatching up the creeping things he found under them. He could catch a scorpion, tweak off its stinging tail, and gobble the rest in a couple of heartbeats.

The asses likewise grazed on the scanty herbage, save when we passed an area of sand dunes, where no natural fodder grew and I doled out hay to them. Fresh water I obtained by digging in the beds of dry watercourses.

Day after day I marched, seeing no other human being. I remember a few days distinguished by some special event, such as the time I drove an ostrich away from its nest in order to steal one of its eggs, or the day I heard a lion roaring and thought the beast was stalking me, or the day I caught a ten-pound fish in the surf and ate fish until it came out my ears, or the day I found the abandoned huts of some fishing clan. I had lost track of time and seasons. I thought the month was Skirophorion, but it might have been a month earlier or later. I could, however, tell roughly how long the journey was taking by watching the phases of the moon.

What with the time I had to spend in hunting for food and caring for my animals, I was seldom able to make more than three leagues a day. As usually happens on a journey into unknown lands, I found that the distance was greater than I had supposed, while my supplies did not last so well as I had hoped. By the end of the first month, the load of food and fodder was down to where one of the asses could carry it alone.

For a while I rode the other ass. This made life easier for me, but then the wretched beast went lame. I resumed my walking, hoping that being without a load would cure the beast; but it only got worse until it could hardly move. So I slaughtered it, cut it up, and smoked its meat. It would have been hard to gather enough desert shrubs to do a proper job of smoking, but I luckily found a log of driftwood.

This journey would have been easy with camels, which can go for ten-days without water and thrive on prickly desert shrubs that other animals spurn. But the camel does not seem to be used in Africa west of the Nile valley.

By the end of the second month, the beach still stretched endlessly ahead; the surf pounded on my left; the desert shimmered on my right; the sea birds squealed overhead. I had eaten all the meat of the ass I had killed. It was as tough as bark, and my teeth were no longer what they had once been; but it sustained me thus far. The dates and the native flour were nearly gone.

I could tell by the stars that I was getting farther north, back towards familiar latitudes. But, without a map and astronomical instruments, I could not measure my distances accurately.

I stretched my food supply by searching tide-washed rocks and tidal pools for edible shellfish. But it takes a fearful lot of shellfish to furnish the strength found in one good, honest roll of bread or pork chop. Besides, I was nearing exhaustion, and so were Satyros and the remaining ass. Their ribs showed. The monkey looked at me from bloodshot eyes, grunting in a puzzled way as if demanding an explanation for our peril and discomfort. Every day, it seemed, we made a shorter distance than the day before. At this rate, we should soon lie down and die from hunger and fatigue.

One day, when I was digging for water in a dry channel, I heard voices. For an instant I thought: this is the end; I am in the delirium that foreshadows death. Then I took a grip on myself and looked around. Half a plethron away stood a couple of men, with two asses and a flock of goats. They seemed to have sprung out of the desert.

The twain approached cautiously, calling out. They were lean, brown men, evidently Moors of some sort, and probably father and son. The younger wore a kilt of coarse cloth and had a goatskin mantle slung around his shoulders. The other, gray-bearded, wore a whole tunic of this cloth. Each carried a spear.

I hauled myself out of the hole I had dug and sat on the edge of the excavation. With a mind-wrenching effort, I remembered what I could of the Moorish tongue and called out a good-day. At once, white teeth flashed against dark skins and beards. The two began to talk. Although their dialect differed from that of Mauretania, I caught a word here and there.

"Where do you come from?" asked the older.

I pointed. "From the land of the blacks, that way. How about you?"

"We heard there has been rain in the South, so we are taking our animals thither for pasture. What are you doing?"

"Digging a well."

The Moors laughed shrilly. "Oh, what a fool! You will never find water that way."

"I have found it before and shall again. Just watch—"

During this talk, I had not noticed that the younger Moor had circled around behind me. Now a frightful shriek made me whip around. The scream came from Satyros, who leaped on the back of the younger Moor just as the latter poised his spear to plunge it into my back. No doubt it had seemed too good a chance to miss, to kill me for my ass and any useful gear and supplies I might have.

With a yell as loud as the baboon's, the young Moor was thrown forward to hands and knees, dropping his spear. As I scrambled out of my hole, an old tavern-fighter's instinct warned me to whirl back towards the old Moor, who was just bringing up his spear. Since my own spear was out of reach, I aimed a terrific, two-handed blow at the base of his skull with my shovel. The skull crunched, the shovel broke with a crack, and the man was hurled to the sand.

I turned back to the other Moor, but he was already on his feet, with blood running down his body from Satyros' bites about his neck and shoulders. He raced away across the sand. I hurled his spear after him but missed. He vaulted on one of the asses and beat it into a gallop, with the other ass and the goats bounding after. They all vanished in a cloud of dust.

I retrieved the young Moor's spear and came back to where I had been working. The old Moor was dead. I petted and praised Satyros, who showed his pleasure by leaping up and down on all fours and grunting.

Then I thought hard. At the best estimate I could make, I had several ten-days more of hiking ahead of me, and my stock of food would never last. But why should I leave the Moor to rot, if he would furnish me with the strength I required?

Such an idea would horrify my civilized contemporaries, but I had seen too many of mankind's queer customs and prohibitions to take any of them very seriously. If one must turn savage to survive, why, say I, turn savage! Besides, the man was already dead—slain in legitimate self-defense—so it was not as if I had gone out and hunted him for his flesh, as did my friends the Mong.

So I smoked that Moor as I had the ass. I used one of his shoulder blades and strips of his hide to make a new shovel. He proved almost as tough as the ass, but without him Satyros and I should never have won through to the mouth of the Lixus.

* * *

It was the third of Boedromion, in the second year of the 167th Olympiad, when I entered Eldagon's warehouse in Gades once more. Eldagon—portly and dignified, with his beard hanging down to his girdle—came towards me with a polite nod, saying:

"What can I do for you, sir?" Then he sighted Satyros, who had now reached his full scarlet-and-blue glory, on his leash. "By Tanith's teats, what is that extraordinary beast?"

"Don't you know me, Eldagon?"

He looked puzzled. "Speak once more, I pray. Your voice sounds familiar."

"What ails you, man? It hasn't been quite a year since—"

"Good Baal Hammon, it is Eudoxos!" He threw himself into my arms, laughing and weeping. "Thrice welcome! Tubal and I had given you up for good, this time. But I might have known you would turn up."

"Why didn't you know me? Herakles! Have I changed so much?"

"Have you seen yourself in a mirror?"

"No."

"Well, have a look."

When I saw my face, I almost dropped the mirror. My skin was as black as that of many lighter Ethiops, while my hair and beard were pure white. I looked older than Kronos.

"By Our Lady, no wonder!" I said.

"What has befallen you? What of your ships and cargo?"

"The blacks got them, and my crew have all either died of disease or been eaten by cannibals. But now I should like you to meet a friend of mine. Satyros, this is Eldagon ben-Balatar, an old associate."

The baboon nodded gravely. Eldagon sent a man to fetch his brother Tubal. Then he asked:

"Did you manage again to amass a fortune on the way home, despite your disasters?"

"*Oimoi!* No. I arrived in Tingis with nothing but an ass, which I sold to pay my passage to Gades. But, knowing how you are about animals, I have brought you Satyros. If he likes you, he may deign to take up residence in your menagerie."

"I knew you would produce something unexpected," he said. "In Tingis, did you have any more trouble with King Bocchus?"

"No. Nobody paid any heed to a penniless old vagabond."

* * *

Well, that is my story. It was six years ago that I returned to Gades from my second assault on the African continent. Eldagon was so grateful for the baboon that he invited me to live with him as a kind of retired senior partner, since the journey had aged me to the point where I was no longer fit for strenuous seafaring. The sons of Balatar could not have been kinder. Instead of blaming me for the loss of the ships and cargo, they attributed my misfortunes to Fate and the gods and praised me for having succeeded in returning at all.

Since then, I have earned my keep by designing rigging for Tubal's smaller vessels. I persuaded him to let me rig a fishing smack with my triangular sail and spent the rest of the summer tacking about the Bay of Gades to show what the sail could do. Although seamen are a hidebound lot, the ability of my rig to beat away from a lee shore at last impressed them. They began to order new ships—small craft like fishermen and coasters—with the fore-and-aft rig. They also commenced to have old ones converted to this rig in Tubal's yard. We put it about that I am the only man who can set the rig up right. In time, they will doubtless discover that the rig is really easy to copy, and that will end the profit we have been garnering from it.

The past year I have spent mostly in dictating my adventures, and this manuscript is the result. I daresay your uncles and other kinsmen will find it interesting, whether or not the public does.

I still think the route from Gades around Africa to India is feasible, although I am no longer up to trying it. The ships should, however, avoid stops along the damp, jungled coast where I met with disaster. If the crew are not devoured by the natives, they will die off from the horrible diseases wherewith this land is rife. How far one must sail to reach a healthier clime I know not. But, if Necho's Phoenicians could do it, we moderns, with all our technical advances, should be able to.

Now, my son, I should like you to do certain tasks for me. As I explained in the introductory letter, one is to edit this manuscript and arrange for its publication. As I think you will agree, mine has been no humdrum life. It is not mere vanity that leads me to wish my successes and failures, my sufferings and triumphs immortalized. I think the tale itself is a worthy addition to the literature of Hellas, making up in excitement and the lore of distant lands what it may lack in literary polish.

Furthermore, if possible, I should like you to do something about the god-detested Hippalos, who is as hateful to me as the gates of Hades. I hear that he is back in Alexandria. The whipworthy trickster has set himself up as the high priest of some weird cult, which he claims is the true scientific religion, based upon his lifelong study of the mysteries of the East.

In addition, he has wormed his way into the confidence of Kleopatra the Wife and her present co-ruler, her son Ptolemaios Alexandros. (As you doubtless know, she quarreled some time ago with her other son, King Ptolemaios Lathyros, and drove him to Cyprus, where he now rules.) Now the dog-faced knave is promoting yearly voyages to India by the route I discovered, from the Red Sea.

To add insult to injury, he has named the half-yearly winds across the Indian Ocean after himself instead of after me. I doubt if you can do anything with the queen, who will still bear me a grudge. But you might send a petition to Lathyros in Cyprus asking him to proclaim me the true and proper discoverer of this golden wind. He may be all the more willing because of his feud with his mother, and he may also some day regain the throne of Egypt.

Lastly, if you ever get a chance to do evil to the polluted Hippalos himself, without untoward risk, I pray and exhort you, as your duty to your sire, to take advantage of it. Avenge both your parents thus.

I had plenty of leisure for thought on my three-hundred-league march along the African coast. I decided that, if Hippalos had made your mother happy, I might by now have been willing to forgive and forget, as old Glaukos had advised. I was not a satisfactory husband to her, either; but at least I never tormented her to the point of suicide. So the greatest pleasure you could give your old father in his last years would be to send him the scoundrel's head, pickled in brine. I know that the chances of your obtaining this trophy are not good, for that temple thief is a fox who can slip through any hole. But the mere thought of it gives me pleasure.

Convey my love to all the kinsmen. Strength to you!

AUTHOR'S NOTE

This story is based upon a passage in the works of Poseidonios the Stoic, quoted by Strabon the geographer (II, iii, 4-5):

4. Posidonius, in speaking of those who have sailed round Africa, tells us that Herodotus was of opinion that some of those sent out by Darius[8] actually performed this enterprise; and that Heraclides of Pontus, in a certain dialogue, introduces one of the Magi presenting himself to Gelon, and declaring that he had performed this voyage; but he remarks that this wants proof. He also narrates how a certain Eudoxus of Cyzicus, sent with sacrifices and oblations to the Corean games, travelled into Egypt in the reign of Euergetes II.; and being a learned man, and much interested in the peculiarities of different countries, he made interest with the king and his ministers on the subject, but especially for exploring the Nile. It chanced that a certain Indian was brought to the king by the [coast]-guard of the Arabian Gulf. They reported that they had found him in a ship, alone, and half dead: but that they neither knew who he was, nor where he came from, as he spoke a language they could not understand. He was placed in the hands of preceptors appointed to teach him the Greek language. On acquiring which, he related how he had started from the coasts of India, but lost his course, and reached Egypt alone, all his companions having perished with hunger; but that if he were restored to his country he would point out to those sent with him by the king, the route by sea to India. Eudoxus was of the number thus sent. He set sail with a good supply of presents, and brought back with him in exchange aromatics and precious stones, some of which the Indians collect from amongst the pebbles of the riv-

8 An error for Necho II.

ers, others they dig out of the earth, where they have been formed by the moisture, as crystals are formed with us.

[He fancied that he had made his fortune], however, he was greatly deceived, for Euergetes took possession of the whole treasure. On the death of that prince, his widow, Cleopatra, assumed the reins of government, and Eudoxus was again despatched with a richer cargo than before. On his journey back, he was carried by the winds above Ethiopia, and being thrown on certain [unknown] regions, he conciliated the inhabitants by presents of grain, wine, and cakes of pressed figs, articles which they were without; receiving in exchange a supply of water, and guides for the journey. He also wrote down several words of their language, and having found the end of a prow, with a horse carved on it, which he was told formed part of the wreck of a vessel coming from the west, he took it with him, and proceeded on his homeward course. He arrived safely in Egypt, where no longer Cleopatra, but her son, ruled; but he was again stripped of every thing on the accusation of having appropriated to his own uses a large portion of the merchandise sent out.

However, he carried the prow into the market-place, and exhibited it to the pilots, who recognised it as being come from Gades. The merchants [of that place] employing large vessels, but the lesser traders small ships, which they style horses, from the figures of that animal borne on the prow, and in which they go out fishing around Maurusia, as far as the Lixus. Some of the pilots professed to recognise the prow as that of a vessel which had sailed beyond the river Lixus, but had not returned.

From this Eudoxus drew the conclusion, that it was possible to circumnavigate Libya; he therefore returned home, and having collected together the whole of his substance, set out on his travels. First he visited Dicaearchia, and then Marseilles, and afterwards traversed the whole coast as far as Gades. Declaring his enterprise everywhere as he journeyed, he gathered money sufficient to equip a great ship, and two boats, resembling those used by pirates. On board these he placed singing girls, physicians, and artisans of various kinds, and launching into open sea, was carried towards India by steady westerly winds. However, they who accompanied him becoming wearied with the voyage, steered their course towards land, but much against his will, as he dreaded the force of the ebb and flow. What he feared actually occurred. The ship grounded, but gently, so that it did not break up at once, but fell to pieces gradually, the goods and much of the timber of the ship being saved. With these he built a third vessel, closely resembling a ship of fifty oars, and continuing his voyage, came amongst a people who spoke the same language as that some words of which he had on a former occasion committed to writing. He further discovered, that they were men of the same stock as those other Ethiopians, and also resembled those of the kingdom of Bogus[9] . However, he abandoned his [intended] voyage to India, and returned home. On his voyage back he observed an uninhabited island, well watered and wooded, and carefully noted its position. Having reached Maurusia in safety, he disposed of his vessels, and travelled by land to the court of Bogus. He recommended that sovereign to undertake an expedition thither.

This, however, was prevented on account of the fear of the [king's] advisers, lest the district should chance to expose them to treachery, by making known a route by which foreigners might come to attack them. Eudoxus, however, became aware, that although it was given out that he was himself to be sent on this proposed expedition, the real intent was to abandon him on some desert island. He therefore fled to the Roman territory, and passed thence into Iberia. Again, he equipped two vessels, one round and the other long, furnished with fifty oars, the latter framed for voyaging in the high seas, the other for coasting along the shores. He placed on board agricultural implements, seed, and builders, and hastened on the same voyage, determined, if it should prove too long, to winter on the island he had before observed, sow his seed, and having reaped the harvest, complete the expedition he had intended from the beginning.

* * *

5. "Thus far," says Posidonius, "I have followed the history of Eudoxus. What happened afterwards is probably known to the people of Gades and Iberia;" "but," says he, "all these things only demonstrate more clearly the fact, that the inhabited earth is entirely surrounded by the ocean."

Poseidonios' account contains obvious errors. For example, Kleopatra III was not out of power upon Eudoxos' second return from

9 Spelled *Bogos* by Strabon but *Bokchos* or *Bocchus* by other ancient writers.

India; she reigned continuously, first with one son and then with the other, down to her death in –89. It is incredible that any tribe on the west coast of Africa should at this time have spoken the same language as another tribe on the east coast. And the island discovered by Eudoxos on his first African voyage was probably Fuerteventura, the easternmost of the Canaries; but Fuerteventura is not "well-wooded." Notwithstanding, the story as a whole may be believed, despite Strabon's own incredulity.

Plinius the Elder and Pomponius Mela cite a garbled version of this story. Plinius (II, lxvii, 169) says: "We have it on the authority of Cornelius Nepos that a certain contemporary of his named Eudoxus when flying from King Lathyrus emerged from the Arabian Gulf and sailed right around to Cadiz ..." Mela (III, ix), citing the same source, uses much of the same wording.

Poseidonios ends his tale ambiguously, without saying what finally became of Eudoxos. Probably the explorer sailed away and vanished. But it is not impossible that he returned to Gades, and I have made this assumption for the sake of the story.

Hippalos is mentioned by several ancient writers, the most informative being the anonymous author of the *Periplus of the Erythraean Sea* (57): "This whole voyage as above described, from Cana to Eudaemon Arabia, they used to make in small vessels, sailing close to the shores of the gulfs; and Hippalus was the pilot who by observing the location of the ports and the conditions of the sea, first discovered how to lay his course straight across the ocean. For at the same time when with us the Etesian winds are blowing, on the shores of India the wind sets in from the ocean, and this southwest wind is called Hippalus from the name of him who first discovered the passage across."

Nobody states when Hippalos lived, or who he was. His date had been estimated by modern scholars at anywhere from that of Eudoxos' Indian voyages (–119 to –116) to that of the writing of the *Periplus* (about +60). My assumption, that he was Eudoxos' first officer, is a plausible guess, which cannot be proved or disproved.

Besides Eudoxos and Hippalos, the historical characters in this story are the various Ptolemies and Kleopatras, the Judaean officers Chelkias and Ananias, the geographers Agatharchides and Artemidoros, the librarians Kydas and Ammonios, the physician Kallimachos,

King Bocchus of Mauretania, King Jugurtha of Numidia, and various rulers alluded to like Mikipsa, Mithradates, and Odraka, who do not appear on stage. All others are fictitious.

Names of people and places in the Mediterranean and Iran are given Greek or Latin spellings, whichever seems appropriate. The name of the Ethiopian king, Tañyidamani, has been slightly Latinized to Tangidamani. Indian names with well-established Greek forms are given in their Greek spellings. Other Indian names are given in their ancient Indian forms, transliterated without the diacritical marks needed for accurate pronunciation. If I tried to figure out how Eudoxos would have spelled these names in Greek, the result would only have been to confuse the reader. Since Greek had no near equivalents of the Indian aspirated voiced plosives (*bh, dh, gh*), or the short *u* as in *put*, Eudoxos might have spelled "Buddha" as Boda, Bodda, Bodtha, Bodta, Boutta, Byttha, etc. The names of Indian places that appear in the text in their Greek forms, with their ancient and modern Indian equivalents, are as follows:

Greek	*Ancient Indian*	*Modern Indian*
Barygaza	Bharukaccha	Bharuch, Broach
Eirinon	Kaccha	Kacch, Cutch
Hemodos Mts.	Himâlaya Mts.	Himâlaya Mts.
Kammonoi, Kamanes		Cambay
Mais R.	Mahî R.	Mahî R.
Modoura	Mathura	Mattra, Muttra
Nammados R.	Narmadâ R.	Narbadâ or Nerbudda R.
Ozenê	Ujjayinî	Ujjain
Palibothra	Pâtaliputra	Patnâ
Souppara	Shurpâraka	Sopâra
Syrastrenê	Surâshtra	Kâthiâvâr

Eudoxos' "giant Indian mouse" is the black rat, rats not having been known in the West in classical times.

The "artemon" was a kind of foresail carried by large classical sailing ships from Hellenistic times on. It was flown from a spar at the bow, which was neither exactly a foremast nor a bowsprit, but something intermediate, standing up at an angle of about 45° to the deck.

The description of the Ptolemies' Nubian gold mines follows the account of Agatharchides, paraphrased by Diodoros (III, 12-14).

There is no evidence that Eudoxos invented the fore-and-aft sail, but he could have. Sails of this kind (either the short-luffed lug, as in the story, or the spritsail) began to appear on small coastal vessels, such as fishing boats, at just about the time of my story. See Lionel Casson's *The Ancient Mariners* (p. 219).

In the West African episode, the Baga were a fishing tribe of former times, mentioned in the legends of Sierra Leone. The other tribes are fictitious. The customs attributed to the West Africans, however, are those found there by Europeans during the era of European exploration and conquest, 1500–1900. The Africans are shown in the story as more primitive than they were during the Age of Exploration, because they undoubtedly were more primitive at the time of the story. The semi-civilized kingdoms of West Africa—Ghana, Mali, Ashanti, Dahomey, and the rest—did not, as far as is known, begin to arise until about the middle of the first millennium of the Christian Era, at the earliest.

The site of Hanno's Kernê has been the subject of much modern speculation. It has been located at several places, from modern Herné at the bay of Rio de Oro to the mouth of the Senegal River. This last assumption is that of Rhys Carpenter, in *Beyond the Pillars of Heracles*. Without wishing to take sides in this scholarly dispute, I have accepted Dr. Carpenter's theory for the purposes of my story.

Made in the USA
Columbia, SC
17 November 2020

24801766R00150